Erasmus W. Jones

# Llangobaith

A story of north Wales

Erasmus W. Jones

**Llangobaith**
*A story of north Wales*

ISBN/EAN: 9783337322366

Printed in Europe, USA, Canada, Australia, Japan

Cover: Foto ©Andreas Hilbeck / pixelio.de

More available books at **www.hansebooks.com**

# LLANGOBAITH;

## A STORY OF NORTH WALES,

BY

## REV. ERASMUS W. JONES.

AUTHOR OF

"THE CAPTIVE YOUTHS OF JUDAH," "THE ADOPTED SON OF THE
PRINCESS," "THE GREAT REVIVAL AT TONVILLE," "THE MAN
WITH THE RUFFLED SHIRT," "SHARP WORDS ON
OLD FLINTROCK CIRCUIT," ETC.

UTICA, N. Y.
THOMAS J. GRIFFITHS.
1886.

# PREFACE.

Midway between the northern and southern ends of the map of England, on the west side, facing St. George's Channel, with its two arms thrown out to embrace the beautiful Cardigan Bay, the waters of which roll over the lost paradise of the "Hundred Lowland Townships," is situated a section of country comprising twelve counties or shires, which, in the parlance of political geography, is called "The Principality of Wales." Here the inhabitants are still using their own Welsh tongue as the language of the home, as the medium of business and social intercourse, and also of religious worship. This little country has figured quite largely in the early annals of modern history, and offers still an inviting field of investigation and study for people of other nationalities and tongues. The scene of the story now offered to the public is in the northern part of this Principality.

The author believes that a large community of readers are ready to greet with a generous welcome any book added to the very few already existing in the English language, that will contribute its quota towards throwing a new light on that country and its people. He was convinced of this by the interest awakened by articles of his touching the peculiar characteristics of his nation, which appeared a few years since in *The Atlantic Monthly* and *The New York Independent.* Hence this story.

For the substance of the legends related by the minstrel at Thrush Grove, the stories told during the evening at Havod, and those subsequently given at Druid's Grove, the author is under obligation to a charming little Welsh volume called " *Cymru Fu,*" (Wales of the Past.)

A word as to the pronunciation of the name "Llangobaith." As our English friends cannot well give the sound of the Welsh *Ll*, let them give it as in *Lloyd*. The accent comes on the second syllable, and the word is pronounced thus: Llân-gob'-aith.

E. W. J.

# CONTENTS.

# LLANGOBAITH;

## A STORY OF NORTH WALES.

## CHAPTER I.

### SCHOOL-DAYS EXPERIENCE.

Those who have traveled in North Wales, will not easily forget that grand chain of mountains extending from "Cader Idris" in the south, to "Penmaen Mawr" in the north, with the Snowdon towering high above its fellows, like a giant monarch among his subjects. Under the shadow of one of these majestic elevations, and not far from the flourishing village of Llangobaith, stood two prominent farm-houses. In harmony with a Welsh custom, these residences, with the respective farms on which they stood, had their proper names, as well as did their owners or tenants. This answers an excellent purpose in a country where the Joneses and Williamses so overwhelmingly predominate. In this way, William Jones of *Brithdir*, is easily distinguished from William Jones of *Ty'n'rallt;* and Richard Williams of *Cae'r-eithin* is not confounded with his namesake of *Bryn-y-gloch.* The two residences were *Glan* 'r *afon*, (Riverside) and *Llwyn y Derwydd*, (Druid's Grove), while their masters were Evan Pugh and Thomas Lloyd. Our story demands the mention of another residence which stood forth prominently among the best buildings in Llangobaith. It was partly a dwelling house, and partly a place of business. In America, the business part would have been called a *store*. In Wales, at that time it was termed a "shop." And for a village, the "shop" was on rather an extensive scale. For many years it had flourished under the careful management of its proprietor, Morgan Edwards.

The family proper, at Druid's Grove, consisted of the parents and an only child. Gwennie was a lovely girl of ten summers, whose sweet disposition and charming face easily won the affection of all who knew her. It was often remarked by the neighbors, that she had richly inherited the loving ways and spirit of her mother, and not those of her father. There was also in the family at this time a child, Mary Humphreys, who had been left fatherless and motherless. Mary was exceedingly comely and bright. Mrs. Lloyd had taken her not only into her house, but also into her heart. Gwennie dearly loved the orphan, and treated her with the utmost kindness.

Evan Pugh, of Riverside, was considered by far the richest man in the vicinity. He was owner of the fine farm which, as an only son, he had inherited from his father. He married his wife in England, and she soon learned to speak the Welsh language with considerable ease. Pugh's wealth, as a matter of course, gave him much influence in the community, but he was really respected by but very few. The peasants viewed him in his true character, an unfeeling, proud, overbearing man. From his English wife these traits received no check. In a large measure, she possessed the spirit of her husband. They had one child, a boy of twelve years, who at a very early age gave unmistakeable evidences of a depraved heart. After an uncle of his mother, he was called Lucas.

Morgan Edwards of the " shop " had been left a widower with two children. Llewelyn was a finely developed lad, of sweet temper and resolute mind. He was eleven years of age. Helen, two years younger, was a sprightly black-eyed beauty, and greatly attached to her brother. Even before the death of their mother, the children had received the tender care of their aunt, a widowed sister of their father, who at the earnest request of her brother, remained to superintend the affairs of the household.

Some years passed away, and the young people were attending a private school of a high grade at Llangobaith. Those traits which had shown themselves in childhood had been more fully developed. Llewelyn, Gwennie and Helen were great favorites, while Lucas,

by his haughty and vicious bearing, repelled all, except
a very few of his own stamp.   The popularity of young
Edwards naturally excited the envy, jealousy and hatred of Pugh, which he manifested on all available occasions.   In point of scholarship, he was left far behind,
and this also increased his spite and malignity.   It became a standing wonder to the school how Llewelyn
could continue to meet the treatment with so much
meekness and patience.

Another cause of Lucas' ill will, was the very high
place the "shop boy" seemed to occupy in the estimation of Gwennie Lloyd.   Notwithstanding his perverse
and depraved nature, Lucas was greatly stirred by the
beauty and accomplishment of this girl, who was now
verging on young womanhood.   Several times he had
made moderate advances, and although the young lady
had treated him with civility, he had readily noticed
the absence of those happy smiles that clothed her countenance while in the society of Llewelyn Edwards.

Attending the school there was also a youth of about
Llewelyn's age, by the name of Taliesin Roberts.   His
parents lived on a small farm in that vicinity, for which
they paid a heavy rent.   For a boy of seventeen, Taliesin, in body and mind, was a noble specimen of devel-
oping humanity.   He was being educated at the expense
of a wealthy widowed aunt, his mother's youngest sister.   For Llewelyn this young person had strong at-

tachment; and no student at Llangobaith stood higher in the estimation of young Edwards, than did Taliesin. Of his age, he was a bright scholar, and David Thomas, the head teacher, was proud of his attainments. For some time Roberts had witnessed the manner in which Lucas and another young fellow by the name of John Spike, treated his friend, and at times his indignation would well nigh break loose. In his ardent love for young Edwards, he would almost forget the insults which he himself received from the same quarters.

One summer noon, during their first term, our two fast friends were sitting together in a shady grove on the banks of a clear running brook, a short distance from the school-house.

"Llewelyn," said Taliesin, "how can you so patiently bear the sneers and insults of those conceited fools, Lucas Pugh and John Spike?"

"It was a little hard at first," replied Llewelyn with a smile, "but I have become so used to it, that it gives me no trouble."

"But is it your duty to become used to it, and pass it by with indifference?" asked Taliesin.

"But what would you have me do?" asked Edwards. "Should I go to the master with tears in my eyes, saying that Pugh and Spike had treated me unkindly?"

"No, not that," was the reply. "You should meet their abusive language with stern rebukes, and make them the laughing stock of the school. And if that would not answer, you should threaten to flog them, which you can do with one hand. If you don't wish to put a stop to this thing yourself, give me permission, and I will scare them into better behaviour without a blow."

"Taliesin," said Llewelyn, "I thank you for your warm friendship, but please let me manage these fellows in my own way."

"So let it be, as far as *you* are concerned," said Taliesin. "But if they undertake to abuse me, I will take matters into my own hands."

At this point, they heard approaching voices; and a few rods up the stream they saw Lucas and his chum approaching, engaged in animated conversation. They soon reached the spot where our young friends were resting.

"Halloo!" cried Lucas in a sneering tone; "we have disturbed your profound conversation. Spike, I'll wager half a guinea, that Llewelyn's theme was Gwennie Lloyd."

"And I'll bet a sovereign that Taliesin's sweet subject was Helen Edwards," said Spike.

"You are wide of the mark," said Taliesin. "The subjects of our conversation were of far less importance. We happened to be talking of Lucas Pugh and John Spike."

"Your opinion of our importance is of no consequence," said Pugh, in an indignant voice.

"Lucas," said Spike, "don't lower yourself by wasting words with that fellow. It would have been better for the good name of our school if his auntie had given another direction to her benevolence, and had left him to the simple teaching of some school of charity."

"Spike!" cried Llewelyn, rising to his feet, "your language is outrageous, and you must take it back!"

"It is the language of a sneaking coward!" said Taliesin. "I will give him three minutes by my watch to take those words back, or suffer the consequence of a refusal."

"And what will the consequence be, may I ask?" inquired Spike.

"I will let you know in just two minutes," said Taliesin, as he divested himself of necktie, coat and vest.

Spike having a full knowledge of Taliesin's physical strength, and noticing the terrible expression of his countenance, found no great trouble in persuading his cowardly self that retreat was the safest.

"You are on your last minute!" cried Taliesin, looking Spike straight in the eye, and slowly approaching him in a threatening attitude. Spike looked at Lucas, and saw in his face signs of fear. He looked on Llewelyn, and in him there was no disposition to interfere.

"Ten seconds by the watch!" cried Taliesin, and his visage was terrible.

"Roberts," said Spike, in trembling accents, "I did not think my words would lead to this. I call them back."

"That settles the matter between us two," said Taliesin; "but while I am in the vein, let me say to Lucas Pugh, that from henceforth if he would avoid a sound thrashing, he must direct no abusive language either to Llewelyn Edwards or myself."

Just then the school bell rung, and the vanquished were glad to find a plausible excuse for escaping from a very uncomfortable situation.

No sooner had they left, than Roberts fell into a fit of laughter.

"It seems to me that the transition from rage to mirth is rather sudden," said Llewelyn.

"It is not such a great transition after all," said Taliesin. "I was somewhat angry, but that excessive rage was a piece of acting."

"Your generalship was admirable, and you deserve promotion," said Llewelyn. "But come, or we shall be late."

Subsequently, the behavior of Pugh and Spike was less insulting, but their hatred was deeper, and their malice more intense.

In about two weeks after this, our two friends were

slowly walking together in the road between Druid's Grove and Llangobaith. This they were often in the habit of doing; during which occasions, as warm confidential friends, they would freely converse together on any and all subjects that might interest their minds. While thus moving toward the village, they were overtaken by a young lass with whom they were perfectly familiar, and of whom they thought much. She was Mary Jones, the youngest of Evan and Margaret Jones's children. Her father was a hard-working, intelligent and pious laborer, living in an humble cot named *Pren y Gog* (Cuckoo's Tree) on the farm of Evan Pugh, to whom he paid a yearly rent that was considered oppressive.

"Good evening, Mary," said Llewelyn in a kind, familiar tone. "You seem to be in a hurry."

"I am going to the village," said the girl. "Uncle Hugh has come from Liverpool, and we want a few things from the shop."

There was something in the girl's voice and countenance, as well as in the appearance of her eyes, that gave Llewelyn to understand that something troubled her, and wishing to render her any assistance within his power, he ventured to say—

"Mary, I am afraid that something is troubling you. Can I give you any help?"

"Oh, Llewelyn!" sobbed out the girl, "our dear Dick

is going way off to Liverpool with Uncle Hugh, and what shall we do at Pren y Gôg without him? He wants to go so much, and father and mother say that he may. We are glad to see uncle, but it will almost break our hearts to lose Dick."

"We shall all miss him, Mary," said Llewelyn, with tears in his eyes. "A nobler boy than Dick Jones never breathed! He is loved by every one."

"Not quite by every one," said Mary. "Lucas Pugh and John Spike abuse him every chance they get, and he bears it all quietly, for our sake! O, my dear Dick!"

"I would be glad to be near by when Dick Jones is insulted by those fellows," said Taliesin Roberts, with a frown gathering on his brow.

"They dare not do it when people are looking on," said Mary, recovering her spirits. "They cowardly insult him when they find him alone. They abuse Robin too; and Jane and I have to listen often to their rough talk. But I must go." And Mary Jones hastened toward Llangobaith.

While our two friends were enjoying themselves in profitable conversation, and in viewing the beauties of nature, Pugh and Spike were indulging in ale-drinking at the "Red Lion." On this day, however, they had left in time to notice from a distance the interview between Mary Jones and her two friends in the road; and it filled their minds with vulgar curiosity.

"I should like to know what that talk was about?" said John Spike.

"And you will know in a few minutes," said Pugh. "She must not pass until she tells us."

"Ha, ha! That will be sport," cried Spike. "But she comes in a hurry, and if we don't look sharp, she will pass us."

"Never you fear," was Lucas's reply. "The Pren y Gôg tribe is pretty well under my direction, and they dare not complain or be saucy."

The girl was now close by, and with hasty steps was about to pass, when the two rowdies stepped in front of her, and brought her to a stand.

"Not quite so fast, my pretty maiden," said Lucas with mock politeness. "I have a number of questions that you must answer before you go any farther."

"Mr. Pugh," said Mary, "I go on an errand to Llangobaith. I am in a hurry. Let me go, please."

"Not a step farther will you go, Miss, until you tell us all about your conversation with the shop boy and Taliesin Roberts," said Lucas.

"Mr. Pugh," said Mary, "you can stop my going to Llangobaith, but you can never make me tell you my talk with Llewelyn."

"I can't, eh?" said Lucas with a pompous frown.

"We'll see about that. Do you know who you are talking to?"

"Indeed I do," said Mary. "You have given all of us at Pren y Gôg good reasons to know you, for many years. Now let me go on my errand." And she tried to pass them.

"Not yet, you saucy brat!" said John Spike, seizing her violently by the arm. "Now tell us what you were talking about with those chaps on the road."

"Never, never!" cried Mary, breaking forth into weeping. "Let go of my arm; you are hurting me! Shame on both of you! Let go of me, John Spike! If Llewelyn or Taliesin was here, you would not dare touch me!"

"Ho, ho!" cried Spike; "just as if we were afraid of the shop boy and his charity chum!"

Just at this time, from a sudden turn in the road, Llewelyn and his friend suddenly stood before them.

"What does this mean, Mary?" asked Taliesin, while his lips quivered.

"O, Taliesin!" cried the girl, "I am so glad you have come! They will not let me go unless I tell them what we were talking about yonder; and John Spike has handled me roughly and hurt my arm."

"She lies!" cried John. "We could not get rid of her. I took hold of her arm to push her off;" still retaining his grasp.

"Take off your hand from that girl's arm, you lying villain!" said Taliesin.

"Not at your bidding," angrily answered Spike, "and you may go to"—

Before he could mention the particular locality, a heavy blow from the indignant Taliesin laid him senseless on the ground.

"Mr. Pugh," said Taliesin, "I leave Spike in your kind care. If there is to be a legal investigation, you know where to find me." Then addressing the girl, he said—

"Mary, we shall accompany you as far as Llangobaith;" and so they left.

"That was the first luxury of the kind I ever indulged in," said Taliesin with a smile.

"It was brief in its duration," said Llewelyn.

"But it was quite enjoyable while it lasted," was the reply.

"Let us hope that there shall be no occasion for another such indulgence," said Llewelyn; and turning to Mary, asked—

"When does Dick intend to start?"

"He starts at an early hour on the day after to-morrow," said the sister.

"We must call and bid him good-bye to-morrow afternoon," said Llewelyn.

They now had reached their destination.   Mary made her purchase, and was soon hastening homeward.

The news of Dick Jones's anticipated departure was soon known throughout the village and vicinity; and all expressed deep regret at losing one who, although poor, was an universal favorite.

John Spike was not seriously injured, nor at all disfigured.   The blow had been accommodating enough to fall just below the right ear, where it left a feeling, but not a visible impression.   After a wonderful display of curses, and vows of vengeance, they pursued their way toward Riverside; and well knowing that they had been overtaken in an undertaking which the people would condemn, they concluded that it was best for them to keep the matter to themselves.

On the afternoon of the next day, a number of youth of both sexes assembled at Pren y Gôg to bid Dick Jones adieu.

" Good-bye, Dick !" said Llewelyn, with tears in his eyes.   "We shall greatly miss you."

"Good-bye, Llewelyn!" said Dick.   "I shall never forget your kindness."   Taliesin and the two girls, Gwennie and Helen, gave him their hands in tearful silence, and with others they slowly went away.

"And they were all here except Mary Humphreys !" said his mother, in a tone of disappointment, after they had all left.   "I looked for her above all the rest."

Had the mother understood the exact state of the case, the absence of sweet Mary Humphreys would have given her no uneasiness.

"I promised to call on Mary for a short time this evening, mother," said the boy, "and that is the reason she was not here."

"Aye, do, my dear child!" said Margaret Jones, "and tell her to come and see us as often as she can."

Soon Richard was at Druid's Grove, to bid adieu to his weeping Mary, and at an early hour next morning he was on his way to Bangor to take the sloop for Liverpool.

———

The young people's stay at school was for a period of three years. Throughout this time Llewelyn had devoted himself to his studies with great diligence, and had made fine advancement. It was the same with Taliesin. The praise he received from the principal on the day he left school was well deserved. He faithfully corresponded with his aunt, and received her thanks and blessings. Spike had left with profane anger, about six months before the rest of the young people. He was openly reprimanded for a malicious falsehood, went home, and explained his movements by resorting to more. His hatred of Taliesin was deep and villainous. The brief affair on the road with Mary Jones, and his unlooked for chastisement, he never mentioned except to Lucas Pugh. But never did he cease to hope for an opportunity that would permit him in some manner to heap vengeance upon the head of one he supremely hated. Lucas, as a student, had been indolent and stupid. Often when his mates were struggling with hard problems, he, mounted on one of his father's horses, was following the hounds. Throughout the years, his jealousy and conceit had been on the increase. He always had a good supply of money, and with those of his own sbrt he would freely spend it. With the landlady of the Red Lion he was a great favorite. There he spent much of his time, and often showed a high degree of drunken hilarity, while coarse profanity broke over his lips. Gwennie Lloyd at the end of the course, was universally loved by her companions. Her accomplishments, amiability and moral worth were un-mistakable. She had a host of warm friends, but her one fondly cherished, confidential companion was Helen Edwards, who was well nigh her equal in everything that constitutes a genuine young lady.

# CHAPTER II.

### JOY AND A JOURNEY.

*Llwyn y Fronfraith* (Thrush Grove) was a beautiful country residence, about twelve miles from Llangobaith, and was the home of Mrs. Parry. Hugh Parry was the only son and child of Col. Morgan Parry, whose ancestors for generations had resided at this charming spot. The young man received all the advantages which wealth could procure. The twenty-first anniversary of his birth was celebrated with unbounded enthusiasm. In the evening. bonfires blazed on the hills, while the booming cannon echoed on the sides of those old Welsh mountains.

His father having been a successful military man, desired his son to follow the same profession. This was in harmony with the young man's mind, and he received his commission as a captain.

Between Hugh Parry and the fair Mary Morgan there had grown genuine affection, and a short time before he left for the army, they were betrothed and pledged to each other their undying love.

In two years from this time an "orderly" rode up to Capt. Parry and handed him a letter. It was from his mother, saying that his father was very low, and re-

2

questing his presence at home as soon as possible. The Colonel was alive when the son arrived, but was fast sinking. He had strength enough to give a few directions, when suddenly he fell back and expired.

The altered state of things at home, compelled the son to resign his commission. It was accepted with much regret. In one year more those hills were again illuminated to celebrate an event in which the accomplished Mary Morgan was arrayed in bridal robes.

The venerable mother did not long survive her husband, and deeply lamented, she was laid down to rest by his side in the old parish churchyard.

In two years after this, the young, noble hearted and pious Capt. Parry sickened and died, leaving a wife and a bright-eyed babe six months old.

For his wife's young nephew, Taliesin Roberts, then about ten years of age, Capt. Parry had manifested great regards. He had noticed in the lad many points of excellence, and in his last sickness he enjoined on his wife to superintend his education and spare no expense.

In about two weeks after the close of their school at Llangobaith, Taliesin received the following from his Aunt Mary:

"LLWYN Y FRONFRAITH, June 15, 18—.

MY DEAR TALIESIN:

Your last letter gave me great satisfaction. The penmanship is excellent, and the sentences finely constructed; which shows that your school days have been well improved. I will say for your encouragement, that I received a good long letter from Mr. Thomas, in which he speaks of you in very complimentary terms. I am glad that at school you have had for a constant companion such a worthy youth as Llewelyn Edwards. He is one in a thousand. The young ladies you mention are charming. You must be careful or one of those beauties will turn your head.

"Now, last of all, I come to the first object I had in view in writing. It would give me and your cousin Arthur the greatest pleasure if you, Llewelyn, his sister and Gwennie Lloyd, would come to Thrush Grove and make us a good long visit. Please make my wishes known to them, and let them consider themselves affectionately invited. Let me hear from you soon. You may appoint the day and I will send my carriage to bring you here. When you get homesick, we shall take you back.

Your affectionate<br>AUNT MARY."

Taliesin at once made known to his young friends the wishes of his aunt. They were highly pleased, and after consulting their parents, they gratefully accepted the invitation. The day was appointed. They would start from the "shop," and a word to that effect was sent to Thrush Grove.

The company was together before the conveyance arrived. Their gay and joyous appearance attracted the attention of three young men that sat around their mugs of ale in one of the front rooms of the Red Lion. These were Lucas Pugh and two jovial young fellows from Bangor, who had turned in on their way homeward.

"Lucas," said Ned Price, "by Saint George, yonder is a scene for a painter! Are they not Miss Lloyd and Miss Edwards?"

"They are," said Lucas, "and I have been watching their movements for some time."

"I was struck with their beauty a year ago," said Price, "but they look far more charming to-day. Tom, just look over yonder, and give us your impression."

"Ned," said Tom, without moving, "you are forever in a glow over some female beauty! Your weakness on that point is astonishing! Here you are all in a flutter over two pretty girls! A hundred of them, all in a row, would not in the least quicken the pulsations of your unworthy friend Tom Jones."

"You may talk that stuff to those that don't know you," said Price. "I'll bet half a guinea that the very sight of those ladies will heighten your heart-beats more than fifteen a minute."

"I'll take the bet," said Tom. "Pugh, take out your watch and count my present pulse."

This was done.

"What is the figure?" asked Tom.

"Seventy-five," was the reply.

"All right," said the young man. "Now let my

mortal vision rest for a while upon those lovely beings that have so disturbed the calm equilibrium of my friend Ned Price."

"This way, Sir Thomas," said Ned, pointing toward the "shop." "Now steadfastly gaze on those smiling, angelic beauties that stand on yonder steps! Mark those symmetrical forms and perfect features; those sparkling eyes and bewitching lips; and—hark! Hear you not those sweet voices breaking forth like the melody of cherubim?"

"Ned," said Tom, "the girls are fine, but none of these things move me. I am as firm as the everlasting rock of Gibraltar! Here, Lucas, take my arm again, and count the throbs, while Ned is in search of his piece of gold."

Here Gwennie, in reply to some remark, broke out in one of her sweet ringing laughters.

"There is a laugh an angel might envy! Let the count begin," said Price.

After a while Tom cried out, "Give us the figure, Lucas."

"Tom," said Lucas, "your pulse has gone up to 96." Ned broke out in a loud "Ha, ha!"

"I believe you are correct," said Tom. "It was that bewitching laugh that did the mischief. Here, Ned, is a guinea; give me the change."

"Keep your money, Tom," said Price. "In all probability I shall lose the next wager, and then we shall be even."

Just then a splendid carriage passed by the door of the Red Lion, and a magnificent pair of horses were brought to a stand in front of Mr. Edwards' residence. The coachman was met by Llewelyn and Taliesin, while the girls had gone in.

The three young men at the inn looked on with a degree of curiosity, and one of them with much astonishment. Lucas was uneasy, if not alarmed.

" What can all this mean?" said he, more to himself than to his companions. " Those two fellows are in their best. I must know where this coach is from, and to where they are going. Boys, let us go and see to this matter."

"To us it is of no importance," said Ned Price. "The coachman, I presume, will give you all the information you desire."

So Lucas left his companions, and in a swaggering style approached the carriage. The coachman had on his lips a sly smile of satisfaction. His name was Richard Rowland. But among his jovial friends he was known as "Dick Roland." Now Dick was very much of a wag. With an air of superiority, Pugh asked—

" Who owns this coach and horses ?"

"They belong to my master," was the answer.

" And who is your master?" was the next question.

"My master is so great a gentleman," said Dick, "that the common people address even his coachman with great civility. But as long as you did not know who I was. I will gladly forgive your unintentional roughness."

"I ask you again, who is your master?" said Lucas, looking at the coachman with a degree of astonishment.

"That is a slight improvement," said Dick with a solemn look, "but it falls far short of that civility becoming my station as the family coachman of one of the greatest men in the nation."

Lucas was getting angry: but knowing that an exposure of his feelings would defeat his object, he concluded that it was best to stoop to conquer, and so he said—

"I am not one of the common people, yet I would be glad to hear who is the owner of this coach and horses."

"That is very much better indeed, my young friend," said Dick in a patronizing tone: "and seeing that you have asked with becoming civility, I will tell you that I have the honor of being the servant of no less a personage than Lord Newboro of Glyn Llifon."

"But why in heaven's name is Lord Newboro's coach in this place? And who is to ride in it, and where to?" asked Lucas, with mingled feelings of anger and astonishment.

"Too many questions in one breath," said Dick. "If
the illustrious person that I have the honor to serve
has sent for these young persons, it is for some worthy
purpose." And lowering his voice to almost a whisper,
and looking exceedingly profound, he continued, "I am
not at liberty to reveal secrets. but in all probability
you will soon hear the names of these young fellows in
connection with very responsible offices in the govern-
ment. Coachmen hear a great deal that never reaches
the ears of ordinary servants."

Lucas was very much disturbed. What his next
question would have been no one knows. Just then the
young people appeared, all ready for the journey, and
Lucas, under the stunning effect of Dick's revelations,
found his way to the parlor of the Red Lion, where
Price and Jones were waiting for further developments.

As soon as Pugh was seated, the carriage. containing
the happy four, swept by at a swift rate, and Tom
Jones noticed that the coachman's face was glowing
with what in modern times is called "fun."

"Well, Pugh." said Ned Price. "who is it that glo-
ries in the full possession of that fine rig?"

"They belong to Lord Newboro," was the answer.

"W-h-e-w!" was the united response from Price and
Jones.

"But," asked Jones, "where are those young people
to be conveyed to?"

"They are to go to Glyn Llifon as guests of Lord and Lady Newboro," was the answer; and Lucas took another heavy drink of ale,

"Lucas, you have been most gloriously sold!" said Tom Jones, bursting into a loud laugh.

Pugh was about to make a boisterous reply, when another gentleman, who held the office of Exciseman, was added to the number. He sat down by a small table, and in a moment his ale was set before him. He drank, smacked his lips, held the glass between him and the light, and remarked—

"No sham about the ale drank at the Red Lion. This is what I call honest. Here is to your health, gentlemen. Well, Mr. Pugh" he continued. "how go things at Llangobaith? I used to know every boy and girl in this vicinity. They have grown up into young men and women. By the way, did I not meet four of your young folks in a coach just now?"

"Yes," said Lucas. "they left a short time ago."

"I knew them readily," said John Ellis. "and a more fine looking four put together you don't often find. That Gwennie Lloyd is a perfect beauty; and if young Edwards gets her he will secure a treasure; and so will she. Dick Roland, the coachman, looked wonderfully well pleased over something. I would be willing to bet a crown that he had just fooled some one with one of his yarns."

"Is that one of his traits?" asked Ned Price.

"Dick Roland?" said the Exciseman, as if astonished at the question. "He is one of the greatest wags in North Wales. He is as good hearted as the day is long, but has a perfect passion for sport; and you will find some of his victims all over. They are generally those over whom the people have no tears to shed. He is a very trusty coachman. He was once in the employ of Lord Penrhyn. For the last three years he has been with Mrs. Parry at Thrush Grove. It is there, I presume, the young people are going."

The two young men from Bangor felt much inclined to indulge in a hearty laugh; but an imploring look from Lucas restrained them, and the conversation took another direction. After Ellis had left, Pugh begged of them to keep his interview with the coachman a secret, which they promised to do. In a very angry mood, he started for home, and Price and Jones, in a pleasant frame of mind, bent their footsteps toward Bangor.

Our young people under the guidance of Dick Roland, were enjoying themselves finely. Everything contributed to make them happy. The day was lovely, the scenery enchanting, their conveyance splendid, and their destination inspiring. On their left stood those famous Carnarvonshire mountains in majestic grandeur, while before them and on their left bloomed the vale of

Llangobaith, promising rich and abundant harvest. The lark warbled its sweetest melody in its upward flight, while the cuckoo chanted her short lay on the high branches.

"Celebrated as our Snowdon is," said Gwennie, "and while strangers by the hundreds come from a great dsitance to enjoy the views from its summit. yet living so near to it, I have never enjoyed that pleasure."

"In that we are both alike Gwennie," said Helen Edwards.

"It is not at all strange that you have never reached those rugged heights," said Llewelyn. "There are but few ladies that have. The ascent is long, tedious, and attended with some danger. It is a shame that the journey is not rendered easier and more pleasurable. when visitors would so gladly pay for the convenience. From the *Wyddfa* we have the finest view in Great Britain."

"The sight of one sunrise from the summit of the Snowdon, repays all the trouble and expense of reaching there," said Taliesin. "It is grand beyond description."

"And yet Taliesin I would be very glad to hear a description of it," said Gwennie.

"My descriptive powers are weak," said Taliesin, "and I cannot do the subject justice. I will simply say that we reached the top of the famous mountain

about three o'clock in the morning. The white vapor
rested thick and heavily on the valleys, which gave the
scene the resemblance of a surrounding sea, while
above the fog, the summit of lower mountains stood
forth like so many islands. The great expectation was
for the signs of the approaching sun. Presently the
eastern sky, just above the horizon, gave unmistake
able indications that the great Regent of day was about
to appear. His shooting forerunners became thicker
and thicker, until the firmament was clothed with un-
describable glory and splendor! We stood in silent
admiration while the grand orb made its advent like a
wheel of crimson fire! The sight is far different from
any sunrise ever witnessed while standing on the plains.
The orb appears much larger; and owing to some op-
tical illusion or something else, it seems to be changing
its form from round to oblong for a few moments after
making its full appearance, and then settling down
into its ordiary roundness. While the rising sun is the
most inspiring sight from the heights of the Snowdon,
on a clear day the Isle of Man and the mountains of
Ireland are clearly visible."

"Thank you, Taliesin!" said Gwennie, "I have been
very much interested."

"And so say we all," said Llewelyn.

# CHAPTER III.



## THE MINSTREL AND A PULPIT ORATOR.

The guests were received at Thrush Grove with all that genuine warmth and affection for which Mrs. Parry was noted. While no one was better versed in all the requirements of etiquette, and the demands of genteel society, she never permitted these requirements when among her friends to restrain the natural spontaneous heartiness of her nature. Her countenance beamed with smiles, while her ringing voice of melody broke forth in sentences that charmed every society in which she mingled. She was universally known and admired by the ever ready encouragement she gave to every charitable enterprise within her reach. Among the poor there were hundreds that rose and called her "blessed." Such, and much more, was the mistress of Thrush Grove, who now, with a face radiant with gladness, stood at the door of her elegant mansion to welcome the young company from Llangobaith.

"Ah, you have come! Taliesin, how finely you look," she said, as she warmly embraced her nephew. Then rushing to Gwennie and Helen, she kissed their beautiful cheeks. After this, she gave Llewelyn such a cordial grasp of the hand that at once made him feel very

much at home. "Is not this a most delightful day? I
know you must have enjoyed the ride. I am so glad
to see you! Arthur, my darling, these are your mamma's friends. Yes, kiss him. He is my great treasure,
for which I daily thank the Lord! Now come in, and
be sure that you are welcome to Thrush Grove! Taliesin has written so much about you that I feel as if
we were well acquainted. I am going to call you
Gwennie and Helen; and this tall, fine looking gentleman I shall call Llewelyn. There is not a more charming name in all the kingdom. "*Llywelyn ein llyw
olaf.*" Here, Gaenor! take the young ladies' things
into their rooms. Gwennie, you have grown tall since I
saw you last. Dear me! it seems but a little while when
you were children, and here you are full blown young
ladies!"

"O no, Mrs. Parry. If I am tall, I claim to be nothing more than a little inexperienced girl," said Gwennie.

"And you must treat us as such," said Helen. "If
we get naughty and unruly, please reprove us and
make us mind."

"And Mrs. Parry," said Llewelyn, "Taliesin and myself claim your motherly oversight and correction,
while we remain on your premises."

"Upon my word," said Mrs. Parry, laughing. "I am
hardly prepared to take under my care four mischiev-
ous, inexperienced little children! I will do the best I

can.    To begin, let me order Taliesin and his little play-
mate to go to their rooms, and get ready for dinner;
while I show these little girls to their apartments.
This way, my little darlings!" and with merry laughter they left the parlor.

Although the family proper at this mansion consisted
of only Mrs. Parry and her young son, it often abounded with visitors.    Her parents were dead.    The distant
relatives of her husband were men and women of fine
culture, while her own kin, although not wealthy, were
highly respectable.    Mrs. Parry had wisely arranged
for her young friends' visit when she would be free
from other visiting friends.

At dinner the conversation naturally turned on the
journey and the joke Dick played upon the heir of Riverside.

"Dick is proud of a joke, and sometimes he carries
it pretty far," said Mrs. Parry    "I suppose they partake of the nature of first of April deceptions, which so
many look upon as innocent.    But unfortunately, Dick's
jokes are not confined to All Fools' Day."

The dinner hour passed away delightfully.    The free
and easy manner of the hostess, served to drive away
all restraint.    Mrs. Parry noticed this ease with great
satisfaction, and was already sure that before her young
guests there were days of pure enjoyment.

After dinner, they were taken through the various

commodious apartments, and they were deeply interested in all they saw. At last they came to a very large room that had somewhat the appearance of a chapel. There were many seats, but the absence of anything in the shape of a pulpit showed that it was not intended as a place of worship. Neither did the decorations, and the numerous mottoes which the walls presented indicate anything particularly devotional. High above the stage, or platform, was a beautiful banner bearing the national Welsh emblems; while beneath it hung a fine picture of the harp. In other parts were found in ornamental capitals, " Oes y byd i'r iaith Gymraeg," (the world's lifetime to the Welsh language), and other patriotic sentiments.

"Col. Parry, my husband's father, was an enthusiastic lover of his nation," said Mrs. Parry, in a manner which showed the deep reverence in which she held the name of the worthy departed. "From the days of his youth, he had proven himself a warm friend of our national *Eisteddfod*. While a great admirer of poetry, especially in the 'restricted measures,' the favorite feature to him at our Welsh festival was harp-playing, together with that feature of vocal melody which we call 'Penillion singing.' He not only encouraged this feature of the Eisteddfod, but twice a year he would have this delightful competition, on a smaller scale, at his own home and at his own expense. This room was prepared for this very purpose. In his last will he made specific provision for the continuance of these meetings once a year, with a prize of five guineas for the best *caner gyd a'r delyn* (singer with the harp), and two guineas and a half for the second best. It is confined to our parish. The company is select. Free admission to all as spectators would overcrowd the room, and ruin the meeting. One of the best harpers in the Principality is selected to play on these occasions, and to select judges. The yearly competition will take place to-morrow afternoon, and I am sure you will be delighted."

"We certainly shall, Mrs. Parry," said Gwennie "The melody of the Welsh harp always thrills my soul, and this 'cann penillion' will be something that I have never witnessed."

Just then the loud vibrations of harp music from an adjoining room fell on their ears.

"I was just going to tell you," said Mrs. Parry, "that Lewis Morris, our harper, had already arrived. He is not only an accomplished player, but he possesses a ripe and thorough knowledge of ancient Welsh lore. He seems to know the history of our people by heart, from the invasion of Julius Cæsar to the present time. His stories, with his manner of telling them, are perfectly captivating. At my house he is always a welcome visitor. I would most gladly have him sit with us at the

3

table. but he insists on putting himself on a lower scale."

"Will he play for us, Mrs. Parry?" asked Helen, who, like Gwennie, was very fond of music.

"Indeed he will, my dear, and sing also," said Mrs. Parry. "Let us go in and it will greatly please him."

His appearance was such as at once to inspire respect, and even reverence. His countenance denoted intelligence and thought. His movements were deliberate and systematic. His eyes were dark; his hair white and long, falling gracefully upon his shoulders.

"Lewis Morris, these are my friends from Llangobaith," said the mistress. "They will be highly pleased to hear some of your melody, both vocal and instrumental."

"At any time while your young friends remain at Llwyn y Fronfraith, it will give me the greatest pleasure to be their obedient servant," said the minstrel in the most respectful manner, as he moved toward the instrument.

The harp was large, and of the old Welsh style, having three rows of strings. In this manner, at that day, the semitones in all the keys were easily reached. While the pedal in this respect is a grand improvement, we fail to hear from the modern harp that full volume of sound that fell on the enraptured ears of our fathers from the old Welsh harp.

The minstrel sat down to his favorite instrument, closed his eyes, gave his face an upward, listening attitude, while his white, delicate fingers swept the well-tuned strings; and at once our young friends were entranced by melody such as they had never heard before! At first it moved gently, like a smooth, running river along the verdant plain ; and again like a mighty torrent rushing impetuously down the cliff.  The music was of the minstrel's own composition, descriptive of one of the great battles of the Welsh with the invaders of their country.

"O we thank you very much for your wonderful playing and superior music!" said Gwennie.  "I never heard the like, and I shall never forget this day as long as I live!"

"The young lady expresses herself in very strong terms," said the harper, gently smiling.

"She gives the sentiments of her companions as well as her own," said Llewelyn.  "I cannot speak as a judge, but my feelings are wonderfully stirred."

"Will our good harper play and sing *Morfa Rhuddlan* for me and my friends, and make some historical remarks?" asked Mrs. Parry.

"With great pleasure, madam," said Lewis Morris.

The Marsh of Rhuddlan is noted in history as the spot where a great battle was fought in the year 795 between the Welsh, commanded by Caradoc, King of

North Wales, and the Saxons, commanded by their prince in person. The fortune of war at this time was with the Saxons, and the Welsh were defeated with terrible slaughter. All that fell into the hands of the invaders were massacred. The battle was fought at low water, and the wounded, dead and dying at the return of the tide were engulfed in the sea, while thousands who endeavored to escape across the marsh shared the same fate. Tradition says that this plaintive melody which I am about to sing and play, was composed by Caradoc's bard after the battle was lost."

He then, to that melody so well known to the Welsh as " Morfa Rhuddlan," sung the following words, into which he threw all the pathetic powers of his harp and voice :

> Dead is Caradoc! The army retreating!
>     Wounded and dying, they lie o'er the plain:
> Cambria, fair Cambria, break forth into weeping,
>     Lost is the day and the chieftain is slain !
> · Fallen are thy heroes--the pride of Eryri,
>     Shouting and singing are hushed evermore,
> Britain's proud emblems all tattered and gory,
>     Lie low with their bearers on Rhuddlan's sad shore !
>
> High were their hopes in the morning at daylight,
>     Each heart was merry and swelling with pride;
> Sad was their fate ere the day's evening twilight,
>     Low they were sleeping by Rhuddlan's dark tide !

Lute, harp and minstrel, in strains soft and lowly,
  Bring forth your tribute and sing of the brave,
Mournfully chant in accents most holy,
  The praise of the heroes that sleep 'neath the wave.


They were about to leave, when the young heir of Thrush Grove put in a plea for his favorite.

"Mamma, I want Lewis Morris to play and sing 'Fab, la, la, la.' I like that the best."

"That I shall do with pleasure. young master." said the harper, as at once he struck into old "*Nos Galan*," (New Year's Eve), each line followed by " Fah, la, la, la." With this Arthur was quite carried away. He ran around the room perfectly delighted, while the venerable minstrel seemed to be much pleased.

About two miles to the south-east from Thrush Grove was a prominent farm-house by the name of " Pen y Caerau." Thomas Lewis, with his family. was a member of the Baptist church. which at that time in North Wales was comparatively weak. In the absence of chapels, their ministers often preached in private residences. The large, old-fashioned " gegin " (kitchen) at Pen y Caerau had often resounded with the flaming oratory of many a Baptist itinerant. On this Monday evening Rev. Christmas Evans, whose fame was already throughout the Principality, was to preach at this house, and an invitation had been sent to Mrs. Parry to come and hear the noted pulpit orator. In this she would be governed by the wishes of her guests.

She found them as anxious to see and hear the celebrated minister as herself. So they took an early start so as to secure seats. Long before the regular hour for service, the large "gegin" was completely filled; and when the meeting commenced, other rooms were crowded, and scores were compelled to remain out of doors.

His opening prayers always partook of the peculiarity of his preaching. and were often attended with wonderful power. It was so here. The congregation was thoroughly stirred, and were in a good mood to receive that which followed. There was a peculiarity about the preaching of Christmas Evans that no one ever dared to imitate. In him it was natural and easy. In others it would have been unnatural, out of harmony, and even ludicrous. At first he was deliberate and conversational. He planned his work, and laid the foundation. His great soul warmed as he went on. Sentences strange in their construction and power fell over his lips. Figures never before heard, startled the ears of his audience.

At this time he chose for his theme, "The evil spirit wandering through dry places, seeking rest and finding none," or Satanic agency defeated in a mind preoccupied by holiness. Said he—

"I see the evil spirit rising from his cavern, bent on the destruction of souls.  He was on a wide Welsh moor, and approaching him in the distance was a poor plow-boy.  'Now,' said Satan, making toward him, 'I will get into that boy's heart, lead him astray, make him vicious, a thief and a murderer.'  But to the devil's astonishment and mortification, the boy, with his face aglow with the love of God, broke out in song—

> 'My God, the spring of all my joys,
>   The life of my delights,
> The glory of my brightest days,
>   And comfort of my nights.'

'Aha!' cried the devil, 'this is a dry place, surely!' He had sought rest and found none.

He next came to a lovely village in a Welsh valley; and there by a cottage door, sat a young damsel spinning flax.  'Here is another chance!' cried the devil. 'I will enter into that young heart.  I will whisper impurity there! I will lead her on to her ruin!  But as he drew nigh, our Welsh girl also broke forth in sacred song, that echoed along the mountain sides—

> 'Should earth against my soul engage,
>   And fiery darts be hurled,
> Then I can smile at Satan's rage,
>   And face a frowning world.'

'Ah!' cried Satan, again foiled, 'this, too, is a dry place!' and off he went.

Satan wandered about, weary and unsuccessful, the whole of that day. Night came—deep, dark night. He passed through a still little hamlet. The lights were out in all the cottages save one. There in an upper room, a faint light was seen, and the devil took courage. 'There,' said he, 'old Williams is dying! If I can get him to doubt, then despair, then curse God and die, that will be worthy of a devil!' and Satan chuckled at the thought. He went up stairs, and as he was crossing to whisper evil thoughts into the mind of the dying man, old Williams roused himself, and in feeble accents, while his countenance became heavenly, he cried, 'Though I walk through the valley of the shadow of death, I shall fear no evil, for thou art with me, thy rod and thy staff they comfort me!'

'Ah!' cried the devil, 'this is the dryest place of all!' and full of rage, he hastened away to the place from whence he came."

The meeting closed, and all went home well convinced that the one-eyed preacher from the south was indeed one of Wales' pulpit celebrities.

# CHAPTER IV.



Among the Welsh, both at home and abroad, the man that disdains his own nation and language is termed "Dick Shon Dafydd." The term originated many years ago with John Jones of "Glan-y-gors," a gentleman of fine poetical talents, unbounded humor, and abundant sarcasm. He wrote a number of ballads, in which those persons who, on the strength of a short residence in England, look with contempt on their native land and mother tongue, were severely ridiculed. In one of these "Dick Shon Dafydd" is the hero. The song in Wales became immensely popular, and hence the term.

Not far from Thrush Grove, there was a farm of some prominence, which at this time was partially known as *Bryn y Waerddydd*, (Daydawn Hill.) For generations it had been known as "Clawdd Cam," (Crooked Hedge.) The old house had recently been demolished, and a fine new mansion stood in its place. Mrs. Jones and her two daughters, Martha and Catharine, insisted that from henceforth "Crooked Hedge" should never be mentioned, and that "Daydawn Hill" should reign supreme. Contrary to the wishes of the unpretending husband and father, this new name had been publicly announced in the weekly papers and the monthly magazines. But Daydawn Hill made very poor progress in establishing its supremacy, and to the utter disgust of Mrs. Jones and her daughters, Crooked Hedge, although repelled at headquarters, would rush unceremoniously into the front.

Ellis Jones had a brother in Liverpool who was a man of much wealth. Daydawn Hill was really the property of this Liverpool brother, who for years had rented it to Ellis on very easy terms. Mrs. Jones of the country, with her daughters, often went to Liverpool, staying sometimes for several weeks at the residence of Richard Jones, where they always found abundant welcome. From England they would come home and astonish, as well as disgust, their neighbors with their extravagant praise of everything that was English, with a corresponding coldness toward Welsh customs. Gradually their native language, with which they were perfectly familiar, was exchanged in their home conversation for a wretched bad English. The father gave unmistakable signs of dissatisfaction with this strange innovation, but being a quiet man, he made no open demonstration against it. He, however, clung to his native Welsh, both in his questions and answers; and at one time he ventured to say that he was sorry for the poor English language that was so terribly tortured and mangled under his own roof.

Let it not be supposed that this mother and daughters were destitute of excellencies. Far otherwise. They were kind, and naturally of an affectionate disposition. They were good to the poor, and correct in their morals. But there was in their nature a degree of vanity, and like many others in Wales, they had imbibed the idea that nothing would add so much to their importance as to become Anglicized: and this feeling led them to abandon their grand native language and pay honor to a foreign tongue with which they had but a very superficial acquaintance. Thus they drew upon themselves the ridicule of some, and the pity of others.

Mrs. Parry was really sorry that a family possessing so many worthy traits, had been overtaken with this weakness. Some two days before the arrival of her guests from Llangobaith, while conversing with Mr. Williams, *Ty Mawr*, a gentleman of wealth and talent, perfectly at home in both languages, she had alluded with a degree of regret to this one great folly of these good ladies.

"If they could only express themselves correctly in the English language it would not be so bad; although even then it would be sadly out of place," said Mrs. Parry. "But they cannot put together one grammatical sentence; and it distresses me to hear them. I know that they can speak Welsh with perfect ease. I do wish that something could be done or said to redeem them from this ludicrous folly."

"Will they be at the musical contest?" asked Mr. Williams.

"They have been invited, and they always attend," was the answer.

"Let us hope that they will hear something on that occasion that will be to their advantage," said Mr. Williams with a smile.

Early in the afternoon, and long before the hour appointed for the vocal competition, the invited friends began to assemble. They were received with smiles of welcome, and given the full privilege of the house, gardens and ornamental grounds. Among others were found our friends from Daydawn Hill. There were many present who could converse freely and correctly in English; but the flow of conversation was in Welsh. Mrs. Jones and her daughters, however, inflicted their spurious foreign production upon all who would have the patience to listen to them.

"My dear Mrs. Parry," said the mistress of Daydawn Hill "I very glad to see you. To-day is a very beautiful weather. There is hundreds of peoples here already. I never see so nice place as Thruss Grove! I am put in mind of Garden of Eden." And thus she went on for some time in her violent assault on the King's English.

Mrs. Parry, in spite of all her efforts to appear calm and unmoved, had to smile; and Mrs. Jones had a vague impression that her effort had not been a perfect success.

Here Arthur saw fit to propound a question in unmistakable ringing Welsh.

"Mamma, what makes Mrs. Jones try to talk English, when she don't know how?"

"Arthur, my child, it is not pretty to talk in that way," said the mother, somewhat embarrassed, while Mrs. Jones' face showed additional color.

"I did not mean to be naughty, mamma," said the boy; "I am sorry. I shall not do so again. I only wanted to know why Mrs. Jones tries to talk English when—"

"Arthur!" cried the mother, interrupting him, and taking him by the hand. "Now run to Mr. Williams, Ty Mawr. There he is." And the boy, with a run and a jump, found himself in the extended arms of his friend, who was near by, and had witnessed the whole with laughing interest.

Mrs. Parry made an apology for Arthur, begged to be excused, and hastened to entertain other friends, while Mrs. Jones mingled in other circles and strove in vain to forget the unwelcome question asked by the young heir of Llwyn y Fronfraith.

The daughters had been formally introduced to our young friends from Llangobaith, and seemed to be delighted with their appearance. While Martha and Catharine were quite deficient in correct English conversation, they were in that line a decided improvement on their mother.

" Miss Lloyd," said Martha (in English of course), " you have learn to talk English quite ready, I suppose."

" I can converse in that language when occasions require," said Gwennie, " but I feel much more at home in my native tongue, which I so dearly love."

" It requires to live some time in England before we can talk proper," said Martha. " We go to Liverpool regilar almost every year. Our cousins don't talk nothing but English, and so my sister and me get a good chance to speak English without the Welsh *broke*."

Here, in mercy to our Llangobaith friends, who had listened to an astonishing exhibition of " Welsh broke," the bell rang for the contest, and the conversation was brought to an end.

The sittings were beautifully arranged in a semicircle from the stage. The room was tastefully decorated with evergreens and flowers worked by artistic fingers into national mottoes. In the centre of the wide stage, were two magnificent harps. At the request of Lewis Morris, in order to add to the interest of the occasion, a noted harper from *Pwllheli*, by the name of Richard Thomas, had arrived on that morning. There were three judges who sat in their respective chairs in front of the platform  Five contestants sat, three to the right and two to the left of the harpers.

The grand opening was a heavy instrumental war-piece called "The Camp," performed as a duett on the two harps.  The execution was brilliant and the effect fine.  The minstrels were absorbed in the theme, and their fingers swept the strings as if by magic.  The highly descriptive piece came to an end: the tumult of war ceased, and victory perched on the banners of the Britons.

Now began the competition in *canu penillion* (verse singing.)  For many generations this musical feature has been in high repute among the Welsh.  It is not an easy matter to make it intelligible to the English mind, nor indeed to any one who has never listened to it.  Among the nations we find nothing like it.  The style must have had a gradual evolution from untutored wildness to a regulated science.  Instead of the harp being an accompaniment to the vocal music, the singing, in some ingenious manner, is rendered an accompaniment to the instrument.  With an astonishing precision, the vocalist not only glides through the different chords, but adapts the words of all conceivable metres to the same melody.  Even the *Englyn*, the

*Awdl* and the *Cywydd* are brought into melodious service, and their huge proportions worked in most beautifully. This is done somewhat on the principle of our modern chanting; but it is quite different in many of its features.

The contestants showed great proficiency, not only in the correctness of their vocal rendering, but also in the almost endless variety of their *penillion* (verses.) Some of these were highly meritorious on the score of composition. Others were so light and comical as to cause bursts of laughter; but nothing was heard approaching vulgarity. This would at once have thrown the singer out of the contest. No *penill* sung by one, could be repeated by another.

At the end of one hour the singers were permitted to rest, and the harpers in unison favored the audience with a number of Welsh melodies which had not been introduced in the competition.

The second part of the contest was brief and highly enjoyable; and to those who were not versed in the technicalities of correct *penillion* singing, it was hard to form any opinion as to who would prove victorious.

Lewis Morris quietly laid aside his harp, bowed to the audience, and said: "While the adjudicators are absent we shall have the pleasure of listening to remarks from a gentleman who is well known to you all, as a lover of his nation and a generous patron of Welsh literature and Welsh music—Mr. John Williams of "Ty Mawr."

Amid great applause, Mr. Williams reached the platform and said, "Ladies and Gentlemen: For this rich music-feast which we have so highly enjoyed, we are chiefly indebted to the noble patriot, scholar, soldier and philanthropist, the late Col. Parry, of Trush Grove. [Cheers.] His memory still perfumes the moral atmosphere throughout this whole region of country. Welsh bards of coming generations shall sing of his noble deeds, while the minstrels of future ages shall gladly strike their harps in honor of his name.

Col. Parry was a *thorough Welshman* in the best sense of that term. That means much more than to be born in Wales of Welsh parents. He was proud of his Welsh birth, his native mountains, native tongue. Welsh music, Welsh pulpit oratory, the Welsh harp and the Welsh Eisteddfod. That is what I mean by the term *thorough Welshman*. [Loud cheering.] The best way to honor Col. Parry's memory is to follow his noble examples. I am sorry to know that in many places there is a disposition on the part of some to discard our noble institutions, and our grand mother tongue, and to fall down and worship at the English shrine. There is among us a foolish aping everything that savors of England. Our splendid Omeraeg is thrust aside by vain ignoramuses before they are able

4

to speak one correct sentence in the language of our English neighbors. The race of *Dick Shon Dafydd* is on the increase; and wherever we go our ears are pained by hearing horribly bad English from "Pigpen Bill" and "Frogpond Nancy." [Tremendous cheers and laughter.] I respect those who from a noble purpose seek a knowledge of the English language; but those are not the people that discard their own, and make themselves ludicrous even to the children. Those who go from Wales to England, remain there a year or two, and come back having forgotten their native language, are more troubled with the lack of good Welsh brains than a Welsh tongue. [Cheers.]

This is a fitting occasion to mention also the name of Captain Parry, who walked in the footsteps of his illustrious father. A mysterious providence took him away while yet young, and his wishes are fully carried out by the lady that we all respect. [Loud cheering.] May Heaven watch over the young heir of Thrush Grove! [Wild and prolonged cheering, with loud calls for Arthur.] Yes, I venture to say that Arthur will oblige us. With the consent of his mother he will come on the stage."

' The boy, nothing daunted, left his mother, and in a moment was on the platform. With a smile on his fair face, he bowed to the audience, and cried out at the top of his voice, "OES Y BYD I'R IAITH GYMRAEG!" (The world's lifetime to the Welsh language.) He then hastened down and joined his mother, while the room rang with loud cheers.

There is no telling what Mr. Williams would have further said. The judges came in, and the orator left the stage. Silence was soon restored, and the following adjudication was read:

"We are free to say that at no previous contest have we witnessed so perfect a specimen of penillion singing as we have to-day. Each of these excellent vocalists has one or more perfections which the others do not possess. We have agreed upon two that in our judgment have presented more of these excellencies than have the other three. The first prize is awarded to William Foulkes of 'Gelli' and the second to Thomas Morgan of 'Brithdir.'"

The announcement was received with loud cheering, in which the vanquished heartily joined.

"I have a word more to say," said the smiling adjudicator, "and it will pay you well to listen. Mrs. Parry, in behalf of her young son, has sent me three half guineas to present to the other three gentlemen who have done so well." Here the audience rose to their feet and heartily cheered, while Mrs. Parry, in harmony with a former custom, decorated the victors with appropriate badges. She then distributed the prizes and the presents.

"I now declare the contest ended," said Lewis Morris. „We hope to meet again in another year."

The reader will be astonished to learn that the mother and daughters from Daydawn Hill were wonderfully pleased with everything from beginning to end. Their vanity was not of the offensive, stubborn stamp, and there was under it a vast amount of real goodness. Had they been favored with such remarks as those of Williams' two years before, they would have been saved from their folly. Arthur had given the mother a preparatory shake, and the superior English of Gwennie, and her warm profession of love for her native Welsh, had in a measure opened the eyes of the daughters. When, in addition to this, the orator had brought his forces to bear upon them, they saw themselves in a new light. A mirror was held before them and the sight was not pleasant. The dispositions of the mother and the daughters were so much alike, that when brought under the same influences they were affected in the same way. They seemed to be cheerful and happy, and in mingling with the company, it was quickly noticed that their conversation was all in good, correct, plump Welsh.

This was the first opportunity for Gwennie and Helen to enjoy a musical entertainment of this nature; and with its strictly moral surroundings it had been to them a season of unmixed pleasure. Their animated countenances plainly indicated the genuineness of their enjoyment, while the remembrance that there was more in reserve increased their delight.

# CHAPTER V.



## "RAVEN'S NEST," AND A TALE OF CADER IDRIS.

John Spike's home was some few miles from Llangob-aith, in rather a secluded portion of an adjoining parish, between two mountains. Some years before the advent of the Spike family into the mountain pass, an eccentric gentleman in Bangor by the name of Pagett, who had abundance of wealth, erected a house in this uninviting locality, and against the earnest protest of his family he moved there, where they lived for two years. The loneliness of the situation told unfavorably upon the health of his wife and children, and to their great relief he abandoned the "Raven's Nest," as he called his mansion, returned with his family to the city, and advertised for sale the house between the mountains.

In a few days, while at his office, he was approached by a person of a forbidding appearance, who said that he had some thoughts of purchasing the house.

"And where do you come from?" asked Pagett.

"It makes no difference where I come from," said the man in a harsh voice.

"That house will cost you a good round sum," said

the owner. "A less costly mansion would better suit your circumstances."

"And what do you know about my circumstances?" was the somewhat angry reply. "I ask for no advice. If your house is for sale, name the price."

Pagett, who did not expect to realize the full worth of the house, said, "You may have the Raven's Nest for five hundred pounds."

"I expected to pay much more," said the man, "but you may have your own way," and pulling from his pocket a huge purse, he counted out in notes and coin the exact sum. He then said—

"There is some furniture left. Do you wish to sell that? If you do, let me hear the figure."

"You can have the furniture that is left for thirty pounds," said Pagett.

"You could have said fifty just as well," said the rough looking man, counting the money. He gave his name, received the deed and went his way.

In about two weeks after this, the few who lived in in the mountain pass were astonished to see the "Nest" entered into by a strange family, consisting of a man, woman, and a boy, who at this time might be about twelve years of age. Their nationality was not known. The man spoke Welsh, with a heavy foreign accent. The woman was of fair complexion, with a countenance denoting sadness. The boy was finely developed in body, but soon showed a disposition badly calculated to win friends whose friendship would be of value. Over his comrades he assumed an air of superiority which secured their utter contempt. The father gave his name as Simon Spike, and was short and uncivil in his answers to all that ventured to make inquiries touch ing his past history or his future movements. Thus he remained a mysterious personage in the vicinity of the "Pass." He would often leave home and be absent for two or three weeks, but no one would ever see him depart, or witness his return.

Young Spike attended school not far from where he lived, where he soon became noted for several traits that were not to his credit. Among these may be mentioned lying, profanity, and backwardness in his studies. His development in the first two mentioned traits was much owing to his home tuition, while the last was more the result of slothfulness than the lack of mental ability.

The neighbors well knew that in the absence of all moral perfection at the "Nest," there was an abundance of gold and silver. Young Spike made a lavish display of these much coveted articles among his astonished schoolmates. His lying propensity often brought him into trouble, and once he was thoroughly thrashed by a spirited boy much younger than himself, who had suffered through his falsehood; and more than once he was publicly reprimanded by the teacher. Simon Spike for some reason was anxious that his boy should acquire a fair degree of education, and after some three years spent at his home school, he was sent to the higher institution at Llangobaith, where he found a booh companion in Lucas Pugh.

Since they had left school they were much together. They were frequently found in merry mood at tippling houses in Bangor; but their favorite resort was the Red Lion at Llangobaith. Occasionally they would join with the drinking crowd, but generally they selected a private chamber, where by themselves they indulged in vile speech and malicious plottings.

When Lucas reached home after that interview with Dick Roland, and the revelation made by the Exciseman, he went to his room and gave vent to his angry passions in a prolonged torrent of oaths and curses. He had been insulted by a *coachman*, and laughed at by the young men from Bangor. But far more painful to him than all beside, was the departure of Gwennie Lloyd, sitting smilingly by the side of Llewelyn Edwards, the one he hated above all others. "No!" said he, "Gwennie will never be such a fool as to reject a fortune and accept the hand of a fellow whose father cannot give him five hundred pounds. And yet this visit to Thrush Grove I don't like. Never mind! Thomas Lloyd will see to his daughter's interest, and

of course I am perfectly safe.    And yet I would give a
pile of gold if the devil or something else would take
that fellow out of the way."    And thus Lucas Pugh,
from the abundance of his depraved heart, went on,
while our young friends, in the innocence and joy of
their hearts, were enjoying themselves to the full amid
the delightful scenery of Llwyn y Fronfraith.

---

The morning following the musical contest, Llewelyn
and Taliesin under the direction of Dick Roland, were
making ready to go a fishing to "Nant y Brithyll"
(Trout Brook), about a mile and a half from Thrush
Grove.

"Now Dick," said Mrs. Parry, as they were starting,
" don't you take these gentlemen through John Moses'
meadows, or in all probability he will abuse them."

"His meadows are the best fishing grounds in the
'Nant,'" said Dick.    "I hope we shall not be under
the necessity of troubling the mean old wretch.    At
any rate, the gentlemen will not go on his land without
full permission."

This John Moses was a very selfish and penurious
man.    He hardly ever fished himself, and would not
permit others to fish on his ground.    The boys of the
neighborhood, not wishing to encounter two ferocious
dogs, were never seen in his meadows.

" Now, my darlings," said Mrs. Parry, after the departure of the young men, "go and come at your pleasure without the least restraint.   While you remain here my happiness, is inseparably joined with yours."

"Mrs. Parry, we have been happy beyond measure !" said Ellen Edwards.

"The pleasure of yesterday I shall never forget," said Gwennie.   "I would not have missed it for anything ; and the good harper said he would give us more."

"Yes, and aside from his music, he will give you capital stories.   As my guests, you may make all the demands on Lewis Morris that you see fit," said Mrs. Parry.   "Arthur, go and ask the minstrel, for me, to come to this room with his harp."

In a few minutes the harper was present, and seemed to be well pleased with the invitation.

"Lewis Morris," said the lady of the house, "my young company are perfectly charmed with your harp melody, and I know that you are always glad to entertain my friends."

"I have no greater delight," was the answer.   He sat down and played the "March of the Men of Harlech," "The King's Delight," "The Dawn of Day," and last of all he sung and  played a minor which he called "The Maid of Talglyn."

"There is an interesting tradition connected with that song," said the harper, " which owing to its length might weary your patience."

"O no! good minstrel!" said Gwennie, "by all means give us the story of the Fair Maid of Talglyn."

"Cader Idris (Idris' chair) as you well know, with the exception of the Snowdon, is the highest of our Welsh mountains. On its summit is a famous rock bearing a strong resemblance to a huge arm-chair. Idris the giant was one of Britain's three great astronomers, and in this rock chair he would sit at night to read and study the stars and planets.

At the foot of the mountain was a palace named "Talglyn," whose proprietor was Gruffydd. He had two sons, noble and manly, and three daughters, accomplished and fair. In these features Gwenlliw, the youngest, excelled. She was the idol of the household. Noble sons of wealthy parents had sought her hand, but no one as yet had disturbed the spontaneous merriment of her young heart. But with all her perfections she had an unbending will. To turn her aside from her purpose was next to impossible.

Gruffydd had a distant relative living in London. This relative's only son Griffin displayed unusual talent, and while yet quite young, was settled with an experienced partner as a lawyer. His parents as well as his partner, became concerned about his health, and in harmony with their wishes he promised that he would pay a visit to his parents' friends at the foot of *Cader Idris.*

At Talglyn they received a letter to that effect, say-ing that Griffin would be with them in ten days.

"Thrice welcome to Griffin, for Evan Ap Gwilym's sake," said the father.

"The young man deserves a hearty welcome on his own account," said Gwenlliw.

"Thou hast wisely spoken, my child," said the father.

"Let one feature of the welcome be an original song from Gwenlliw, accompanied by her harp," said Bron-wen.

"I can sing and play," said Gwenlliw, "but I am sadly deficient in poetry, although I covet it above all other gifts."

"Nay, but my sister writes verses with ease," said Blodwen.

The ten days were soon over, and young Griffin was a most welcome guest at Talglyn palace. Joy and gladness danced on every countenance, and the young London lawyer had never experienced so happy a day.

"Ah!" said he, "and here is the famous Welsh harp, the praise of which is so often on my father's lips! I hope to hear its rich melody. Which of you fair ladies will greatly oblige your city friend?"

"We all play some," said Blodwen, but at this time Gwenlliw will entertain us. Come, sister dear, go to thy harp."

With much ease and grace, the young sister took the

instrument, and in a voice of exquisite richness she sung—

> Cheerful are our hearts to-day,
> Strike the harp and join the lay:
> Welcome, stranger, to old Wales !
> Welcome to her hills and vales !
> Gaze upon her mountains proud,
> As their summit reach the clouds ;
> Climb the sides of Idris' Chair,
> View the landscape far and fair.
>
> > Welcome ! welcome ! welcome !
>
> Welcome to our humble walls,
> From the city's crowded halls,
> Cast away all anxious care,
> Chase the fox and hunt the hare ;
> Speckled trout call from the stream,
> Scale the heights where eagles scream:
> Listen to the birds so gay,
> Warbling at the close of day.
>
> > Welcome ! welcome ! welcome !

"Many thanks to Gwenlliw for her wonderful performance," said Griffin, with much feeling ; "and more than all, for the hearty welcome which in the name of the family she tenders an unworthy stranger."

In his bed chamber the young lawyer on that night, in looking over the state of his affection, found himself deeply in love with Gruffydd's youngest daughter.   In her own apartment sat Gwenlliw alone in a meditative

mood. Her cheeks were somewhat flushed, and her
heart throbbed with strange pulsations, which took her
not long to define.

After a suitable interval, our young friend from London made known to Gwenlliw his feelings, and was
happy to find that his love was reciprocated. The consent of their parents on both sides was readily given,
but owing to Gwenlliw's tender years, it was thought
best to defer the ceremony for a time. So Griffin returned to London and followed his profession for a
year. When they met again, their love seemed to be
more intense than ever. She was swift of foot, and she
would climb the rugged steeps, and dance on the edge
of projecting rocks where the mountain goats would
not dare stand, while her lover would look at her with
mingled feelings of admiration and fear.

One night after returning from a pleasant walk, they
joined a merry company at the palace, engaged in re-
peating stories and old Welsh traditions. Last of all
came Gwenlliw's turn, and she went on with unusual
animation.

"Whoever will venture to spend a whole night in
Idris' Chair will in the morning be a poet, a maniac or
dead. Taliesin and Myrddin had courage enough to
undergo the test, and they became famous poets. So
did a lady of noble birth in the thirteenth century, but
she was less fortunate. Her friends put forth every

effort to persuade her to forego the experiment, but she was fully determined to reach the chair.  One night amid the wailing of the storm, without the knowledge of her friends, she ascended the rugged heights.  When on the next morning they went in search of her, they found her pale and lifeless in Idris' Chair.  There is for you a tradition of woman's courage!  Was it not glorious?

"It is consoling to know that it is simply a tradition, and not a fact," said Griffin.  "There is no danger that any one will ever put the matter to a test."

"As yet you do not know the strength of a woman's resolution," said Gwenlliw, with some feeling.  "You may think differently some day."

The company retired to their respective bed chambers.  The young lover's mind was not tranquil, for Gwenlliw's countenance in the room below had indicated some inward agitation.  The night had become tempestuous.  He laid down and soon feel asleep.  In his dream he saw himself wandering around the famous Chair of Idris.  From this he awoke with a frightened, beating heart.  He slept again, and was troubled with the same vision, only in a worse form.  Now he saw that in the chair sat a lady, and by the lightning's glare, he saw that the apparition was none other than Gwenlliw, his own beloved, in whom rested all his hopes! He awoke and slept no more.

It was soon broad daylight. He went down to the room below, where he was joyfully saluted by all present.

"Betty," said Gruffydd to the servant, "go and call 'Gwen;' it is strange that she sleeps so long."

The servant returned and said, "Master, Miss Gwenlliw makes no answer, and her door is locked."

This was indeed strange. The father ran quickly to the door of the room and cried: "Gwen, my darling, come down!" But there was no response. The door was forced open, but the daughter was not there. It was evident that she had gone out through the window to the roof of a lower building, and from thence to the highway.

While all was confusion, Griffin was thinking of his dream; and with a pale contenance, and in words terribly solemn, he said:

"My Gwenlliw is in Idris' Chair, a maniac or dead! In a dreadful dream last night I saw her there."

"My young friend," said the father, "that cannot be possible. Your great anxiety has disturbed your reason."

"I tell you Gwenlliw is in Cader Idris!" cried Griffin. "Did she not admire the courage that made it a test? Follow me!" and he started.

Seeing that he was in such earnest, they followed him. He rushed up the steeps as if assisted by miraculous power.  Onward they went through winding pathways, until at last they reached the famous rock.  There they found Gwenlliw dead, and cold as the chair in which she sat.  Her fine dress and striped mantle were soiled by the rain, the earth and the tempest.  Her beautiful hair, blown by the wind, covered her pale face, while her small delicate hands were firmly clasped.  The young man rushed forward and clasped her to his bosom with terrible lamentation  He loudly called her by name, but there was no answer.  Her tongue was chilled in death, and the once merry heart had forever ceased to throb.

She was interred near her father's palace, by the side of her mother, amid the convulsive sobs of the family, and the bitter agony of the almost distracted lover.

The young man with a sorrowful spirit left for England, while on his heart deeply graven was "Cader Idris," with its dead Gwenlliw.  He bade to Wales an eternal adieu.

"That is the tradition of 'The Maid of Talglyn,'" said Lewis Morris.

"It is thrillingly interesting, and very sad," said Gwennie.

"A little too sad for your young minds," was the reply.  "I will give you a little relief."  He took his harp and played that charming Welsh melody, "The Bells of Aberdovey."

5

# CHAPTER VI.


### A STRATAGEM, AND THE "GYMANFA."

Taliesin and Llewelyn, although not experts as anglers, had had some experience in that line. Their respective luck in fishing had varied. Past success had not been sufficiently uniform to create in their minds at this time a full confidence that their effort would prove a happy one. For some reason, or reasons, perhaps known to themselves, the trout of "Nant y Brithyll" on that day were in such a mood as not to be charmed by the alluring deceptions thrown before them by those gentlemen from Llangobaith and their expert guide. Occasionally a wandering fellow, who had left the society of those older in years, fell a prey to the gay deceivers on the bank of the stream, but the fish as a body, treated them and their ornamental cheats with supreme indifference, and two o'clock in the afternoon found our fishermen's baskets almost empty. The situation seemed to trouble Dick Roland much more than it did the other two. He was a skillful angler, and had been somewhat more successful than the two visitors; but he was very reluctant to return with such a meagre display of trout. Now they had reached the border of John Moses' green pastures, and Dick well knew that if they could fish through those grounds they would be successful.

"Now, gentlemen," said he in the most respectful manner, "so far we have had poor luck. The day has been too clear. Now it is getting cloudy, and we shall have trout. I shall go to John Moses' meadow. I am very sure that he will gladly consent to have us fish there. You will please remain on this side of the hedge until I shall give you a signal to come on. I ask of you one favor. While old Moses is near, please drop your Welsh and talk English. When you see me taking this red handkerchief and wipe my face, like this, you may know that all is well, and come into the meadow. Gentlemen, will you consent to this?"

"Most gladly," said Taliesin.

"And we shall deal out our best English," said Llewelyn.

"Thank you," said Dick, and with a broad smile on his countenance, he jumped over the hedge into Moses' meadow, with his fishing rod in his hand, but did not fish.

He was soon seen by the tenant, who walked towards him with hasty footsteps and in a threatening attitude.

"Now, see here, Dick Roland," said he, "if you think that because you are Mrs. Parry's coachman you can come and take away my trout, you are very much mistaken, and the best thing you can do is to go back as soon as

you can. If you don't I will set the dogs on you·
Clear out!"

"John Moses," said Dick, in a very cool manner,
"you are a mean, contemptible wretch, and it would
give me great pleasure to give you a tremendous flog-
ging. I did not come here after your trout, but to tell
you something that would be to your advantage, and
keep you from getting into an awful scrape. But since
you order me away, all right; I shall go," and he
started.

"Stop, Dick! I was a little too fast," cried Moses,
who was always glad to hear of anything to his advantage. "What is it?"

"Well," said Dick, "of course you don't know that
the young Ashton Smith, of Vaenol, and another young
gentleman, are guests at Thrush Grove. You don't
know that in a few minutes they will be in this meadow
fishing for trout."

"Young Ashton Smith?" cried Moses in amazement.
"Good heavens, his feather owns this land."

"I know that, John Moses," said Dick. "Now get
your old mouth into perfect order and shape to give
 them a regular cursing. Order them from your grounds;
and if they don't start at once, set your dogs on them,
and next week when you go to Vaenol to pay your rent,
they will kindly remember and properly reward you.

Little as I respect you, John Moses, I thought I would give you this warning."

"Dick, you have shown me a great favor!" said John Moses. "I consider it a great honor for those gentlemen to fish in my meadow."

"It is rather a warm afternoon," said Dick, as he flourished a very large red pocket handkerchief and wiped his brow.

The young men were already in the meadow, and at once they found themselves in luck. Splendid trout, in quick succession, were deposited in their baskets, and the English flowed over their lips in commendable abundance.

"Is Ashton Smith the one with the straw hat?" asked Moses.

"No," said Dick; "his name is Mr. Taliesin."

The parties soon came together. "Gentlemen," said Dick, "this is Mr. Moses, who is very happy to welcome you to his most excellent fishing ground."

"Is indeed truth!" said Moses, faintly comprehending what was said, and using nearly all the English in his possession.

"We shall always remember Mr. Moses' kindness," said Llewelyn.

"What did he say, Dick Roland?" asked John.

"*Dywedodd y cofient am byth eich caredigrwydd,*" said Dick.

"Dick, give me your rod," said Moses; "I know where there are some fine fellows, and we shall soon fill the baskets."

About half an hour sufficed to give them abundance; and the young men, after giving the tenant a warm grasp of the hand, *in English*, left the meadow. Under the direction of their guide, they soon reached Thrush Grove, where they were congratulated upon their grand success.

The next week, at the yearly rent-paying at Vaenol, the senior Ashton Smith was present and in a very happy mood. When John Moses paid his rent, the estate owner pleasantly remarked that he had been very regular in his payments, kept his farm in good order, and that it was reported that he raised the best trout in Nant y Brithyll, and ordered the steward to return to him five pounds.

This was done by the steward, who, in Welsh, gave what the master had said, laying particular stress on the trout part of the speech.

John Moses reached home at an early hour, and his wife was astonished at the good quality of his temper. His usual growls and curses had given way to smiles and pleasant words.

"Nelly!" he cried, "'*D a'i byth o'r fan yma*, (I'll never move from this spot), if those trout young Ashton Smith got in my meadow the other day, did'nt

bring me five pounds!  Ha, ha!  See here, woman!"
and he showed her the glittering gold.  "But we must
say nothing about it, or the neighbors will be jealous.
After this, Dick Roland is welcome to all the fish he
wants."

----

The guests, with Mrs. Parry and Arthur, were again
in the carriage which was to convey them to the yearly
preaching meeting, or the "Gymanfa," at *Pen y Groes*.

Ever since the great revivals under George White-
field, Daniel Rowlands, Howell Harris and others, there
has been more preaching in Wales, in proportion to its
population, than in any other country on the globe.  In
no part of our world has the gospel been held in such
reverence by the masses.  No meetings are half so popular as their preaching anniversaries.  They regard the
"Gymanfa" with a reverence akin to that with which
the ancient Jews regarded the feast of the Passover.

At these meetings, eight sermons are preached: two
on the evening of the first day, and two at each of the
three public services on the day following.

Calvinistic Methodism was planted at *Pen y Groes*
at an early day, and now they had a strong church and
a commodious chapel.

The morning of the second day was fair and cloudless, and the heat quite moderate.  At the first service the
house was well filled, and in the afternoon and evening

it was thronged. The singing was congregational, in which all heartily united. It swelled "like the voice of many waters." The preaching was of a high order, in which the old doctrines of grace were handled in a masterly manner by pulpit champions of the old style. Those were the days of hearty responses. The "Amens" were abundant. "Diolch i'r Arglwydd!" (Thank the Lord,) broke forth from grateful lips; and "Gogoniant!" (Glory) sweetly vibrated in a heavenly atmosphere.

At this meeting, some of the ministers excelled in that one peculiarity connected with Welsh preaching —the *hwyl*, or the variety of their intonations. The effect produced by this is often astonishing. It differs entirely from any tones ever heard in English pulpits, or any chromatic chanting of the mass within Papal altars. It is a difficult matter to impart to the English mind a clear idea of the genuine "Welsh hwyl," or that musical style in which the minister pours forth his pathetic passages when under "full canvass." A clergyman who has no ear for music, can never charm his hearers with this melodic peculiarity. The best description we can give is this: It is the application of sentences, in a chanting style, to portions of the minor scale. The minister is never at a loss how to apply the words to the melody, or the melody to the words. They run together as by mutual attraction. The sentence may start on E minor. The minister has his own melodic style. It ranges here and there from the first to the fifth, often reaching the octave; then descending and ending in sweet cadence on the key note. This was most impressively illustrated at Pen y Groes in the afternoon of the second day. The minister's wonderful, pathetic eloquence carried his audience clear above terrestial objects, and for a time they seemed to be basking in the sunlight of the celestial world.

In the evening the interest was still deeper. The last sermon was by a young minister, who could be a son of thunder or a son of consolation, as occasion required. He took for his text the words of Elijah on Mount Carmel—"Choose ye this day whom ye will serve." In the most graphic manner he portrayed the service of the two masters. The vast audience was completely wrapt in attention. The closing part of that sermon will never be forgotten. It will show the English reader the peculiarity of some of those Welsh pulpit giants of the olden times.

"Well, my fellow travelers to the eternal world," said he, "this is the best description I can give you of the two masters. *Let us now divide the house,* and let each choose his favorite. Everything must be conducted honestly, and I will see that Satan has fair play. Let him have the first chance, and let every one that would be his follower acknowledge him fairly and open-

ly! Now, are you ready? 'Blessed forever be thy
name, O Prince of Hell!' Let each of his servants in
this assembly respond to that a hearty *Amen!* [A
long silence.] . Ah! what is the matter? Now or never own your master! I will give you one more chance.
Now be ready with your response! Be men! Acknowledge your master here as well as in the fair and
frolic, or abandon him forever! Now for it; 'Blessed
be thy name, O Prince of Darkness! On thy head be
the crown, and let Jehovah be dethroned!' Hurry,
now, with your Amen! [Great solemnity and long
silence.] "Well, now," said the preacher, "we s all
try the other side. Followers of the Son of God, I
know that *you* are ready to acknowledge your Master.
Now polish your old Amens! Let us begin—'Blessed be the God and Father of our Lord Jesus Christ,
who, although he was rich—" [Here the preacher was
interrupted with an united Amen that shook the chapel.]
"There is for you, servants of Satan! The old family
here at Pen y Groes are not ashamed to show *their*
side! But that is nothing to what you will hear presently. That 'Amen' was only just to clean the throat
for another one that will be strong enough to split your
master's head. Now ready! 'Blessed be thy name
forever, O Saviour of men!'" [Amen from hundreds,
mingled with shouts of joy and cries for mercy.] The
scene was beyond description. To bring that meeting to

a close was not an easy achievement, but at last it was
accomplished by the singing of an ever memorable
stanza to an immortal melody—

> Pa le,
> Y gwna'i fy noddfa 'dan y ne'
> Ond yn e'i glwyfau anwyl E' ?" etc.

The moon in cloudless majesty had risen above the
Carnarvonshire mountains, and the friends from Llwyn
y Fronfraith enjoyed a delightful homeward ride.

# CHAPTER VII.



FUNERAL CUSTOMS.

On Monday of that week, a well-to-do farmer, who had lived about three miles from Thrush Grove, died, and was to be burried on Friday. That long interval between the death and burial may seem strange to the American reader, as our short intervals may seem to a newly arrived foreigner. Griffith Edmund was highly respected, had been a regular attendant at the parish church, and blameless in his moral character. Mrs. Parry made it a practice to attend nearly all the funerals in the surroundings, and inasmuch as she was well acquainted with the family, she purposed to attend this also; and so, on Friday morning, the carriage was again at the door, and with her guests she started for "Craig yr Eryr" (Eagle Rock).

"For one, I hope that, as a people, we shall forever abandon some of our funeral customs," said Mrs. Parry, with much expression. "I shall do what I can to bring them into disuse. While they are kept up we can hardly afford to ridicule Irish wakes."

"What particular customs would you abolish, Aunt Mary?" asked Taliesin.

"I would begin with the vulgar custom of feasting

and smoking at the close of the "wylnos," or the prayer meeting held at the house on the night before the funeral," said Mrs. Parry. "To me it is disgusting, on these occasions, to see the coffin adorned with a huge plate of tobacco, and a dozen pipes. Again, I would abolish the unseemly practice of passing around spiced hot ale at the house before leaving for the church. Such things, in my opinion, are not becoming the solemnity of a funeral."

"And so it seems to me *now*, after having listened to your remarks," said Llewelyn. "But such is the tremendous power of custom and habit, that absurd as they really are, I have never before given the subject a serious thought. I most heartily join with you in hoping that these usages may soon come to an end."

"My mother looks upon them as does Mrs. Parry," said Gwennie, "and has positively declared that such vulgar performances must not be seen at her funeral. Dear mother, I hope that day is far away!"

"Surrounded, as we are to-day, by gospel light, such relics of the dark ages ought to disappear," said Mrs. Parry. "I am glad to know that already in these parts people begin to look at them in their true light. The Welsh pulpit, by its plain utterance, has well nigh banished the 'interludes' of 'Twm o'r Nant.' For this we are thankful. I hope our ministers will next attack these demoralizing funeral customs which make us a laughing-stock to our English neighbors."

"I have noticed that at Llangobaith a large funeral at the church is invariably followed by a drinking crowd at the Red Lion," said Llewelyn. "They generally become boisterous, and often end in a fight."

"It is so, more or less, throughout the principality," was Mrs. Parry's reply, "and it is a shame! Twm o'r Nant's plays, with all their rudeness, had many redeeming features; but these funeral dissipations are evil, and only evil."

"Mrs. Parry," said Gwennie, "many of our ministers call at your house. Have you ever called their attention to this thing?"

"Yes, I did venture to speak once to Mr. John Elias on the subject in very plain Welsh," said Mrs. Parry.

"And how did our great preacher view the subject?' asked Llewelyn.

"At first he looked steadily at me without saying a word, until I began to fear that I had done wrong," was the answer, "but to my great relief, he at last said, 'Mrs. Parry, I thank you for calling my attention to a glaring evil. I will remember your words, and by God's grace, though young among my brethren, I will lift up my voice against these ungodly customs.'"

"Aunt Mary," said Taliesin, "you could not have introduced the subject to a more proper person. John

Elias is bold and fearless, and what he considers as morally wrong will be denounced in his ministry."

The subject was now changed, by a remark from Helen Edwards, who said :

"My father thinks that John Elias is the greatest preacher in Wales."

" He is so considered by thousands," said Mrs. Parry. " We have our different tastes and temperaments, and we are differently affected under the same preaching. We measurably judge of a minister's talents by the effect it produces upon our own mind. When I listen to John Elias I am led to ask, 'Can it be possible that Wales can show anything equal to that?' I am led to ask the same question when I sit under the ministry of Williams, of Wern, and Christmas Evans."

"And the Wesleyans, despised as they are, have men of very brilliant talents," said Llewelyn. " Some weeks ago I was asked by old Shon Dafydd, a very zealous 'Wesla,' to go with him to a private house called 'y Fachell,' about a mile from our house, where a young man by the name of David Rogers was to preach on a certain night. I went, not expecting to hear anything in the line of superior talents. I was greatly astonished, as well as pleased. It was one of the most eloquent and affecting sermons I ever listened to. I went home greatly benefited and happily relieved from some wrong opinions I had formed in regard to the

views of the Wesleyan Methodists.  If you ever have
an opportunity, be sure and hear this David Rogers."

"I will, Llewelyn," was her answer, "and I am very
glad to hear you speak in such terms of praise of
a minister that belongs to a people so much
spoken against.  Some of their views may be errone-
ous, and it may be possible that some of our views are
not perfectly correct.  As far as I can see, these people, in common with the Calvinistic Methodists, believe
the great fundamental doctrines of our holy Christianity.

They were now drawing near Eagle Rock.  The people were seen gathering from all directions, and it was
evident that the funeral was to be large.  Mrs. Parry
and her company were ushered to favorable seats with
a show of much respect.  Presently the fashionable
drink made its appearance, and was served in regular
order from a large communion tankard borrowed for
the occasion from the parish church.  The spiced ale
was poured into a smallish cup, and aside from the
four from Thrush Grove, there were but few that did
not partake of the beverage.  This custom was confined to those families who were in easy circumstances,
and there were but few, comparatively, who could
afford to furnish the " diod boeth."

"When the coffin was well fastened to the bier, the
" clochydd " (parish clerk) rehearsed a few ritualistic

sentences before " codi'r corff," (lifting the corpse), the bier was lifted on the shoulders of four bearers, who slowly led the procession, while the singers chanted a solemn melody. Along the road the bearers were relieved by others, until the journey was ended. At the porch they were met by the surpliced rector, who led them into the church, reading a part of the burial ritual. At the close of the service he went into the altar and stood behind a table facing the congregation. This was the sign that he was ready to receive the " offrwm." (offering). First the relatives of the deceased marched forward and deposited their contribution on the table. Others followed who felt disposed to contribute. The clergyman then carefully counted the money and publicly announced that on this occasion the offering was four pounds, six shillings and four pence half penny. He then put the same in his pocket, went before the bearers, and all marched to the grave, where a hymn was sung in addition to the usual service. While the parish clerk, who was also the sexton, was filling the grave, his little boy, who was well known, stood by with a wooden bowl in his hand ready to receive "arian y rhaw," (spade money). Into this depository the friends again threw their offering, which was small compared with that at the church. It is true there were a number of shilling and sixpenny pieces, but the bulk of the offering at the grave was in pennies and

6

half pennies.  The funeral was over, the people scattered, the majority started for their respective homes,
while dozens found their way to the "Cross Keys,"
close by the Llan, to indulge in drinking ale.

# CHAPTER VIII.



The time had nearly arrived when the company must return to Llangobaith. The only drawback to Gwennie's perfect happiness was the remembrance of her mother's feeble health. On this point, however, her hopes were far stronger than her fears, and for that reason she was not despondent.

On Friday evening our young friends sought the minstrel's room, where, as usual, they found a hearty welcome.

"Mr. Morris," said Llewelyn, "to-morrow we intend to leave for home, and we have come to thank you for your kind favors."

"Mr. Edwards," the minstrel replied, "I shall greatly miss the merry sunshine of your presence. If these young ladies would be pleased with a little more of my harp and vocal melody, I am their humble servant."

"Nothing can please us more," said Gwennie with a radiant smile.

He played a number of Welsh melodies that he had not played before, and ended with a minor which he had composed himself, called "Fair Meinir of the Pant."

"There is an interesting tradition connected with

that song," said the minstrel, "and if you are not in haste I will relate it."

"We are not in the least haste, good minstrel!" said Helen. "We will most gladly listen to the story."

"About one hundred and fifty years ago, there lived near together two families midway between *Clynog Fawr*, and *Nefyn*, by the name of Meredith. Rees Meredith lived with his two sisters, the father being dead. Evan Meredith, an invalid widower, lived with his only child, Meinir. These children were cousins. Rees was fine looking, amiable, intelligent and industrious. Meinir was fair and lovely. Their childhood attachment had grown into strong affection, and in the course of time, the day was appointed for their matrimonial union.

On the afternoon of the day before the appointed ceremony, hand in hand they lovingly wandered along until they came to a familiar retreat where they had often sat together for many happy hours. This was on a smooth stone by the side of an oak, nothing of which now remained but a heavy trunk, which reached about ten feet from the ground. Behind this and touching it was a high stone wall. There they sat and thought of the morrow. While conversing, Meinir's eyes fell upon her own name cut in the bark of the oak by Rees, under which were also the words.

"MARRIED JULY 5."

" My dear Rees," said Meinir, " was not that presumptuous?  Perhaps that, after all, we shall not be married."

" My dear girl !" he cried with a laugh, " surely, you will be mine to-morrow."

The morrow arrived and Meinir, attired in her bridal robes, stood by the side of her invalid father, expecting the young men's appearance who were to lead her to the church.  Then it was the custom for the bride, in a playful way, to hide and escape from her pursuers. This Rees understood, and she was to meet him at a certain spot behind the old church.

The young men soon made their appearance, and reached the house, but the bird had flown.  They made a diligent search, and after a while they saw her in a field near by.  They raised a shout, and pursued her.  With a laugh, off she went and disappeared in the thicket.  They made a long search, but all in vain.

At the church a throng was waiting for the bridal party, while the pathway from the porch was strewn with flowers.  With a throbbing heart, at the place appointed, Rees was looking for the appearance of his betrothed.  At last the young men arrived, but without the bride.

" In the name of heaven," he cried, " where is Meinir ?"

" We hoped to see her here," they said : " we have

looked for her in every available spot, and she cannot be found!"

"I will go myself!" said Rees, and off he started with the utmost speed. Her father assured him that the lost one was not there. The young man ran to and fro, loudly calling the name of his darling, but there came no answer. He soon met his friends, with sorrowful hearts, returning from the church. He fainted and fell to the ground, and in this condition he was carried to his own home. During all that night, and for days and weeks following, there was a constant search for the lost maiden, but not the least trace of her could be found. Rees grew worse, and before long the sister's most painful fears were realized—their brother was insane! He became a wild wanderer, and avoided the society of all, except when driven by hunger. And yet, at times, he was conscious of his awful fate. His favorite spot was on the stone by the old oak. Here he would remain by day and by night, sometimes sitting down, then running around. Now praying, again cursing. Here the sisters, with the tenderest love, fed him and did what they could for his comfort. Thus things went on for years.

At intervals he would become a little more rational, and converse with a degree of intelligence.

"Why stay here more than in any other place, my dear Rees?" asked the sister.

"Here I can better dream of Meinir!" was the reply.

Occasionally he would accompany his sister as far as the house, but would not sit down or eat. During a storm he would never remain indoors, but always hasten to his favorite spot, near the old oak. And a more dangerous spot, during a tempest, could not be found, for no less than three times had the tree been struck by lightning. One of these terrific storms was approaching, and his sister hastened after him. She found him sitting indifferently on the familiar stone, while the heavens were clothed in threatening blackness. When the first lightning flashed, he loudly laughed ; and when implored to come and seek a shelter, he replied:

"My dear Gwyneth, return home, and leave me to enjoy the storm."

"Rees, I cannot leave you in this dreadful tempest!" said the sister.

There was another lightning flash, accompanied by a terrific thunder.

"O thou that knowest all things," said Rees, with a gleam of restored reason on his pale countenance, "listen to the cries of a poor wretch! O my lost Meinir! In dust, or as an angel, I ask. I implore, I pray that I may see her but for a moment—one glimpse! then will I lay my head on the cold earth and die!"

Scarcely had he concluded the sentence when another lightning, with a touch of its wing, laid him prostrate at the foot of the tree. The crash was terrible; and when the sister opened her eyes she beheld a sight from which she turned away in horror. The old oak trunk had been split from its top to the ground, which showed a hollow inside. Through the opening she saw a human skeleton standing erect in the interior. Some remnants of Meinir's wedding dress still remained. The unfortunate bride, in playful glee, had reached the top of the trunk from the stone wall. The top, covered over with leaves and loose materials, gave way, and she fell into the depths below."

Gwyneth endeavored to hide the dreadful sight from her brother, who, by this time, had revived. But he arose and saw it all! He spoke not a word. With his finger he pointed to the skelton and cast one strange look at his sister. A melancholy smile played on his lips. The mystery was at last revealed. He fell to the ground, and in a few moments his troubled spirit had found rest. The two were buried side by side in the cemetery of the "Pant," while hundreds freely wept over the sad fate of Rees Meredith and his fair Meinir."

"With a deeper sense of our obligation than ever, we again thank you and bid you good bye," said Llewelyn.

Each took the harper's hand, and they parted.

———

The remembrance of having been duped by Dick Roland was galling to the proud, conceited spirit of Lucas Pugh. The more he thought of it, the more angry he became, and he swore that such an insult would not go unpunished. He would watch his opportunity, and Dick Roland would yet rue the day on which he took such undue liberties with a person who soared so far above him.

At a late hour, one night, in company with his companion in mischief, Lucas was returning from Llangobaith, where, with a number of others, he and John Spike had indulged quite freely in the proverbial strong ale dealt out at the Red Lion. These potations had rendered them highly courageous, and ready in their utterance, and had added much to the strength and height of their conversational pitch. Whispering is not one of the characteristics of intoxication in any of its stages. They were about half way between Druid's Grove and Riverside, and having much to say before reaching their destination, they sat down by the road-side.

" You are right, Lucas," said Spike. " For the lying devil to treat a gentleman in that way was outrageous! I would pay him back in his own coin, in a manner that he would never forget."

" That is what I am going to do, if I can ever get at him," said Lucas, " but how to go about it, is not so clear. John, you must help me in this. I would give twenty pounds to see that cursed coachman fooled ten times worse than he ever fooled any one else."

" We can bring that about easy enough," said John. " I have been thinking the matter over a good deal for a day or two; and if I have had some help from older heads, the scheme is none the worse for that."

After indulging in a plurality of profane adjectives, qualifying a number of proper nouns, their out-of-door conference came to an end, and they moved onward toward Riverside.

# CHAPTER IX.



Saturday morning was pleasant, and in good season our young people were ready for their homeward journey. The parting, like the meeting, was affectionate in the full sense of the term. A few warm embraces, and the chariot wheels were whirling toward Llangobaith. The journey was delightful, and before noon they had reached the "shop." The coachman had his horses well seen to at the stable of the Red Lion. He was warmly invited to take dinner at Mr. Edwards', but he preferred to remain at the hotel.

Early in the afternoon, as he was sitting alone in one of the rooms, a well-dressed gentleman of a very pleasing appearance approached him, and asked if his name was Richard Rowland.

"That is the name I received at my baptism, by my god-father and god-mother," was the reply. "But, my friends, in order to save time, call me 'Dick.' "

"Mr. Rowland," said the stranger, with a most engaging smile, "my name is Warren—Charles Warren. I have the honor of being an agent of the Marquis of Anglesea of *Plas Newydd*. For years he had in his service a most trusty coachman by the name of Jones, a man that the Marquis highly valued. Two weeks ago Jones died, and I am in search of a person that will fill his place. In conversation with some of the dignitaries at Penrhyn Castle the other day, your name was mentioned to the Marquis in such favorable terms that he has determined to secure your services, even if he has to pay you twice the sum paid to the generality of coachmen. I was on the point of starting for Thrush Grove, on purpose to see you, but I accidentally learned that you were to be at Llangobaith to-day. I have no desire to discommode Mrs. Parry, who, as I learn, is a most excellent lady, but I must stand by the interest of the Marquis. Mr. Rowland, I would not be too inquisitive, but I will ask you how much wages do you get at Llwyn y Fronfraith ?"

"She pays me fair wages," said Dick, "but I would be glad to get more. I get forty pounds a year."

"That is not bad," said Warren, "but I am fully prepared to assure you that the Marquis will gladly pay you eighty pounds in solid gold, with many valuable presents."

"I am exceedingly obliged to you, Mr. Warren," said Dick, somewhat affected. "I shall ever remember your great kindness. Mrs. Parry has been very good, but she will gladly say to me, 'Go,' when she knows that I am to get such grand wages. Eighty pounds! Bless my soul! Yes, Mr. Warren, I will gladly come."

"Every man should study his own interest," said Warren, "and I am glad that you view things in their true light. There is one thing more. The Marquis' daughter is now at Penrhyn Arms, in Bangor. She instructed me, if you accepted the offer, to ask of you to come to Bangor so that she can get a sight of her new coachman, of whom she has heard such favorable reports. They can give you a full week to arrange for your new situation. Can you grant the lady this favor!"

"I certainly can, sir," said Dick. "and that on this very day. I drive as good a pair of horses as the parish can show."

"Very well," said Mr. Warren, "I will send the boy with my horse and carriage to Bangor, and will ride there in your coach."

"I thank you for that favor," said Dick, with a proper bow.

Just then Lucas and John Spike came in.

"As true as I live, here is Lord Newboro's coachman!" said Lucas. "Roland, that was rather a hard joke you played on me that day. I was a little angry at first, but I soon got over that. and I have had many a laugh over it since; so we will call it all right and have a little ale."

"I owe you an apology for that joke, Mr. Pugh," said Roland. "Somehow it is in me, and it is hard to get rid of it. I hope Mr. Warren here will not think that I am guilty of anything that is very bad."

"The gentleman seems to be satisfied, and that is enough," said Warren. "As for myself, I never had the ability or disposition to carry out a joke."

Here a man on a horse suddenly appeared in front of the Red Lion. He jumped from the saddle, hastened to the room, and handed Lucas Pugh a letter that seemed to cause him some astonishment.

"My presence is demanded at Bangor at four o'clock, on important business," said he, "and here I am two miles from home without a horse. I don't see what I am to do."

"I can relieve you from that embarrassment," said the coachman, in the politest manner. "By a streak of good fortune, which I never dreamed of, I am called to Bangor myself, and will be there before four; and if you have no objection to ride in Lord Newboro's carriage, and if Mr. Warren does not object to your company, I shall consider myself honored in being your coachman."

"I shall be very glad to form the gentleman's acquaintance," Mr. Warren said.

"Richard, I am deeply obliged to you for your kind offer," said Pugh. "How soon will you be ready?"

"In just half an hour," was the answer. "I have not

much time to spare. My horses will find it a good long
pull from Bangor to Thrush Grove."

" I really envy these gentlemen the pleasure of their
ride," said John Spike, " and I am greatly tempted to
ask Roland the favor of being one of the number "

" You are a thousand times welcome." said Dick.
"More the merrier," and with a bow, he left the
room.

Then a more joyful three were never seen together.
When they had closed the door they laughed and
clapped their hands. The scheme was to be a grand
success.

" Ha, ha!" cried Lucas. " Yes. it *is* a good long
pull from Bangor to Trush Grove."

" How they will stare at him at Penrhyn Arms when
he inquires for the daughter of the Marquis of Anglesea !" said Spike. and again they laughed.

They soon brought themselves down to a suitable
seriousness, and waited for the end of the half hour.

Presently Dick appeared with his magnificent greys.
A finer appearing, or a faster traveling pair were seldom found. They were entirely safe, and the coachman's control over them was almost magical. A word
would bring them to a sudden stand. trot or run. To-
day they seemed to understand from Dick's voice that
some extra service would be required, for which they
were thoroughly prepared. The coachman came down

from his seat and opened the coach door. The three schemers hastily took their seats.

"This door, like my mouth, has a disposition to swing open when it ought to remain shut," said Dick. "I will therefore, to save you trouble, lock it."

"Thank you, Mr. Roland," said Mr. Warren.

The charioteer was again in his seat. He took the reins in his hand, cast a sly glance and a meaning bow toward the "shop" where the young people sat in a laughing group, spoke *the* word which the horses understood so well, and off they went at a full galloping speed, not toward Bangor, but directly toward Thrush Grove. The road was smooth, straight and level, and the proud grays swept along at the rate of twenty miles an hour. Within the coach there was a terrible commotion. They soon found that Bangor was not Dick's objective point, and that they themselves were three imprisoned fools. They cursed, swore, pounded and threatened, while the laughing coachman was the very picture of enjoyment. They were already three miles from Llangobaith, and at the foot of a hill the horses were permitted to walk.

"Open this door, you mean devil!" cried Lucas in a perfect rage.

"Peace, troubled soul! thou need'st not fear," said Dick.

"Let us burst the door open!" said John Spike.

"Do it if you dare!" said the coachman. "The first one that shows his head out of this coach, without my consent, will feel the full weight of the heavy end of my whipstock. Now mind that, John Spike! I shall let you out when you beg for it in a proper spirit. Now we have reached the top of the hill, and here we go for Bangor. How I long to see the bewitching smiles that play on the ruby lips of the Marquis' daughter!" Then *the* word, and the horses went at full speed for some two miles farther. Here they stopped. Dick left his seat, bearing in his hand a huge whip. He first, in his own comical way, looked at them through the thick glass door. Lucas and John were terribly angry, while Mr. Warren broke out in a hearty laugh.

Here Dick opened the door and said, " Shall we have a few words from the agent of the Marquis of Anglesea?"

"Roland," said the agent, " from the first, I entered into this as a joke, without the least ill will. You had played a good one on Pugh, and he sought my assistance to pay you back. We have been completely worsted, and I take my defeat most cheerfully. I think these boys will be wise enough to do the same. Roland, how far are we from Llangobaith?"

"Just five miles," was the answer, "and perhaps that is far enough to carry a joke. You were entitled to the trial, and it was prepared with much ingenuity. And

7

now, Pugh and Spike, are you ready to accept this in a pleasant way, or do you wish to ride a little farther?"

"For heaven's sake, let us get out of this!" said Lucas, "and don't say anything about it."

"Then come out," said Dick. "Go in peace, and sin no more. But for fear that you may give Dick Roland too much credit, and yourselves too little, let me say, the next time that Lucas and John deliberate together, touching matters of this nature, let it not be out of doors and in a loud voice, at a late hour of the night, sitting by the side of the hedge in the road between Druid's Grove and Riverside; for there is no telling who there may be listening on the other side of the hedge."

"Ha, ha, ha!" cried Warren," that tells the whole story. Come, boys, let us go." And they parted.

John and Lucas secretly cherished much wrath. The coachman took his seat, and for the rest of the journey he permitted his horses to move at a moderate rate.

Dick said nothing about the joke, but it was soon understood at Llangobaith; and many a time after this Lucas had to listen to the remark, "I wonder if the Marquis of Anglesea has yet found a coachman!"

To the great joy of our young friends, on reaching home they learned that the noted pulpit orator, Rev.

William Williams, of "Wern," was to preach at the Calvinistic Methodist Church on the morrow, at half-past ten. This famous Congregationalist came to the vicinity at the beginning of the week to pay a short visit to his cousin, Thomas Williams, who was one of the church officials. A delegation waited on the reverend gentleman, and he kindly consented to remain over the Sabbath and preach. The news had spread in all directions, for his fame was not second to that of Rev. John Elias.

The congregation was immense. He took for his text, "And that repentance and remission of sins be preached in His name among all nations, beginning at Jerusalem." There was a magnetism about his preaching that is indescribable. For about ten minutes, in the most ingenious manner, he arranged his subject. He entered into his theme, warming up as he advanced, while every eye was fastened upon his illuminated countenance. The sermon abounded in the most striking illustrations. When he came to the last part of his text, showing why the preaching of the gospel should begin at Jerusalem, after many other reasons, he said—

"And last of all, it was *to test its power*. At the village of Bersham, where I now reside, there is a foundry for casting cannon. After they are cast, they are tested by the founders, who first of all put in a single charge, and if they bear that, then a double charge. If they bear that without bursting, then they are pronounced fit for the deck of a man-of-war, or the battle-field. In this the casters act wisely, for if there should be a flaw in these engines of war, it is better that it should be detected in the foundry-yard, than in the act of being fired against the enemy in the far distance. The gospel was a new and untried instrument. It was first to be tested; and where on the face of the whole earth was there a more fitting place than Jerusalem for making the first experiment? If the gospel proved itself instrumentally equal to the conversion of *Jerusalem* sinners, no misgiving could ever be entertained concerning its fitness to do execution in the land of the Gentiles. Peter was the man appointed to test this new gun. He charged it, and fired. Three thousand were converted on the first trial! After this, the fishermen of Galilee went every where boldly preaching the word, fully assured that the gospel, which had proved to be the power of God in the salvation of Jerusalem sinners, would answer in every other part of the globe."

The service closed; and all the people were astonished at his doctrine.

# CHAPTER X.



Of Gwennie's parents we have said but little.  The father, as already intimated, was an avaricious man of the world, fully bent on the accumulation of wealth. It is strange that such a person had been able to secure the heart and hand of the pure-minded and accomplished Sarah Williams.  His ardent professions of love, and the bright colors in which he portrayed the future, won her consent.  At that time Thomas Lloyd presented several favorable traits.  His love of gain had gradually crept upon him until at last he became a most ardent worshiper at the shrine of Mammon.  There was in the family no visible signs of unhappiness.  Mrs. Lloyd sweetly smiled on all her neighbors, and bore her griefs in silence.  She was a devoted Christian, and contrary to her husband's wishes, had united with the Methodist church at Llangobaith.  She was in a declining state of health, and was fully conscious that her "earthly house of this tabernacle" would soon dissolve.  Gwennie, under the training of this pious mother, had, from her infancy, loved to pray, and daily she walked in the humble footsteps of the Man of Nazareth.

In Liverpool, Dick Jones found employment in a large provision store, near the dock. Here ships were furnished for long voyages. He received good wages, much of which, again and again, he sent to his parents with an assurance of his most earnest love. In this place he remained for nearly three years, holding regular correspondence with Mary Humphreys.

One day a captain of an East Indiaman, who had often noticed his activity, asked him if he would not like to be a sailor. The young man said that above all things he desired it. The captain told him that he might come aboard of his ship, which was to sail for Bombay in two weeks; he would give him an easy berth, ranging between the forecastle and the cabin. Without delay, Richard wrote home a most affectionate letter, begging in the most earnest manner for permission to go to sea. With tears, they wrote to their son that he might go with his parents' blessing. The sailing day arrived, and the noble ship Bombay, before a favorable breeze, started on her long voyage. Gayly the colors waved, joyfully the sailors chanted their merry choruses, as the proud craft plowed the waves of the Mersey on her way to the broad ocean. But alas! never again would the voices of those jolly tars vibrate in the sky of old England! The vessel encountered terrific gales in the Indian Ocean, and was wrecked. As far as could be gathered, all on board had perished except a negro cook and one sailor, a native of India.

The news almost crushed the parents, while brother and sisters joined in loud lamentation. Mary Humphreys sought a secluded spot, and there poured her young heart in weeping over the sad fate of her own dear Dick. Hundreds in the parish of Llangobaith, besides near relatives, shed tears of affectionate sorrow over the heartrending calamity. Chief among these sorrowful ones were the four young persons so well known to the reader.

A short time before the sailing of his vessel. Dick Jones had written the following :

" My Dear Friend, Llewelyn Edwards :

"In a few days, Providence permitting. I start on a long voyage. My long cherished desire is about to be realized. and I am to be a sailor. I have the full permission of my parents, and am happy. I may be as safe on the sea as on land. but not knowing what may transpire, I will write to one who was the genuine friend of my early years.

" At Pren y Gôg we were poor children, and our garments were of very cheap materials. Some few laughed at us and injured our feelings with unkind words. But on your countenance we always found friendly smiles, and your kindness made us happy. I said a *few* laughed at us. Yes, thank God, the number was small. The abuse I received at the hand of Lucas Pugh, ever since I was a small lad, no one on earth fully knows but myself. I hid much of it, even from my parents, in order to spare their feelings ; and what they did know of his cruel conduct, they begged of me, for their sake, to bear in silence. I look upon him as one of the vilest wretches that ever cursed the footstool of God. He has often, when we were both young, without the least provocation, cut me cruelly with his whip, in the presence of his mother, who looked on and laughed at my agony! When I became fifteen or sixteen years old, he was not quite as venturesome, but on every available occasion he would do what he could to injure my feelings. Since then I have often asked, 'Shall not the Judge of the whole earth do right?' Lucas Pugh may yet find, even in this world, that 'the way of the transgressor is hard.' But my early misery was often relieved by the tender hearts, comforting lips and generous hands of dear Mrs. Lloyd and her sweet little Gwennie, together with the members of the family at the 'shop.'

"Although I am delighted with the thought of my voyage, I am at times a little sad when I think that possibly I may never again see my native land and the faces of those I so dearly love. I commit my all to the Lord, whose 'ways are in the sea and his paths in the great waters.' I send my grateful regards to your father, sister and aunt. Do what you can to cheer the minds of my dear parents. The consent they gave me cost them a struggle, and my love for them is intense. I hope, by the blessing of God, to be the support of their declining years. I have no higher ambition. In hopes of meeting again, I remain your sincere friend

RICHARD JONES."

It was about one year after Gwennie's visit to Mrs. Parry, and in the parlor, at Druid's Grove, in an easy chair sat Mrs. Lloyd.  Her face was pale and thin, but there were yet strong traces of her former beauty.  Her large, dark eyes flashed with intelligence.  On a low stool, almost touching her feet, sat her daughter, with a sad countenance and tearful eyes.

"But, my dear mamma," said Gwennie. "don't talk in that way !  Dr. Evans, I am sure. can give you something that will stop that cough. and in a few days you will be better."

"My darling is ever hopeful," said the mother. "but. Gwennie, my time on earth is very short. and while I have a little strength I must improve it for your benefit.  I have a few things on my mind that I must tell my child before I join the saints above."

The daughter buried her face in her mother's lap and loudly sobbed.

"My mind is as calm as a summer eve," said the mother.  "It will only be to depart and be with Christ. For your sake, I cling to earth ; otherwise, I long for my release.  Gwennie, there are secret powers at work which at last, if not frustrated by a determined spirit on your part, will involve you in temporal and spiritual ruin."

"My dear mamma," replied the daughter, "whatever may meet me, I shall be governed by the fear of the

Lord, my moral convictions and the wishes of my mother."

"That is just like my good, devoted daughter!" said Mrs. Lloyd. "Gwennie, from frequent remarks of your father to me when alone together, I find that at Glan'rafon they expect that you are to be the wife of Lucas Pugh!"

"Mamma," said Gwennie, "I will presently open to you my whole heart. Please go on. How does the thing strike my father?"

"Alas, my child!" was the reply, "he is completely carried away with the thought, and will do all within his power to advance the scheme! To me the Pughs are repulsive. They have never a smile for the poor, nor a gift for the needy. They 'fear not God, nor regard man.' Lucas is a depraved, malicious young person. And this is the one they select as a husband for my dear, sweet girl! May Heaven forbid it!" And the mother wept.

"Oh, my dear mother!" cried Gwennie, clasping her hands, "Heaven *will* forbid it! If the time ever arrives when on this point it will require courage, let my mother know that it will not be wanting."

"God bless my dear child!" said Mrs. Lloyd, while a sweet smile of peace rested on her pale face. "I fear that you will meet with stormy times. You are not a stranger to your father's iron will. Thomas Lloyd was once a better man.  Let us confide in God and seek directions at the throne of grace.  You have moved in good, intelligent, and godly society, and it is very possible that you have seen some *one*, who, in your own secret heart, you more than highly respect.  I trust that before my daughter there is a happy future.  Gwennie, Llewelyn Edwards is one of God's noblemen, and is to be an eminent minister of the everlasting gospel.

Here Gwennie's face turned crimson, while in some confusion she replied :

"My dear mamma, these are strange words to which I listen!  Why mention the name of a person who has never whispered to me a word touching love or matrimony ?"

"Has he not, my dear ?" replied the mother, as she gazed on the tearful, laughing eyes of Gwennie.  "Perhaps not yet, in so many words.  The language of love is not confined to the tongue.  I am getting weary; kiss your mother and leave, and may God give you grace to act well your part in the stern battles of life."

The daughter kissed the mother with stronger affection than ever before, and hastened to her own chamber where she freely indulged in a flood of tears.  But they were not all those of sorrow.

———

The chamber was still and solemn.  The hour which Gwennie had fondly hoped was far away had already arrived, and her dear mother was in the " swellings of Jordan." Pillowed high on a soft couch, the amiable and pious mistress of Druid's Grove was fast sinking into the shades of mortality. There were present many of her neighbors, while their tearful eyes and heaving bosoms testified how dearly they valued the one who was about to leave them. Mrs. Owen, of the "shop," stood by and gently fanned the pale, sweet face of the dying saint. Gwennie was graciously nerved for the occasion, and did not distress her mother by any outward demonstration of grief. She knelt by the couch, with her mother's hand in her own, and gazed on the sufferer with a look of intense affection. Her uncle Morris, from Carnarvon, stood with quivering lips near the couch, while her father looked on with deep solemnity.

" The valley is beautifully lighted," said the mother in faint accents. " I have no dread of Jordan's waves. Jesus meets me on the shore! I want Gwennie and Mary Humphreys to sing together once more my favorite verse,,

> " Cyfaill yw yn afon angeu,
> Ddeil fy mhen yn uwch na 'r don."
>
> [Christ, my friend, in death's dark river
> Holds my head above the wave."]

Gwennie and Mary, both divinely assisted, sung in soft, sweet accents, the eight lines in an old pathetic minor melody, and with the ending cadence, the happy spirit, without a struggle, left its clay mansion, and amid the songs of angels reached the "Bright Forever."

The funeral services at the house were conducted by Rev. Thomas Lewis. The Pugh family attended with all their usual display of pomp and vanity. Mrs. Pugh was attired in that superfluity of apparel which, especially at funerals, shows a weakness of mind. Her husband blustered about with an imperious air.

At the parish church Rev. Hugh Rowlands not only read the burial service, but delivered a fine eulogy on the pious and benevolent life of the departed.

At the grave the chapel choir sung the familiar funeral hymn that begins,

> " Ni ddaw 'ngbyfeillion teg eu gwedd,
> I'm hebrwng ond hyd lan y bedd."

> [Kind friends with all their ardent love,
> Must leave their dear ones in the tomb.]

It was sung in that thrilling old long meter tune, " Bampton," which can never be forgotten by any lover of minor melody who ever heard it. The " dust to dust, earth to earth, ashes to ashes," were committed, and such was the great solemnity produced, that a far less number than usual on such occasions, visited the parlors of the Red Lion.

# CHAPTER XI.



Gradually Gwennie resumed much of her former cheerfulness, and things at Druid's Grove moved with much regularity. Her father was seemingly affectionate—more so than formerly. But the daughter had her misgivings that under those extra shows of kindness, there lurked motives and purposes at the thought of which she shuddered. The frequent visits of Lucas Pugh were highly pleasing to Lloyd, and Gwennie, under a sense of duty to her father's guest, always treated him with civility. This ladylike deportment was construed by her father and Pugh into an evidence of a fair degree of regard for the heir of Glan'rafon.

Gwennie and Llewelyn, as is well known, had been much in each other's society from early childhood. When children they had loved each other with that affection peculiar to that juvenile period. During subsequent years this early attachment had glided into a stronger and more earnest type. Llewelyn was sure in his own mind that there was not a person in the wide world for whom he cherished such feelings as those he had for Gwennie. And the young lady knew that there was but one young man on the face of the earth that could make her heart throb with affectionate emotions. They seemed to understand each other's feelings, and each had equal anticipations. The young man had of late wondered at himself for delaying what he firmly purposed to do, while the young lady occasionally innocently wondered at the same thing.

It was well known to young Edwards that Lucas was greatly taken up with Gwennie's beauty and accomplishments; and he thought it possible that in his conceit and vanity he might go so far as to ask for her hand. Of one thing, however, he was in blissful ignorance; he was not aware that her father was endeavoring to bring about such a union.

He was now about to leave home for the Bala Theological Institute, to prepare himself more fully for the work of the Christian ministry. He had already preached repeatedly at Llangobaith and at neighboring chapels, and had astonished the people with his eloquence and ready utterance. He would not leave without revealing to Gwennie in plain words the honest feelings of his heart. He had given her to understand that on a certain evening he would call at her home, to bid her good bye. Fortunately, her father on that day would leave for Pwllheli, and would not return for several days.

Gwennie, with a beating heart, was in the parlor waiting for the coming of Llewelyn; and thus she mused, " He said he was coming ' to bid me good bye.'

Is that all?  That look he gave me when he spoke the words was peculiar; and his voice trembled.  Noble Llewelyn! little do you know of the depth of that love that in this heart is cherished for you *alone!*  Dearer than ever are you to me since  you  have been called  to be an ambassador of the Prince of Peace!  You come 'to bid me good bye,' and—"

Footsteps were heard close by; Llewelyn knocked at the door, and soon the twain were seated in the parlor.

"And  you  have  come  to  bid  me  good  bye," said Gwennie in as steady a voice as she could command. "There is indeed a sadness  in  those two words, and I need not tell you how much we shall miss one whose society we so highly value.  But for one, I am glad that the friend of my childhood has already consecrated himself to the work of preaching the gospel.  Llewelyn, I bid you God-speed!"

"Thank  you,  Gwennie,  for  your  kind,  cheering words," said  the  young  man.  "To-morrow  morning I start for Bala, and I am here to bid Gwennie Lloyd good bye!  But  before  we  pronounce  those  thrilling, parting words, I have something to tell  you  that  has been  long  cherished  in  my  heart.  I have  been  much in your company, and in you I have found a perfection of moral worth that is superlative.  My speech at this time will be plain and brief.  This is no time for a display of words.  You have known me from the days of my childhood. I have some learning, but very little wealth. For a long time I have greatly loved you, and now, in the fear of the Lord, I ask, Will you promise to be my wife at some suitable period in the future, if our lives are spared?"

With some embarrassment, Gwennie replied, " Llewelyn, I thank you for your plain, honest words. I consider myself honored in being the object of your affection. If you have not known it before, be it known to you now, that for years you have been the only earthly being on whom my peculiar affection has centered. I thank you for your love. To me it is worth more than all beside. With unspeakable pleasure, I promise to be your loving, devoted wife, and share in the joys and sorrows of your ministerial life."

"Gwennie, dear," said Llewelyn, "my cup of earthly enjoyment is full and running over! The period of my study at Bala will be rendered delightful with the thought of my betrothed darling."

"Llewelyn," said Gwennie. "I most joyfully accept your heart and hand, with the full knowledge that the step will bring upon me the frowns of my father, who, as my mother informed me, has purposed in his heart that I must be wedded to one whose presence I loathe."

"Can it be possible that your father favors the approaches of Lucas Pugh?" asked Llewelyn with much astonishment.

8

"He surely does," she said, "and the time is not far away when he will force upon me this offensive subject. His will is imperious, and he may resort to harsh measures. But you may rest assured that I am yours forever. No earthly power can ever change my purpose."

"Gwennie. I am sorry to be the means of leading you into trouble," said the young man, touched by the maiden's heroic language.

"The trouble would be all the same, independent of you," was her answer. "My father is bent on my union with the heir of Riverside. I have no great anxiety for myself. I fear that when Lucas comes to know the whole truth, his malice will invent some mischief against you."

"On that point, Gwennie, let us borrow no trouble," said Edwards. "I have the sweet assurance that our betrothal is well pleasing to God, and that before us there is a happy and useful future."

The conversation that followed was long and happy; and in parting, never did true hearts beat with purer love. With a light heart, Llewelyn sought his quiet home, and Gwennie Lloyd, with her bosom heaving with peculiar emotion, went to her chamber and gave vent to her feelings in a flood of joyful tears.

------

Friday at Bangor was "*Dydd y Farchnad,*" (market day), and the farmers of the surrounding country, with hundreds of others, gave to the streets on that day a lively appearance, while the public houses reaped a benefit. Late in the afternoon of one of these market days, Evan Pugh and Thomas Lloyd were closeted together in a select little parlor at the "Harp." Their good-natured smiles and the freshness of their countenances indicated that they had been there for some time, and the bar-maid's entrance with another quart, was a sign that they were to remain together a while longer.

"Yes, Lloyd, as I was telling you." said Evan Pugh, "he is 'a chip of the old block.' He is father every inch. He is none of your blubbering, so called, philanthropists, who fool away their money on worthless paupers, that are too lazy to work, or on ranting, dissenting ministers. who ought to be shut up in madhouses."

"That is the kind of young man for me!" responded Lloyd. "May he ever follow in the worthy footsteps of his father?"

"And by the way, Lloyd," said Pugh, "my boy, when he is ready for a wife, does not intend to go far away from home in search of one. Ha, ha! Lloyd, let us drink on that."

"Here is to the noble heir of Riverside," said Lloyd, rising; "and to the fortunate maiden who shall be honored with the offer of his heart and hand!"

"And," said Pugh, rising also, "here is to the beautiful and accomplished Gwennie Lloyd, of Druid's Grove, who, above all others, the heir of Glan'rafon admires, and who, before many days, he will select as his bride!"

Here they brought their glasses together, drank, cordially shook hands, and sat down. Pugh would have called for another quart, but Lloyd gently remonstrated, and they were soon on their way homeward.

For once at least, Thomas Lloyd was exceedingly amiable. To even Robin Jones, who took care of his horse, to whom he seldom addressed a polite sentence, he was civil, and actually pleasant. That young Welshman was startled by the gift of a shilling, which caused the serious inquiry in his mind whether he was really "in the body" or not. This question was soon decided in the affirmative. The next question to be decided, was, whether the man who had given him the shilling was Thomas Lloyd of Druid's Grove. This also had to be answered in the affirmative. But had he really given him a shilling? He put his hand in the depth of his pocket, and there, sure enough, was the coin. He took it out and looked at it, and there seemed to be no mistake. He next put the coin between his teeth and bit it. He at last concluded that it was all reality, but exceedingly strange. So he led the pony into the stable, humming as he went, a part of an old Welsh "penill."

"Well, said Robin Jones to himself, "last Sabbath the parson preached on the millennium. Who knows but that this is a piece of it? I am well pleased with it as far as it goes. I am sure it is a grand improvement on the old dispensation. But will it last for a thousand years? A shorter one will answer my purpose just as well." And Robin once more felt of his silver coin.

---

In their favorite drinking chamber at the Red Lion were found Lucas and John. Their intoxication had reached that point which rendered their tongues exceedingly ready of utterance, and their spirit light and gay. They had been together for some time, and we must take the conversation as we find it.

"Her big piety and Methodistic notions, of course. I don't fancy," said Lucas, with an air of self-complaisance, "but when she comes to Riverside, she will throw aside such foolish nonsense."

"If she comes to Riverside I think she will," said Spike with a slight smile.

"But why do you say 'if?'" asked Lucas with some emphasis.

"Pugh," said Spike, "I have some fears that her

'big piety and Methodistic notions,' as you well term them, will lead her to reject your offer."

"Never!" cried Pugh, bringing down his hand on the table with tremendous force. "She will not dare to disobey her father's orders."

"If Gwennie Lloyd does not see fit to accept your offer of her own free choice, her father's orders will not stir her an inch," said Spike.

"John!" said Lucas, "I deserve more encouraging words from you. Gwennie treats me with much kindness, and she is not the girl to throw away such a grand chance. As sure as you and I are at the Red Lion to-night, so sure shall Gwennie Lloyd be mine! On that let us drink."

"There is one thing in your favor," said John. "I think Gwennie thinks more of that contemptible shop boy than she does of any one else, but the blind fool does not see it. To-morrow morning he leaves for Bala, to prepare himself for Methodist howling; and so *he* will be out of your way. I have long watched for a good chance to avenge the insults he and Taliesin heaped upon me while at school. They have escaped me thus far, but my time will yet come."

"I am with you there, every time, my boy!" said Lucas. "I have insults to avenge as well as yourself."

Here the conversation ended. Lucas started for home, and Spike remained at the Inn. The night was somewhat dark, and between the village and Druid's Grove, Pugh passed some one, and had the impression that the person was Llewelyn Edwards. Where had he been? A thought struck him, and the reflection was not at all pleasant.

The intended departure of Llewelyn for Bala was well understood. The time also was well known, and on that morning many of the villagers had assembled at and around the " shop " to bid him good bye. Tears gathered in his sister's eyes, but under those tears there were feelings of joy, chiefly from the knowledge of how things stood between her brother and Gwennie Lloyd. The different sects showed their respects, and Mr. Rowlands, the rector of the parish, volunteered to take the young man to Bangor in his carriage, to meet the coach. He left amid a shower of blessings, while handkerchiefs waved as long as he was in sight.

# CHAPTER XII.



A QUESTION AND THE ANSWER.

With considerable assurance, Thomas Lloyd entered into Gwennie's room on an errand that for a long time had been uppermost in his mind. The door was open. The daughter arose and with a smile said:

"This is a fine morning, papa; I hope that you are feeling as well as you did yesterday?"

"I feel finely," said he. "Gwennie, I have good news to tell you."

"Have you, papa?" said the daughter. "Are you sure that I shall regard it as good news?"

"We shall see presently," said Lloyd. "I hope that you are ready to admit that my judgment is not to be despised."

"And I hope that my papa is ready to admit that what one person may consider good news, may not be so considered by another. When I am told what it is, I shall be my own judge," said Gwennie.

"I trust that there will be no occasion for us to differ," said the father.

"Please don't look so grave, papa!" said the maiden. "Let me hear what you call good news."

"Well," said the father, "you are about to be offered

the heart and hand of our young friend, Lucas Pugh.
This is what *I* call good news.  This grand offer will,
of course, be gladly accepted."

"When Mr. Pugh himself shall be ready to ask me
any question touching that matter, I shall be ready to
give him a prompt answer." said Gwennie in a firm voice.
"He will not be kept in suspense, for even one minute.
Papa, I hope this is satisfactory."

"Gwennie, the manner in which you receive this news
is not satisfactory!" said her father in a stern voice.
"Let me give you fair warning that my wishes in this
matter are not to be thwarted.   Think of it well!"

"I will think of it well, papa," said Gwennie.

The father left the room with very ill grace : pulling
the door after him with a force that was entirely un-
necessary.  The next minute his voice was heard on
the balcony, crying—

"Robin ! Robin Jones!"

"Here I am, master!" cried the servant, hastening into
the imperious presence.

"Why do you let me call you so many times, you
careless fellow ?" said Lloyd.  "Go and saddle Dick,
and don't be all day about it!"

Robin Jones hastened to the stable.  At this time his
soliloquy had to be brief.  "Just as I feared!" said he,
as he took down the saddle.  "Gentlemen, the Millen-

nium is closed for the season. This is what I call 'short meter.' Come on, Dick."

The master jumped into the saddle and was soon out of sight.

———

"Good morning, Lloyd," said Pugh. "It is fortunate that you have found us both at home."

"I am very glad to know that my preference for your daughter meets your approbation," said Lucas.

"It is the realization of my fondest hopes," said Lloyd.

"The manner in which she receives me," said he again, "means more than common civility."

"Gwennie makes no undue approaches," said Lloyd. "I trust, that as a person of good sense, she will accept your noble and generous offer "

"Lloyd, have you any fears in regard to this matter?" asked Evan Pugh.

"In the end all will be well," was the answer. "What she calls her 'moral convictions,' may cause her to hesitate a little, but when the offer comes in a proper form from the lips of the young man himself, it will be all right."

"That will be attended to without delay," said the heir. "I swear by everything that is holy and sacred, Gwennie Lloyd must be my happy bride."

"There, Lloyd," said Pugh, "didn't I tell you that he was a 'chip of the old block?'"

"Please inform your daughter, Mr. Lloyd," said Lucas, "that to-morrow afternoon I wish to see her on particular business."

"I will gladly inform her," said Lloyd, "and I can assure you that Gwennie will be at home waiting for you."

After some further conversation, the master of Druid's Grove left. He reached home early in the afternoon, in a state of mind much more calm than when he left.

Soon after breakfast, on the following day, the father, full of his favorite theme, entered Gwennie's room.

"Gwennie," said he, "yesterday I was instructed by Mr. Lucas Pugh to inform you that to-day, in the afternoon, he wished to see you on particular business. You will, therefore, receive him with that civility due his station."

"You may be sure, papa, that I will do so," said the daughter with a calmness that somewhat puzzled the father, and he left.

The afternoon came, and from her window she saw Pugh on a fine horse nearing the house. He was soon within the enclosure, where he was cordially received by Thomas Lloyd. The young man had evidently taken all pains to appear attractive; and if judged by his hilarity and swaggering style, he had no misgivings in regard to the result.  Mr. Lloyd conducted him to the spacious parlor, and went up stairs to inform his daughter.

"Tell Mr. Pugh, papa, that I will be down in a few minutes," said the daughter.

This he did, and immediately left the premises.

Quick footsteps were heard on the stairs, and the next moment Gwennie, with as much composure as she could command, entered the room.

"Good afternoon, Mr. Pugh," said she, with a slight bow.

"Good afternoon, Miss Lloyd!" replied Lucas, his face clothed in smiles.  "Upon my word, you look perfectly charming!  Of course you expected me?"

"My father gave me your verbal message," said Gwennie, "and I am here at your request."

"Thank you!" said the young man.  "I knew that you would be glad to see me."

"In meeting you, Mr. Pugh, I do no more than I would for any other person," said Gwennie.

"That is noble independence!" said Lucas, striving to appear pleased.  "I believe you know the object of this visit?"

"I shall know it better when I learn it from your own lips," was her reply.

"Miss Lloyd," said the heir of Riverside, with some

embarrassment, " ever since I was a boy, I have adored your beautiful face and graceful form. I always got angry when I thought other boys were trying to win your affection. I swore years ago that Gwennie Lloyd would be my wife. Other fine ladies have tried hard to win my love. In my opinion, you outshine them all. You are well worthy the heir of Riverside. I am here this afternoon to ask you to become my wife." And Lucas wiped his heated brow with a very costly handkerchief.

"Mr. Pugh," said Gwennie, in a firm voice. "I shall never be your wife."

Pugh looked at her in perfect astonishment for a few seconds, and then said: "You certainly cannot be in earnest."

"I never was more so," was her answer.

"Am I to understand that you deliberately refuse this offer?" asked the suitor, with a degree of resentment.

"That is the very thing I wish you to understand," was the reply.

"You are foolishly throwing away a valuable chance," said Pugh.

"I threw nothing away that I consider of the least value," said Miss Lloyd.

"You will change your opinion before many days," said young Pugh.

"Never!" said the maiden, looking him in the face.

"But, surely, you would not disregard your father's wishes?" said he.

"I would, when they are contrary to my sense of duty," was the reply.

"But why am I thus rejected?" asked the heir of Riverside, with a degree of importance.

"My reasons to me are sufficient and conclusive," said Gwennie.

"Miss Lloyd," said Pugh, with much bitterness, "I came here for a purpose, and I am not to be thrust aside. I ask again, why am I thus treated?"

"Then, in a few words, I will gratify you," said the young lady. "You cannot command my respect, much less my affection. I look upon your moral character as decidedly bad."

"You will yet be glad to embrace what you now spurn," said Lucas.

"Let me warn you against that delusion," said Gwennie. "Go your way, Mr. Pugh, and remember that you are never to trouble me with this matter again."

"Miss Lloyd," cried Lucas, losing all control of himself, "I swear by all the powers of heaven that you must be mine! Has not another, more in harmony with your religious notions, worked himself into your graces?"

"If there has, it is simply our own business," was the answer.

"Miss Gwennie Lloyd," said Lucas Pugh with a wicked look, Llewelyn Edwards shall never be your husband! I have my settled purpose, and woe be to that man that will dare, in this matter, stand between me and yourself."

"Those are the words of a malicious coward," said Gwennie, in a fearless tone. "Llewelyn Edwards will dare do anything that he considers honorable, and so will I. To me your presence is exceedingly offensive, and this interview must close."

In a few minutes the heir of Glan'rafon, pale with rage, was riding toward home at a fearful rate.

At Riverside, in a room fantastically furnished, sat Evan Pugh and his gay English wife, engaged in a lively conversation. The subject seemed to be agreeable to both, and the master and mistress appeared to good advantage. It was said by those who professed to know, that at other times those countenances had indicated angry passions, and that things had often gone so far as for the head of Evan Pugh to be made a target for a certain spry little woman to prove the accuracy of her aim, by firing at it a loaded China teapot. If such pastimes had ever been indulged in within the walls of that mansion, there were no evidences of it now.

"Aside from her Methodistic notions, she is a fine

young lady," said Evan. "In regard to her beauty, there can be but one opinion."

"But, Evan," said Mrs. Pugh thoughtfully, "is it not possible, after all, that she will stubbornly refuse Lucas' offer ?"

"Moonshine and nonsense!" cried the husband in an elevated voice. "The girl is no fool, and she will not throw away such a grand opportunity."

"That is the common sense view of it, Evan," said the mistress, "but girls are not always governed by it."

"Lloyd is governed by it, and that will answer our purpose," said Pugh. "The idea— But yonder he comes! Good heavens, how he runs that horse! I fear that everything is not pleasant."

By this time his son was by the house. His face denoted terrible wrath, and while a servant led away the panting steed, the late rider joined the astonished parents. He threw himself into a chair and gave vent to his feelings in a plurality of sentences too vile to be chronicled.

"Be calm my son!" said the father with as much composure as his own anger would permit. "Thomas Lloyd will subdue her stubborn will."

"Never!" cried Lucas. "Words have passed between us that leave me no hope! I was ordered out of her presence, while her lips were full of the praise of that sanctimonious shop boy."

"Shop boy!" cried the father in evident amazement. "That penniless, dissenting ranter, in preference to the heir of Glan'rafon!"

"I am perfectly satisfied that the shop boy is her accepted lover," said Lucas, wiping his face.

Then followed from the lips of the father a torrent of oaths; and after having relieved himself thus, he left the room, while the mother and son remained together.

"Lucas, I feel this insult to the quick!" said the mother with compressed lips and flashing eyes: "and it will be bitterly avenged! Let us swear together, on this spot, that the shop boy shall never be her husband!"

"Mother, I do so swear!" said the son, rising: "Riverside has brains enough to work the wires, and if we need safe and powerful helps, I know where they can be found."

The interview closed, and the mother and son went their way to invent hellish plots against the innocent.

# CHAPTER XIII.


## A COVERT FROM THE TEMPEST.

Gwennie was in her room. Before her stood her father, who had come in rather abruptly. The daughter, in spite of her resolution, showed a degree of nervousness. She was somewhat pale, and no wonder, for she was well aware that a storm was about to pour its fury upon her head. From her behavior, her father was not able to satisfy himself as to the exact situation. The last words he had heard from his daughter had given him some hope, but still his fears predominated. He would soon know, and he was prepared for the discovery, whatever might be its nature.

"Gwennie, I trust that your interview with Mr. Pugh was pleasant, and that his presence was highly agreeable to you," said the father.

"No, papa! I know of no person on the face of the whole earth whose presence to me is so offensive," said Gwennie, in a low, but firm voice.

"And you rejected his offer?" said Lloyd, with a frown on his countenance.

"Yes, papa, without the least hesitation," said Gwennie.

"And thus you have discarded my wishes, and disobeyed my commands?" said the father.

"Yes, papa," said Gwennie, "but ‚I have a dear mother in heaven whose wishes I have not disregarded."

"None of your Methodist nonsense!" cried her father. "I am master in this house, and my wishes must be respected. You must undo this mischief, repent of your folly, and let me invite the young man to another interview."

"Papa, I know that you are master in this house," said Gwennie, "but you are not the master of my conscience and religious convictions. Lucas Pugh and myself have had our first and last interview. No influence on earth can change my mind. I am of proper age to act for myself, and it is not within the power of even my father to frighten me from my purpose."

"Those daring words, unless soon retracted, will not go unpunished!" said Lloyd. "For years I have looked forward to your union with this young man. Your foolish Methodism has run away with your reason, and you have madly rejected a grand offer."

"I am highly pleased with my action, papa," said the daughter. "Mr. Pugh can easily find a lady much more in harmony with the moral taste and the domestic atmosphere of Riverside. My taste runs in an opposite direction."

"So I see," said the father with a sneer. "I suspect

that that bawling dissenter, Llewelyn Edwards, has of late worked himself into your graces. I warn you, Gwennie Lloyd, against giving encouragement to that religious enthusiast, who cannot command one hundred pounds."

" Llewelyn commands something of much more value than an hundred, or an hundred thousand pounds!" said the daughter with some spirit. "His blameless life, piety, amiability, scholarship and splendid talents command the universal respect of the community."

"As your suitor, let him never dare to darken my door!" said Lloyd.

"In that capacity he will never darken any door," said Gwennie with cheeks aglow. " Let not my father speak in disdainful terms of Llewelyn Edwards in the presence of his betrothed!"

" Betrothed, eh?" cried the father. "Curses on your heads! Is this the reward I receive for bestowing upon you expensive advantages? You have rendered yourself unworthy of my protection, and unless you renounce your crazy purpose and do my bidding, you must leave this house. I give you two weeks to make up your mind."

"You are very indulgent, papa!" said Gwennie with a smile. "Two hours will do just as well. Be it then two weeks."

"What I say is not an idle threat," said the father. I fully mean it all."

"I believe you, papa," said Gwennie, "and I am fully prepared for the emergency."

Morris Williams lived at Carnarvon, and was a man highly respected on account of his upright dealings and deeds of charity. For years he had been engaged in successful merchandise, and was the possessor of much wealth. About three years before this he had lost a most amiable wife, and was left a childless widower. Soon after the death of his companion he left his fine mansion, with all its rich adornments, in the care of a person who would well see that every thing was kept in order, and took rooms at the "Goat Inn." at that time a prominent hotel in the town.

While for Gwennie, Morris Williams had always cherished a strong attachment, his nobleness of soul would not permit him to entertain very favorable opinions of her father. When his sister consented to become Lloyd's wife, he was much grieved, because he saw even then that his mind was avaricious.

From whom, therefore, in this emergency, could Gwennie naturally expect help and advice but from her dear "Uncle Morris?" She sat down and wrote to him a long letter, reviewing the whole situation. It ended thus:

"And now, my dear uncle Morris, I have told you all.

I have rejected a wicked, swearing, drinking and Sabbath-breaking person, with abundance of gold, and have accepted the heart and hand of a respectable, pious and scholarly young man who is comparatively poor.  For this I am about to be disowned by an enraged father.  I am sure that you will honor my judgment.  But oh! my dear uncle, where shall I go?  My probation at Llwyn y Derwydd will close on the 25th.

Your own loving niece,

GWENNIE LLOYD."

Morris Williams, on his way from his place of business at the close of the day, called at the post office, where, as usual, a number of letters were waiting for him.  Without even looking at the address, he put them in his pocket, walked to his room at the hotel, and here they were examined.

"Ah!" said he, "here is one from Llangobaith, and from Gwennie at that."  It was soon opened.  The uncle's countenance while reading it underwent several changes.  He began with a smile; then came astonishment, then an unmistakable frown, and ending again in a smile.  He carefully refolded the letter and put it in his pocket.  He then rose and paced his room in silence, while his mind was powerfully agitated.  At last he gave utterance to his thoughts in low speech.

"Disown her, eh?  Disown *Gwennie*, the pure-hearted and accomplished *Gwennie*, the loving daughter of my sister Sarah!  *Gwennie*, the pride of Llangobaith, and the pet of the community! *Disown* her, eh? Oh! Tom Lloyd, at last you have reached your lowest degradation! Yes, Lucas Pugh has *money*, and that is all that Tom admires. Lucas Pugh for *Gwennie!* An *angel* put into the bosom of a swearing tippler! Of course she rejected him, and she clings to her noble Llewelyn, though threatened with expulsion. Noble Gwennie! 'But oh! my dear uncle, where shall I go ' cries my darling. Thank God! I know exactly where you shall go."

At once he sat down and wrote to his niece the following:

" DEAR GWENNIE:

Your letter has created in my mind peculiar emotions. I will not indulge in harsh language against your father. I fully justify your action, both in your choice and rejection. From what I know of Thomas Lloyd, I think he will carry out his mad threat. Be not dismayed, my dear Gwennie. On the afternoon of the 25th, at 2 o'clock, I will be at Druid's Grove with a carriage. Have all things in readiness for your departure. Say nothing to your father in regard to my coming. You may rest assured that, Providence permitting, I will be there at that hour. My house, in which I have not lived for three years, will be in perfect order to receive you. This letter will be sent in harmony with your directions.

Your own

UNCLE MORRIS."

The two weeks probation had come to an end, and the 25th was as beautiful a day as ever dawned on the vale of Llangobaith. Gwennie, wholly unbeknown to her father, had fully completed the preparation for her exit. During the two weeks, she had worn a cheerful appearance, and even the maid-servants until this day, had not suspected that anything was wrong. From her easy behavior, the father was inclined to think that his threatening had produced the desired effect. With her cheerful countenance, the uncle's letter had much to do.

It was half-past one in the afternoon, and Gwennie was in her room making mental preparation for what she knew was close at hand. Her father's well-known footsteps were heard, and presently he was in the room.

"Gwennie," said he, "this is a most lovely day, and the view from your window is charming."

"It is indeed delightful," was her reply, "and I have enjoyed it for many a happy year."

"And I hope you will enjoy it for many years to come," said the father; "if not from that window, yet from some window where the view of the vale of Llangobaith will be equally delightful."

"I have no desire to change this window for any other, at least for many years, papa, if you should be pleased to have me remain."

"You know the conditions I gave you, and I trust

that, like a sensible girl, you have concluded to comply
with them.   This day ends the two weeks within which
you were to make up your mind."

"I told you then, papa, that the period was altogether
too long," said the daughter.   "Your conditions are of
such a nature that I cannot comply with them."

"And you tell me that to my face again, do you?"
said the father in a stern voice.   "Do you remember
what I said would be the consequence of your disobe-
dience?"

"Oh yes, papa! I remember well what you said.   I
could not possibly have forgotten that."

"And don't you believe that I was in earnest?" was
the next question.

"You were certainly in earnest, papa, and so was I."
said Gwennie.

"And I fully purpose to carry out my threat." said
the father.

"And I fully purpose to. be the happy wife of Llewelyn Edwards," said the daughter.

"Now, miss, no more of this impudence under my
roof.   Pick up what belongs to you and get ready to
leave this very day!"

"My things are all packed. papa, and I am ready to
go," she said.

"But where in heaven's name are you going?" asked
Lloyd.

"That certainly cannot concern the man that turns his only child out of doors," said Gwennie with much feeling.

"Conquer your stubbornness, and accept the hand of Mr. Pugh with my blessing," said Lloyd.

"I have accepted the hand of another, whose shoes Lucas Pugh is not worthy to carry. I receive the blessing of God and the smiles of my sainted mother," said the maiden.

"Confound your religious nonsense!" said Lloyd. "I will no longer listen to such twaddle. You must leave my—"

Before the sentence was finished, an elegant carriage drawn by two spirited horses, came into the yard, right beneath the window of the daughter's room. The driver left his seat, opened the carriage door, and to the utter dismay of Thomas Lloyd, Morris Williams appeared, and entered the house. He warmly embraced his niece, and paid but little attention to the master of the house.

"Well, Tom," said Morris, "I have heard, by the way, that you have a disobedient daughter."

"You have heard the truth," said Lloyd.

"And I have heard, also, that you have given this disobedient child timely warning that unless she would change her mind, you would banish her from your house."

"That is the correct story," said Lloyd.

"Now, Tom, you are a very bad specimen of humanity!  Gwennie is perfectly right in rejecting that rough, brainless booby, and she acts wisely in accepting the hand of one of the finest young men in North Wales.  And for this she is disowned by her father!  Shame on you, Tom Lloyd," said Morris Williams.

"I am not to be thus abused in my own house!" said Lloyd.  "If you have any business here, you had better attend to it and leave."

"Gwennie," asked Williams, "are you ready?"

"All ready, uncle," was the reply.  "My trunks are up stairs"

"Ned," said the uncle, addressing his coachman, "go with this lady and bring down her trunks."

This was done in a few minutes.  The two entered the carriage. the door was closed, and at a rapid rate they were on their way toward Carnarvon.

----

The next meeting of Lucas Pugh and John Spike was in the same private room at the Red Lion.  The countenance of the former had undergone a change, but not for the better.  The haughty assurance of the last meeting had disappeared to give room to stormy passions and malignant rage.  He poured out a violent stream of vile language. With clenched hands, he vowed vengeance on the heads of very innocent persons. His companion was much more composed, and was secretly well pleased with the way things were shaping. Ever since he had left school, John Spike had wickedly longed for an opportunity to empty his mean revenge on the heads of two persons. Had Lucas realized his monstrous anticipations touching Gwennie Lloyd, the "shop boy" would have soon been dismissed from his mind, and Spike would have to bring about his revenge alone. But since his friend had met a decided repulse, his favored time seemed to be drawing nigh; and under a cover of pretended sympathy, he inwardly laughed at Pugh's calamity.

"Lucas," said he, "things have turned out as I feared they would, and it is no wonder that you rip and tear. If it had been my case, I presume I would have gone on just as you do. But this bellowing and frothing, pounding the table and smashing tumblers, are not the best things to do under the circumstances. Now stop your raving, and let us look the matter over and decide upon our future movements. That fellow has been plotting against you for years, and now he thinks the job is finished. I know that you have too much spirit to submit tamely to such an outrage as that."

"I will have revenge as true as my name is Pugh!" said the rejected Lucas, trembling with anger. "My one great hope is blasted. But, John Spike, that Llewelyn Edwards shall never be the husband of Gwennie Lloyd !"

"That's the right kind of talk !" said Spike. " Give me your hand on that, old fellow! Now let us drink. Here are curses and bad luck to Llewelyn Edwards and Taliesin Roberts !" and their glasses were emptied.

" Lucas," continued Spike, " to upset their calculation requires a good deal of ingenuity. When among these Llangobaith people, we must hide our wrath and keep our mouths closed. Then in case the ' shop boy ' should come to grief, the source of his trouble would not be suspected. Lucas, you may count on my hearty assistance, and if one Spike is not enough, you well know where a stronger and a heavier Spike can be found. Ha, ha !"

" My mother feels this insult, and is fully determined on revenge," said Lucas. "She will gladly stand by us ; and when money is needed, she knows where to find it."

There in that little drinking parlor those two depraved wretches remained for hours plotting mischief, and if some of their measures lacked ingenuity, they were never wanting in malice.

# CHAPTER XIV.



Although Gwennie had found at Carnarvon a sweet asylum, and in her uncle a most affectionate protector, yet the peculiarity of the situation rendered her at times somewhat despondent. No effort on the part of Morris Williams was wanting to cheer her mind and cause her days to pass away pleasautly. With this in view, and from the high esteem in which he held Helen Edwards, he sent his carriage to Llangobaith with an earnest request to the young lady, with the consent of her father, to accompany his servant back, and spend a few days with Gwennie at Carnarvon. This being in perfect harmony with Miss Edwards' mind, the two maidens were soon in the sweet enjoyment of each other's society.

Among the warm friends of Mr. Williams was a family living in a farm-house, a few miles out of town. It was called *Hafod* (Havod). This household was justly celebrated for its musical talent. It consisted of the parents, three sons and two daughters. The interests of the farm did not suffer from their love of music. The sons were ever faithful to their agricultural duties, while the daughters were diligent in all the requirements of the home. In his younger years, Evan Hughes, the father, was considered the best singer in the parish, while Mary Lewis, his wife, who still retained her maiden name, was famous for the purity and compass of her voice. In the line of instrumental music, the father had aspired to nothing higher than the *Jews-harp*. On this he was indeed a master, and his celebrity was extensive. At an early age the children, one after the other, had given unmistakable evidence of musical genius, and in this they were encouraged by their parents. Owen played the harp, William the violin, and Henry the flute; while Sarah and Miriam were content with their fine powers as vocalists. Oftentimes the good music-loving neighbors would visit the old mansion for an hour or two on an evening, when they would always find a hearty welcome. Occasionally, Evan Hughes would invite a number of choice friends, well knowing that his boys and girls never failed to make such evening gatherings highly enjoyable. To one of these entertainments, Morris Williams had received a most cordial invitation from the head of the family. "Come without fail," he had written, "and if you have any particular friends that are lovers of music, bring them with you."

"Girls, are you lovers of instrumental music?" asked Morris Williams one morning, with a pleasant smile.

"Indeed we are, uncle!" promptly answered Gwennie. "At Thrush Grove we were perfectly charmed with harp melody, and I long to hear more."

He then gave them a brief history of the musical family at the *Havod*, and read to them the pressing invitation, remarking, "I would much enjoy such a musical feast, and if my two young ladies will accompany me, I shall be glad to be their guide."

" We shall most gladly accept your kind offer." said Helen, " not only for the sake of the music, but it will be a rich treat to see such a family."

"The parents are of the old genuine Welsh stamp," said Mr. Williams, "and it may be well for you to understand the situation before we go.  They have well-furnished rooms, but Evan Hughes' kingdom is in the old commodious "gegin," (kitchen).  Here he always entertains his friends, and here, I presume, will be the entertainment to-night."

"To me it will be all the better," said Gwennie.  "I am sure that it is going to be grand!"

They were soon on their way to the Hafod, and after a delightful ride they reached their destination.  It was a large, old-fashioned farm-house.  A great, heavy oaken door, which had never tasted of paint, opened into a wide hall, on the left of which was the large kitchen, with great, closely-matched slate slabs for a floor.  At the farthest end of this room was a large, open chimney, with a fire-place, and hearth extensive enough to seat two dozen persons. On one side of this old "gegin" was a long eating-table, scrubbed into perfect whiteness. Then there were rows of shelves, on which were placed in regular order a large number of wooden trenchers, as white as the before mentioned table. A little farther on was the old Welsh "dressel." This was of oak, black with age, and highly polished. On its upper part the pewter plates shone brightly in the light of the blazing fire. There were abundance of oaken chairs and three-legged stools. Into this genial, cheerful, old Welsh farm kitchen, our friends from Carnarvon were ushered, and received by the family with such a spontaneous welcome that at once made them feel perfectly at home.

There were many present, and ranging in ages from childhood to old age. Soon Owen was heard tuning his harp. The flute was the standard of pitch. Then Henry put his violin in harmony with the others.

"I move that our kind host Evan Hughes be respectfully asked to give us one of his wonderful Jewsharp solos," said Thomas Jones of *Glan 'Rhyd*.

This pleased the company, and as Evan Hughes had no objection, he took out of its case the ancient instrument.

"You are very kind," said the old gentleman. "My poor playing will take but little of your time." To me there are sweet and peculiar associations in the tones of

this simple instrument.  They carry me back to the
scenes of  fifty years ago, when around the May pole,
the lads and lasses merrily skipped in harmony with its
vibrations.  There are but few of us left!  But this is
no time for sadness, and I will give you something
lively."  And so he did, with an accuracy, volume and
expression that was truly astonishing.  He was heartily
cheered by all  the strangers present,  and with evident
satisfaction Evan Hughes put his "ysturmant" in its
case.

The company was next entertained by several harp
solos.  Owen was a master player, and felt the inspiration of his own music.  Next came several duetts on the
harp and violin, producing a fine effect.  Then the three
instruments united in a grand chorus, which was loudly
cheered.

The order was now changed into "canu penillion,"
(singing verses), that feature of  harp and vocal melody
to which  the reader was  introduced at  Thrush Grove.
There were many present aside from the family, who
were well at  home in this  scientific branch.  The two
daughters entered heartily into this feature, their voices
beautifully blending with the harp in harmony with
the technical rules of " penillion " singing.

After this there was a season of story-telling.  There
were  those present who were  experts in this rare ac-

complishment.    The first called upon was Robert Cyffin, the weaver.    He chose for his subject—

ROBIN DDU DDEWIN, (Robin the black magician.)

" We know next to nothing of this strange man except by tradition.    He was believed by many to be in possession of superhuman knowledge.    He made such pretentions, when in reality his success was only the result of his keen penetration.    He was of very dark complexion, and this was the reason that he was called 'Black Robin.'

The wife of a nobleman in South Wales lost some very valuable pearls, the gift of a departed sister.    The palace was thoroughly searched. and all the servants closely examined. but all without avail.    The conjurors and witches of the parish, and those surrounding, were consulted, but the pearls could not be found.    At last a servant with suitable conveyance was sent to North Wales after Black Robin, and it was not long before he stood in the presence of the nobleman.

'Robin Ddu Ddewin,' said the master, "only restore to us the pearls, and fifty pounds will be thy reward.'

'That is not the way I do business,' said Robin. 'In all probability I shall find the lost treasure: but I must be paid for my services whether I succeed or fail.'

•But I must have some test of your knowledge before I can promise you such a sum." said the gentleman.

'Very well, bring forward your test,' said the black magician, although he had but faint hope that he would be able to stand it.

'You may now leave,' said the man of the palace, 'Return to this room in half an hour.'

In the magician's absence, the nobleman went to another part of the palace and brought to the room a tame robin red breast, and put it under a pan on the table, and waited for the magician, who soon made his appearance.

'Now,' said the master, 'you may give me a proof of your superior powers by telling what is under that pan.'

The black pretender saw at once that there was no hope for him, and said:

'Ah, you have caught Robin this time.'

'Correct!' cried the nobleman, clapping his hands with delight. 'It *is* a robin! I no longer doubt your superior power." Here is your money, and now go in search of the pearls.'

Robin went to his room and pondered the matter over. He was well persuaded that the theft was committed by one of the maid servants.

The next morning, in company with a man-servant who was given him as a guide, he went into an old church-yard near by where the sexton was engaged in digging a grave. He threw up a skull. Robin instantly picked it up, extracted all the teeth and put them in his pocket. The servant looked on in horror! They returned to the palace; Robin to his room, and the servant to the kitchen, where he revealed to the maidens the skull story, to which they listened with pale countenances. Soon Robin came in, looking as grave as a ghost, and spoke:

'To-night, at 9 o'clock, let all the servants belonging to this palace meet me on this spot. Any one disobeying this order will suffer punishment. Remember the hour!' and he departed.

At the appointed time the servants, from the lowest to the highest, stood in the solemn presence of Robin Ddu Ddewin.

'Men and women,' said he, 'hearken ye diligently to my speech! I am about to call three legions of spirits to assist me in my search for the lost pearls. To the guilty one this will be a terrible night! That person will be dragged from the palace by infuriated, invisible goblins, and ground to powder.'

They trembled in his presence, for fear that those terrible goblins might perchance seize the wrong person.

'But,' continued Robin, 'all this may be avoided if the pearls are brought to my room before midnight, and no one need fear that I shall ever say a word in regard to the guilty person. That will be kept a secret for ever.'

He then went to his room, wondering how his scheme would succeed. In about an hour his door, which was not locked, was very gently opened a few inches, and a hand appeared, containing paper. Robin took the small package, the hand disappeared, and the door was gently closed. In the paper were found the lost pearls.

Of course, the gentleman of the palace knew nothing of Robin's movements, and the schemer was determined to keep his promise to the girl sacred. At dead of night he was taxing his brains as to how he should proceed so as to add to his own fame. At an early hour he saw from his room, in a field behind the palace, a number of geese. He secured the pearls in a piece of bread, and went out. He selected from the rest a peculiar looking fowl, threw before it the precious morsel, which was immediately picked up and swallowed.

On returning to the palace, he met the owner, who said, 'Well, magician, how about the pearls?'

'Come out with me,' said Robin, 'and I will show you where your treasure is kept.'

They both went into the field. Robin, pointing to the particular bird, said, 'There, secure that goose; kill it, examine it and find the pearls.'

Of course the treasure was found. The lady was overjoyed, and Robin was overwhelmed with kindness. No suspicion rested on any of the servants. The wife easily believed that they were dropped, and with other sweepings thrown out of doors. On the morning of his departure, Robin was presented with a splendid horse, with saddle and bridle, on which he rode home with fifty pounds in his pocket; and that is my story of Robin Ddu Ddewin."

The story was well received and applauded.

The next called upon was Thomas Davies, of "Cefn," who said that he would give them.

### ELLEN OF "CAE 'R MELWR."

"A great while ago, in the vale of Llanrwst, there lived a family, consisting of father, mother and one daughter, on a farm named Cae 'r Melwr. Morgan Jones was considered very rich. Ellen was a beauty, and almost idolized by her parents. In one of the little cottages on the farm lived a poor widow with her only child, a bright, active lad they called Jack. These two children played together, and were fond of each other.

Ellen was sent to a select school at Llanrwst, and seeing she was rather timid, the father, by the consent of the widow, sent Jack to a free school at the same place, in order to be a companion for his daughter in going and coming. Thus things remained for some two years. After this the boy was employed at Cae 'r

Melwr. He was wonderfully active and efficient in everything pertaining to farming; and by the time he was twenty years of age he was the '*hwsmon*,' or head servant of the farm. He was noted for his intelligence and fair personal appearance, and without any effort, had made a very favorable impression on the mind of the daughter.

Ellen, in order to perfect her accomplishments, was sent to England, and when she returned at the end of two years, she found that Jack was the most competent *hwsmon* in all that region, and she looked upon him with pride.

The people began to whisper that something beyond common friendship existed between Jack and Ellen, and the rumor did not at all please the parents. They thought much of Jack, but it would not do for their accomplished daughter to marry her father's head servant. No, Ellen must marry a gentleman. This talk became more general, and the father was perplexed.

One day, at Gwydir, a village near by, Morgan Jones met a gentleman from England, who had spent some time in the vicinity. This English farmer begged of Mr. Jones to let Jack accompany him to England to superintend his farm; declaring that he was the most promising young man in that line that he had ever seen. The master of Cae 'r Melwr was very unwilling to part with his head servant; but, after all, was it not

the best thing?   It would end this  courtship business,
if there was anything in it.   He  mentioned the thing
to Jack, and, to the old man's  astonishment, the servant gladly accepted the offer.   There were but two days
to prepare for the journey.   His mother silently wept,
and committed her boy to the care of the 'Father of
the fatherless and the Judge of the widow.'   The
young man's heart was deeply affected, in view of leaving his mother, and the other one that was more dear
to him than all beside.

Time passed away, and Jack was well nigh forgotten,
except by his mother, and—who?

At the end of some four  years after Jack's departure
from Wales, there came to Gwydir on a pleasure tour
a young gentleman from England, a son of an Earl.
On one evening, at this village, there was a grand dinner, and the surrounding gentry were all invited; and
among others was the beautiful heiress of Cae 'r Melwr;
and she, above all beside, attracted the attention of
the young Englishman.   Before the festivities were
over, he had fallen over head and ears in love.   This
could not pass unnoticed, and before many days it was
whispered among the neighbors that Ellen of Cae 'r
Melwr and the fine gentleman from England were lovers.   This rumor greatly pleased the young lady's parents.   The young man became a regular visitor at their
residence, and without the consent of the daughter,

and against her protestation, the father gave the young nobleman to understand that it would be all right; and the day of the wedding was appointed. The son of the Earl went back to England, in order to make preparations for the happy event.

On the day before the wedding, mounted on a fine horse, the young Englishman with several servants started from Llangollen, where they had arrived the evening before. · They overtook another gentleman. The young bridegroom, after some conversation, asked the stranger how far he was going. He replied by saying that he was going to *Capel Garmon*. 'I am going a very little farther, and on a most delightful business,' said the bridegroom. He was quite communicative; he told all, and lavished upon Ellen Cae 'r Melwr superlative praise. They reached Capel Garmon soon after dark. Here they shook hands and parted. The Englishman pursued his way toward Gwydir, while the other put up at the hotel of the village, where they parted. He inquired for a clergyman of the church of England. The rector was soon in his presence, and for a little time they conversed about different subjects, among them, the grand wedding expected on the morrow at Cae 'r Melwr.

'I have heard,' said the parson 'that this young lady is not a willing party to this engagement. . I hope however that this is not true.'

'Mr. Rector,' said our friend, 'I also wish to be married at the church to-morrow morning before daylight, for which service I will pay you ten pounds.'

'It will be somewhat irregular,' was the answer' 'but seeing it is a pressing case, I will comply with your request.'

The rector left for home. At a late hour of the night our gentleman also left, and after an absence of about one hour, returned in company with a lady closely veiled. At a given hour he went out the second time and soon reached Cae 'r Melwr. He knocked vigorously at the door. The old gentleman rose from bed, and soon recognized the voice of his old servant Jack.

'I beg pardon for disturbing you at this untimely hour,' said he. 'but I have my master's daughter at Capel Garmon and we are to be married there at the church at four o'clock. It is now near three. Will you come with me, and give away the bride to your old *hwsmon ?*'

'Heaven bless you, Jack! I will with the greatest pleasure!' said the old gentleman, quickly dressing himself. 'I know you are worthy of her, I care not how good she is."

On they went toward Capel Garmon, while the old gentleman revealed to Jack the wedding to be at his own house on that day, and gave him a pressing invitation to be present himself with his new English wife.

They reached the hotel, and there found the priest and the parish clerk. They soon started for the church. For the bride's sake the ceremony was in English. It was over, and the twain were made 'husband and wife together.' The old gentleman said that he must hasten home to Cae 'r Melwf, and again enjoined on the young pair to be present at the wedding.

'Jack has a splendid wife,' said Morgan Jones, after he went home. It was rather dark, and I did not really see her face. But only think of it, she gave me a hearty kiss at the church door when we parted ! You will see her yourself before long.'

At Cae 'r Melwr on that early morning they were all busy. It was high time for Ellen to be up, but she did not appear. They waited long and listened, but her footsteps were not heard above stairs. The bride's maids had come; six of them, as fair as the dawn. They went into her chamber, but she was not there! All were astonished. Some shed silent tears, others sobbed aloud, while the parents sat dumb.

'Well,' said the old gentleman at last, 'I now see how it is! Yes, I now see *exactly* how it is ! As sure as my name is Morgan Jones, with my own tongue and with my own lips, this morning, at the church at Capel Garmon, I gave my daughter away to Jack!'

'Never mind! never mind!' cried the old lady, jumping to her feet, 'let us thank the Lord that it is no worse! If she didn't get the son of an Earl, she got a grand specimen of a MAN!'

The couple was sent for, and received a hearty welcome home. On the part of the guests, the festivities were ten times more joyful than they would have been if Ellen had wedded the gentleman from England. The young pair led a happy life at Cae 'r Melwr, and Morgan Jones never regretted his work on that early morning, in giving away his only child to his former faithful servant."

"Good!" cried Evan Hughes, clapping his hands. "Now, boys, give us, in chorus together, 'The March of the Men of Harlech.' Play with a will!" No sooner were the words spoken, than the walls of that old "gegin" rung with the sound of that famous Welsh melody.

In less than five minutes that long table was set with the richest dainties the farm could produce, and a merry company partook of a rich repast.

At somewhat of a late hour the company from Carnarvon started for home. The evening was charming, and the maidens declared, again and again, that never would they forget the genuine pleasure they experienced on that night at the "Havod."

# CHAPTER XV.



Llewelyn, at the Institute, was progressing finely. Among the students he was already a favorite, and much respected by the community at large. On several occasions he had preached at the town with great acceptability. In the country around, wherever he spoke, the chapels were always filled with delighted hearers.

When not at the school building, he would often retire with his books to some favorite retreat on the shore of "Llyn Tegid" (Tegid Lake), which has always been one of the attractions of this inland town.

During one of these out-of-door enjoyments, a gentleman of very pleasing exterior slowly came up in front of his bower, and politely bowed. A pleasing smile rested on his countenance, while he said—

"Pardon me, sir; I fear that I have disturbed the sweet quietness of your study. Being a stranger, I hardly knew which way I was wandering."

"Your apology is needless," said Llewelyn. "These grounds are free to all, and strangers are specially invited to avail themselves of their charms."

"I have traveled quite extensively," said the stranger, "and I have gazed on fine scenery; but I have seldom seen a spot surpassing this in quiet beauty and loveliness."

"This is the universal testimony of those who visit Bala." said Llewelyn. "How long have you been here ?"

"I arrived last evening,' was the reply. "My health is not the best  I have thought that a few weeks spent in this inviting portion of Merionethshire might add to my physical strength. My mother is dead. My father and sister at present live in Cardiff. There are but two children of us, Helen and myself; and when we are home together, our cup of happiness overflows."

Llewelyn was touched by this simple statement of the stranger, whose family relation was so much like his own ; and at once he felt a strange nearness to the young man who had lost a mother, and had a beloved sister Helen.

"I suppose you remain at the hotel," said Llewelyn.

"My trunks are there at present," was the reply ; "but I would much prefer a room in a respectable boarding-house. The noise and confusion connected with an inn does not at all suit my quiet disposition."

"I have a most excellent boarding place, kept by Mr. and Mrs. Ellis, a gentleman and lady of undoubted respectability." said Llewelyn; "and I know there is a

commodious room adjoining mine that is not occupied,
which, if it would suit, you might secure."

"I feel greatly relieved," said the stranger, "and I
must see Mrs. Ellis at once. If you will assist me in
this matter you will place me under lasting obligation."

"I will do it with much pleasure," said Edwards.
"We can attend to it at once."

"I gratefully accept your kindness," was the reply;
and they slowly walked together toward the town.

The matter was soon settled to the satisfaction of all
concerned; and Mr. John Jenkins was numbered
among the boarders of Mr. and Mrs. Owen Ellis.

For Llewelyn the stranger seemed to have particular regard. He was much in his society. This, on the
part of the student, was fully reciprocated. They entered freely into each other's rooms, and were soon fast
friends. In the art of conversing, Mr. Jenkins was very
happy. His knowledge of common events was credita-
ble. On weighty questions he conversed but little, either from a want of information or a lack of taste. The
boarders in all numbered about a dozen, and in the
opinion of each he was a young man of very pleasing
manners.

Among these was a young lady, amiable accomplished, and possessing much wealth, by the name of
Martha Thomas, who seemed to regard Mr. Jenkins
with much favor. He was often admitted into her par-

lor, and sometimes went with her to chapel. Thus some weeks passed, while the gentleman from South Wales continued to rise in the estimation of all the boarders. He would often receive letters from his sister, breathing pure affection. Parts of these he would at times read to the company, while his voice trembled with emotions of love.

One day Miss Thomas made the startling announcement that her valuable gold watch was missing—that she had left it on her desk in the morning, and that some one had stolen it. She could not believe for a moment that it was anyone with whom she was acquainted. It was a gift from a dear friend, and she would rather have lost an hundred pounds. Mr. and Mrs. Ellis were almost distracted. The honor of the house was at stake. Never before had anything of such a nature happened beneath their roof. The boarders and lodgers looked at each other in mute astonishment. The proprietors insisted that a thorough search must be made at once by a proper officer of the law. To this no one objected, except Miss Thomas, who said it was of no use; that she was perfectly satisfied that a stranger had slyly entered the house, found the watch, and had departed for parts unknown. But Mr. and Mrs. Ellis insisted; two officers with a search warrant were soon secured, and all were required to submit to the searching process. Notwithstanding Mrs. Ellis' agita-

11

tion, the rest of the company, Miss Thomas included, could hardly abstain from bursts of merriment in view of a process that seemed to border on the ludicrous.

Trunk after trunk was examined, but to no purpose. Llewelyn's was the last to undergo the search.

"Mr. Edwards, please unlock your trunk," said one of the officers, smiling as he spoke.

"With pleasure, sir," said the young man.

"Mr. Edwards," said Miss Thomas, "I am thoroughly ashamed of this whole proceeding; and you must remember that I am not responsible for it."

"I would as soon suspect the angel Gabriel!" said Mr. Jenkins with much feeling.

"Such language is not becoming!" said Llewelyn; "proceed, Mr. Officer."

Article after article was removed, until the bottom of the trunk was reached, and there, carefully folded in a piece of paper, was something that took the officer's particular attention. He took hold of it with evident embarrassment, while his hand trembled. He opened it in the presence of the whole company, and there was a gold watch!

"Mr. Edwards," said the officer, "do you claim this watch as your rightful property?"

"I do not, sir!" said the young man, "and God is my witness that I have no knowledge of the manner in which it found its way to my trunk."

" Miss Thomas," asked the officer, " is this your watch ?"

" I am sure that the watch is mine, and I am just as sure that Mr. Edwards never touched it." said Miss Thomas.

Above all the rest Mr. Jenkins was affected.  He was moved even to tears ; while in words eloquent with indignation he cried out, " This is a devilish plot to injure as pure-hearted a young man as ever breathed the air of Bala!  Ho, ho! the plot is as silly and clumsy as it is malicious : for who out of Bedlam will believe that Llewelyn Edwards is a thief !"

" Miss Thomas," said the officer. " shall I take Mr. Edwards in custody ?"

" May Heaven forbid !" cried the young lady. " This matter is either a cruel joke or a villainous plot.  I have recovered my treasure, and am satisfied."

" Let this matter go no further," said Mr. Jenkins. " Mr. Edwards is above suspicion ; and let him be assured that he never stood higher in our estimation than he does this moment."

And thus it ended.  The more Llewelyn thought of the matter, the more it became involved in mystery. He revealed the thing to the officers of the school, and they assured him that he had their unbounded confidence.  He called the attention of the church officials to the same matter. and without a dissenting voice they gave him the same assurance.  By this he was greatly relieved.

At that day there was in Carnarvon one weekly paper, *The Carnarvon Herald*, in which was found correspondence from various parts of North Wales.  In about two weeks after this watch trouble, the following appeared in the columns of that paper as an item of news from Bala :

### "A THEOLOGICAL STUDENT COMES TO GRIEF.

The other day our usually quiet town was thrown into intense excitement by a case of theft, attended by peculiar circumstances.  A very worthy young lady by the name of Thomas, remaining at the well known boarding-house of Mr. and Mrs. Owen Ellis, lost a valuable gold watch.  Two officers of the law made a thorough search, and the missing watch was found at the bottom of Llewelyn Edwards' trunk.  This young man is from Llangobaith, near Bangor, a candidate for the ministry.  Through the influence of friends the thing has been measurably hushed up.  It is understood that Miss Thomas will not prosecute.  Young Edwards heretofore had sustained a good character, and it is lamentable that by yielding to temptation he has blasted his reputation, and caused his friends to hang down their heads in shame.        SILAS EVANS."

Gwennie's heart was greatly cheered by the presence of her fast friend Helen Edwards.  Much of their time was spent in confidential chats touching the future, and they were happy in each other's love. They would often loiter amid the magnificent ruins of Carnarvon castle, and converse of those years gone by when their ancestors so nobly fought against foreign invaders and home oppressors. Together they would climb those winding stairs, and stand on the giddy heights of "Twr yr Eryr" (Eagle Tower), from where they had a magnificent view of all the surrounding country. At the close of day, arm in arm, they would promenade the length of that beautiful quay, and view the harbor with its many sails of commerce. From one of these delightful rambles they had just returned. They found Morris Williams in his usual seat, looking with much solemnity at the Carnarvon *Herald*.

"Why, my dear uncle Morris," said Gwennie, "you look as if something serious had attracted your attention."

"It is serious enough, my dear!" said her uncle.

Mr. Williams would occasionally indulge in a rich joke, and Gwennie at first thought that this was the nature of his solemnity. But looking at him again, and noticing a certain unsteadiness in his voice, she made up her mind that her uncle was in earnest.

"What is it, my dear uncle?" she asked in a low voice.

"It is something touching Llewelyn," he replied. "He is neither dead nor sick, and is the same noble man that he ever was. But some infernal agencies are at work to destroy his character, and they try to make the people believe that he is a thief!"

"Ho, ho!" cried the girls, in a mixture of weeping and laughing, while Gwennie continued, "My fright is over! Llewelyn is safe!"

"Heaven bless my dear brother!" said Helen.

"You have behaved nobly," said Mr. Williams. "I will now read the strange paragraph, which in part may be true. It has been written by some one who desires Llewelyn's ruin."

After reading the article, he said again, "Let us wait one week, and we shall have something from Bala that will show the matter in its true light."

The week was soon past. The *Herald* was again out, and the best brains of Bala had met for the vindication of young Edwards.

### "A VILE SLANDER.

*Mr. Editor*—In your last number you published an item from this town that does cruel injustice to a most worthy young man. The paragraph is partly true, but it was conceived in malice, and is the production of some lying villain. The watch was taken, and it was found in Mr. Edwards' trunk; but no one believes that it was put there by the young student. Your correspondent signs his name 'Silas Evans;' we have no such a name in Bala. When he wrote of Mr. Edwards 'yielding to temptation,' he knew that he was penning a falsehood. Miss Thomas never thought for a moment that Mr. Edwards was guilty. The authorities of the school and the officials of the church have passed resolutions of entire confidence in the young man. The vile plot did not originate at this place. Let not the friends of Mr. Edwards be disturbed in the least. Here he is respected by all.

In behalf of the Theological Institute,

THOMAS LEWIS.

In behalf of the Calvinistic Church,

ROBERT GRIFFITHS."

In reading this article, Morris Williams several times had to surrender to his emotions, while the young ladies shed tears of joy and affection. The faithful uncle procured twenty copies of the *Herald* for distribution in the vicinity of Llangobaith.

# CHAPTER XVI.



Thomas Lloyd, after the departure of Gwennie, sat down and endeavored to comprehend the situation. She was actually gone! Yes, *Gwennie* had gone, and in spite of his unbending will, he felt a choking sensation, and faintly heard the voice of a long ago banished conscience crying as if from far away, in distinct accents, "THOMAS LLOYD, YOU ARE WRONG!" That voice he dreaded, and from that empty room he hastened to another of much smaller dimensions, poured into a glass a liberal quantity of some reviving liquid, and thus, for that day at least, he was well delivered from the accusation of the troublesome meddler.

"Jane," said Lloyd to one of his most responsible maid-servants, in about two hours after Gwennie's departure, "for a while I wish you to take the responsibility of housekeeping. Gwennie is gone."

"Yes sir, I saw her going," said Jane, "and without wishing it, sir, I heard some of the conversation. You have turned my dear young mistress from her own home because she was faithful to her true lover. And now, sir, that Miss Gwennie is gone, there is no pleasure for me in this house, and I am going too."

"Nonsense, Jane! That will never do," said Lloyd, curbing his feelings. "She dared my authority, and I sent her away."

"It is not for me to dispute with my master," said the servant, "but you commanded your daughter to marry a very bad man. He has plenty of money, but he swears, and breaks the Sabbath, and gets drunk. And for refusing to be the wife of that bad man, you have turned Miss Gwennie, who is the very image of her mother, out of doors! No, this house is no longer a place for Jane Lewis, and I cannot stay."

"Jane, you are both foolish and saucy," said Lloyd. "You are a good servant, and if you want higher wages, you can have it; but you must not leave me."

"I find no fault with my wages, sir," said Jane, "but I will not be the housekeeper of a man who has so treated my young mistress. If you can get your sister Grace or some other lady relative to come and take charge of things, I will remain your servant for a while longer."

"Jane, you have put a new idea into my head," said Lloyd, while his countenance brightened. "This very day I will write to Grace. If she comes, you need not tell her anything about this trouble. I can do that myself."

Here the conversation ended. Jane went her way, wondering at her boldness, and Thomas Lloyd hastened to write a letter.

About two weeks had passed since the stolen watch excitement at Bala.  Llewelyn was a favorite at school, in the church and among the citizens; but no one seemed to enjoy his society more than did Mr. Jenkins, who still remained in town, and was very attentive to Miss Thomas.

"Mr. Edwards," said Mr. Jenkins one day, "I envy the ease with which you can manage a boat."

"In that I had some experience years ago," said Mr. Edwards.  "Since I came to Bala I have taken much pleasure on the lake."

"In that line I never had any experience, and I am exceedingly timid in regard to the water," said Mr. Jenkins.  "I am almost ashamed to confess it.  And yet I have a strong desire to go on that beautiful lake.  If I was a good swimmer in case of an accident, it would be different; but you see I cannot swim at all."

"Neither can I," said Llewelyn with a smile, "but with a good boat there is nothing to fear on this bit of a lake."

"Then you are just the man for me to trust." was the reply.  "If you will indulge me in this matter, I will most gladly pay for the use of the boat, and thank you most heartily in the bargain."

"It will give me great pleasure to be of any service to you, Mr. Jenkins," said Mr. Edwards.  "Your warm sympathy when I was in trouble a few weeks ago has laid me under great obligation to you."

"Oh, don't mention it!" said Mr. Jenkins. "But when shall we go?"

"Let us go this evening at six o'clock. Shall any one go with us?"

"Oh no!" said Jenkins with a hearty laugh, "I should be so afraid the boat would sink."

At the appointed time they started; Llewelyn took the oars, while Jenkins timidly sat in the stern. The boat was soon skimming along at a rapid rate.

"This is delightful," cried Jenkins. "It is a shame that I have not been on this lake before. Hereafter I shall not be so silly."

"I will row you to any part of the lake or shores you may wish," said Llewelyn.

"Thank you, Mr. Edwards, you may go where you choose. It is all the same to me."

And thus they chatted away indifferently for a long time, until they thought it was time to give their boat a homeward direction.

"Mr. Edwards," said Mr. Jenkins with a most pleasant smile, "your movements seem to be so easy and graceful, that I would give a great deal if I could boast of such proficiency in the same line."

"A very little practice, Mr. Jenkins, would give you all the proficiency you desire," said Edwards, "and I would advise you to begin at once."

"I am inclined to make the trial now," said Mr. Jenkins, "and you are at full liberty to laugh at my blunders."

"There will be no occasion for laughing," said Llewelyn. "Now let us change seats."

They both stood up; and Mr. Jenkins, in changing his location, stepped on the extreme end of the rowing seat, the boat leaned over, he lost his balance, fell heavily into the water and sunk from sight. He soon came to the surface, reached out his hands and wildly cried, "For God sake, save me!"

Llewelyn stooping over, gave him both hands, when Jenkins in the most frantic manner gave such a jerk that instantly pulled the young student into the water. Not knowing how to swim, he went down. When he came up, Jenkins was at some distance, clinging to the stern of the boat. Llewelyn made a desperate struggle to keep his head above the water, but soon again sunk out of sight.

Fortunately, this was seen by two men from the shore, who at once started to the rescue; and when the student came up the second time, they were on the spot with their boat, and he was saved.

Seeing that Mr. Jenkins was in no immediate danger, they paid their attention to Llewelyn, who, although much exhausted, soon revived.

"Is my friend safe?" was the first question.

"He is safe," was the reply.

The two men now slowly pulled toward Mr. Jenkins and took him into their boat.

"Gentlemen," said Mr. Jenkins, "your timely arrival seems like a miraculous interposition of Providence in saving a most worthy young man from a watery grave."

"But your behavior in the premises seems to us as strange," said George Griffith.

"To tell you the truth," said Mr. Jenkins, "I was so alarmed and bewildered that I did not know what I was about. But we are in no condition to stay here any longer, and so we will take our own boat and start for the town."

"Mr. Edwards is not in a fit condition to row," answered Thomas Phillips. "You had better remain in this boat, and let us take you home."

"I am fully recovered," said Llewelyn; "I can row without the least difficulty. We most heartily thank you for your assistance. Mr. Jenkins explained to me before we started, his great timidity on the water, and that fully explains his behavior. You will do me a great favor by keeping this unfortunate thing to yourselves. If the students should hear of it, it might cause me much annoyance, and it might be embarrassing to Mr. Jenkins, who on all occasions has proved to me a most excellent friend."

"Mr. Edwards," said Mr. Griffith, "we shall do as you desire."

They again went into their own boat, reached the town, sought their respective rooms, changed their garments, and all passed off without drawing any particular attention.

That evening Mr. Jenkins came to Mr. Edwards' room, and said—

"I have just received a letter from home, and my sister is so anxious to have me return, that I have concluded to start in the morning. While I have been here, your society has been to me very agreeable. And better than that, I trust that your moral influence has told favorably on my mind. I see more beauty in Christianity than I ever have before. I am sorry that my behavior on the lake was not more manly. For the time being I lost my senses. Never again will I venture on the water in a small boat. To-night I will stay at the hotel, in order to take the coach at an early hour. I will now bid you good-bye, in the hope of seeing you again in a few weeks. I would advise you to be on your guard against secret enemies. That silly gold watch plot convinced me that there are those who are bent on doing you an injury. I think it will yet be brought to light, and that the guilty wretch or wretches will be punished."

The two then parted, and Llewelyn felt that he was indeed losing a true friend. Mr. Jenkins, in a most honorable manner, settled all his bills, and made several nice presents to Mr. Ellis' children.

Miss Thomas was evidently affected, but her good sense was a sufficient guard against any demonstration. The popular young stranger departed next morning, and the impression he left upon the inhabitants of that quiet town, with but very few exceptions, was decidedly favorable.

# CHAPTER XVII.


### THOMAS LLOYD'S SISTER.

Grace Lloyd was a lady of forty years, whose heart, as yet, had never throbbed with any particular emotions of affection for any male member of the human race. In other years she had caused many hearts to flutter. With imploring looks, more than one had begged of her in touching poetic strains, to save them from destruction. But with an expression on her fair countenance that only quickened their pulsations, she had given them to understand, that hitherto she had not met a man for whose society she was willing to exchange her single blessedness; and in accents plain she had bidden them to depart, and seek balm for their wounded spirits in some other quarters. And thus she had reached this age without a single wound from Cupid's arrow.

Grace possessed an independent mind; but in her manners there was nothing haughty or imperious. She was somewhat abrupt in her expressions, and often severe in her remarks; but she was always found on the right side of all moral questions. She had means of her own, and for several years had lived with some of her Welsh friends in Liverpool.

Of her brother's trouble with Gwennie she was in blissful ignorance. The letter, urgently requesting her presence at Druid's Grove, gave her no reason for the daughter's absence ; and under the impression that her niece would soon return, she had consented to superintend the household duties.

Several things, in different parts of the house, indicated to her keen perceptions, that Gwennie had not left home under the ordinary circumstances of a person paying a transient visit to a distant relative, with the expectation of soon returning. There was a strange absence of almost everything that belonged to the daughter, with a suspicious silence on the part of her father in regard to her departure; and several times, to questions relative to Gwennie he had returned evasive answers.

"I don't know what it is," said Grace to herself, " but I am sure that something of a serious nature has of late taken place under this roof. I am not going to remain in the dark any longer. As Tom's sister, and Gwennie's aunt, I have a right to know how matters stand; and I *will* know, or my name is not Grace Lloyd. Jane!"

That person was soon in her presence, and manifested in her countenance a thorough readiness to do the housekeeper's bidding.

"Sit down, Jane," said Grace in a cheerful tone. "I

12

wish to ask you a few questions in regard to matters in this house."

"If Miss Lloyd wants to know anything about flour, butter, cheese, meat and cooking, or anything else in my line, I will tell her with great pleasure," said Jane.

"Those are not the things I care about just now," said Miss Lloyd with a slight smile. "I wish to know what were the circumstances under which Gwennie left home. You need not answer unless you are perfectly willing."

"I could tell you much, Miss Lloyd, but I am not at liberty," said Jane in trembling accents.

"I honor you for your faithfulness," said Grace. "But Gwennie is the last person on earth that I would have suspected of doing anything wrong!"

"May Heaven save us!" cried Jane, wringing her hands. "Don't you suspect for one moment that my dear young mistress did anything wrong! She is as pure and good as the angels in heaven!" and she burst into violent sobbing. Then resuming, she said, "Let Miss Lloyd go to her brother. He is the one to answer her questions."

"You are quite right, Jane," was the answer, "and I will follow your advice." And the housekeeper and the excellent servant went about their respective duties.

"I have never made much of an ado over the girl,"

said Grace again to herself, "and it may be possible that she thinks that I care but little about her. If she does, she will one day change her opinion."

The next morning, after breakfast, Grace requested her brother to come to her room up-stairs, that she wished to consult him in regard to some household movements. And Thomas Lloyd having no objection to being consulted, found his way to Grace's room.

"Grace, you are getting along finely. If you wish to get any information in regard to housekeeping, Jane will tell you all about such matters."

"At present I am in search of information that should not come from a servant, but from the head of the family," said Grace. "Tom, I want to know in the first place, what were the circumstances under which Gwennie left this house?'"

"O bother!" said her brother, "why should you trouble your head about that? Gwennie is away, and will stay away, and I beg of you not to mention the subject again."

"Your begging is in vain, and the subject *will* be mentioned again," said Grace. "Your letter to me was misleading and deceptive. I came here under the impression that Gwennie had left on a visit to friends. The looks of her rooms appeared to me mysterious, and I soon became convinced that there had been some trouble. Why did you not tell me the whole truth?"

"I told you as much truth as then answered my purpose," was the short reply.

"And I intend that before you leave this room, Tom
Lloyd, you will tell as much as will answer *my* purpose," said the sister, in a way that the brother pretty
well understood. "Please bear in mind that I am not
a dependent on your charity. I would advise you to
be a little careful in regard to the manner in which you
answer my questions. As your sister, and Gwennie's
aunt, I have a right to know these things in regard to
which I am in the dark. If you prove stubborn, I give
you fair warning that to-night will find me at Bangor,
and that in less than forty-eight hours I will be in my
own rooms in Liverpool. I ask you again, what were the
circumstances under which Gwennie left this house?"

Thomas Lloyd well understood the nature and temper of that person before whom he quailed, and replied:

"Gwennie defied my authority, as a parent, and
utterly refused to obey my commands."

"When I hear what those commands were, I shall be
able to judge whether she did right or wrong," said
Grace. "What did you command her to do, Tom?"

"I commanded her to accept the hand and fortune
of a worthy young gentleman, who sought her for a
wife, and she disregarded my command, and rejected
his generous offer," said Thomas Lloyd.

Here Grace burst out in a peculiar laughter in which were mixed in equal quantities, scorn. auger, and ridicule. After the laughter came a certain *look*, which Thomas Lloyd had often witnessed in other years, and before which he could never stand. And now. penurious as he was, he would have given a good round sum of money to escape that peculiar stare. But to run away, at this stage, would have been disastrous.

"Grace, for Heaven's sake. don't look at me in that way!" he cried. "Your words are hard enough. and your laugh is worse, but give me anything rather than that look!"

"Well, brother." said Grace, with somewhat of an altered countenance, "I am deeply interested in the narrative. Now proceed, and give me the name of this worthy gentleman, as you call him, that your daughter, contrary to your command, rejected."

"He is none other than Mr. Lucas Pugh. of Riverside," said Lloyd.

"And you call *him* a worthy gentleman!" said Grace.

"And why not?" asked the brother.

"For the best reason in the world." was the answer. "He has not one worthy quality, nor a single gentlemanly trait. And, Tom Lloyd, you know it! And yet, with that full knowledge, you commanded your pureminded daughter to unite herself to that vile specimen of moral corruption!" And again she gave her brother that *look.* "Of course, she disobeyed your command," she continued. "It could not be otherwise. Oh, I feel humiliated to think that I have a brother that could pollute his lips with such a monstrous order!"

"Grace!" said Lloyd, jumping to his feet, "such language is hard to bear!"

"We cannot tell how much we can bear until we are put to the test," said the sister. "I have much more to say before you leave this room, and I am going to say it in my own way. But let me hear more of the narrative. Why did Gwennie leave her home? Answer me that question."

"I commanded her to leave," said the brother, with as much assurance as he conld command. "In addition to rejecting Mr. Pugh, she has accepted the suit of a fellow whose father caunot command a thousand pounds."

"And who is this 'fellow,' as you call him, that was so bold and daring?" asked the sister in feigned wonder, and with a smile which Lloyd well knew did not indicate that the storm was subsiding.

"It is Llewelyn Edwards, of the 'shop,'" said Lloyd. "He has of late become a ranting Methodist, and is now at Bala preparing to be one of their ministers."

Without replying to his last remark, the sister said: "At last I understand the situation, and I am somewhat relieved. At first I had some faint fears that

Gwennie had been guilty of some imprudence and had, without reason, left her home. Now I see that she has been perfectly blameless, and that her actions have been those of a pure-minded lady. Never has she stood so high in my estimation as she does this moment."

" And by the same rule, I never stood so low in your estimation as I do this moment," said Lloyd.

" Tom, thou hast said it," said Grace. " I have known for years that the love of money was the great ruling passion of your soul. But I had no idea that you could ever stoop to such a depth of degradation as this. I shudder to think of it!"

" Then let us drop the subject," said Thomas.

"No! The subject is of too serious a nature to drop," said Grace. " You have committed a great wrong. I hope that this awful sin against God and your daughter is not yet known. Tom, this matter must be righted, and that without delay, or you will be hissed even by the children when you pass by. What is your candid opinion? I think you have seen the time when you had a degree of conscience. Tom, is there any left? I am very anxious to know whether there is anything in you that is worth saving. Are you satisfied with your treatment of Gwennie?"

" Well, Grace," said the brother, " seeing we have gone into the subject so deep, I may as well admit that

I am not satisfied with what I have done. I have been too severe."

"Ah, Tom," said Grace, "I am sure that that is the voice of a good conscience, and is a positive proof that it still lives! I will give you all the assistance in my power. This conscience, if you will but listen to its voice, will tell you that Lucas Pugh is a person that no Christian girl can admire; that your commands were cruel and wicked; that Llewelyn Edwards is full worthy of your daughter, and that you should ask Gwennie's forgiveness and bring her home. All this conscience will tell you."

For a few moments there was silence, while the sharp eyes of the sister rested on those of the brother. Lloyd, from the moment when the conversation began, felt that he was brought before a terrible tribunal with whose judgment he could not trifle. During each additional minute he felt that his defence was weakening, until at last he clearly saw that he was indeed the unkind wretch so plainly described by his sister, and more so by the voice of conscience. His pride and stubbornness fought desperately, but that terrible voice came nigher and stronger, ringing in the ear of his soul, "*You have done wrong!*" until at last, in words marked with agitation, he said:

"Grace! it is both foolish and wicked for me any longer to hide my real feelings and convictions. I know that your severest sentences are all true. I felt that I was guilty, but I tried to defend myself with weak sophistry. From that fatal moment when I drove Gwennie from her home, I have been one of the most miserable of men. I have not enjoyed one quiet hour by day or by night. A heavy load has been pressing me down. All the arguments I could gather have appeared weak and foolish. Several times I have been on the point of starting for Carnarvon after Gwennie, and to ask her forgiveness. But pride triumphed over conscience. When I wrote to Liverpool, I ought to have been honest. I promised myself that I would give you the information on your arrival. Since you came, the more I thought of it, the more I shrunk from approaching the subject. I am astonished at the change that has come over me, and I am tempted to doubt my senses. My eyes have been opened to see the past, and the sight is shocking! I have been governed by one ruling motive—money-making. For the first time the awful conviction comes upon me with crushing weight that had I been a different man, my wife would not have died! I am well convinced that Lucas Pugh is a bad young man, and I am very glad that Gwennie refused to comply with my mad request. Llewelyn Edwards is a worthy person, although I have no sympathy with his Methodism. Grace, I have told you all; the effort has almost prostrated me. I feel as weak as a ch ild, both in body and mind.   I will leave this matter in your  hands, and I will  abide  by your  instructions."

Grace, while delighted, was not demonstrative.   She simply said—" Tom, in regard to your bodily strength, I cannot say.   But in my opinion, you have manifested more  strength  of  mind  than  ever  before.   We have reached a favorable point, and before many days Druid's Grove will smile again under a brighter sunshine than it has seen in many years."

# CHAPTER XVIII.



It was a delightful evening. The sun had disappeared beyond the hills of *Sir Fon*, and the western firmament was covered with golden splendor. Gwennie and her uncle had just returned from a pleasant walk on the beach fronting that fine harbor, and were seated in one of Mr. Williams' parlors. Helen Edwards had returned to Llangobaith some days before.

"Uncle Morris," said Gwennie, "to me this has been a day of deep meditation. Past events have crowded upon my memory."

"And most of them have been pleasant," said her uncle.

"They have," she replied. "My school days were one perpetual stream of enjoyment. My church relation has been happy, and I have rejoiced in the affection of a most loving mother."

"And yet you have passed through some severe trials, Gwennie," said Mr. Williams.

"Yes," said the maiden, "but worse than all, my father turned against me and banished me from my home!"

"His conduct was very bad!" said Mr. Williams.

But, Gwennie, he will yet look at the matter seriously, be heartily ashamed of his conduct, and ask your forgiveness."

"Oh, my dear uncle!" broke out Gwennie, with tears. "Do you really believe that my father will again be good and kind, and that I shall get home to Llwyn y Derwydd?"

"Yes, my dear," was his answer. "I am almost sure of it."

"And why do you think so, Uncle Morris?"

"For several reasons," he said. "First, no person, unless utterly depraved, can go as far as he did without meeting a tremendous reaction. I think he has some conscience left after all, and that he will yet try to atone for his cruel treatment. Another thing, Grace Lloyd has taken him in hand before this time, and if she has not scattered the live coals of truth upon his naked heart, I am mistaken. Yes, Gwennie dear, you will go back to Druid's Grove. I shall miss your society much, but I don't wish it to become known that your father has treated you so unkindly."

"My dear uncle, are you not too hopeful?" cried Gwennie. "But may my father in Heaven grant that it may so prove!"

Here one of Mr. Williams' clerks brought in the mail and presented it to his master.

He looked the letters over, and quietly smiled. Gwennie watched him with a throbbing heart.

"Is there anything for me, uncle Morris?"

"It looks very much as if there was, Gwennie," said her uncle, as he handed her three letters.

"Oh, uncle!" cried the girl, "a letter from papa! Is not that astonishing?"

"Not as I view things, dear," was the reply.

"I am afraid to open it, uncle Morris!" she cried again.

"I think there is nothing in it that will hurt you."

She opened it and read the first sentence. "My dear abused child." She jumped to her feet, uttered a loud cry of joy, fell upon her uncle's neck and kissed him.

"Oh, uncle Morris, I am almost too happy to live! Papa calls me his 'dear abused child!' This is too good to come all at once! Where is the letter? I must go by myself or you will be ashamed of me!" and she ran to her room. A calmness came over her, and she read the following:

"My Dear Abused Child:

Ever since that day when I so cruelly and wickedly ordered you to leave your own home, I have been a deeply wretched man, continually tormented with guilt and shame. I tried to get Jane to take charge. She refused, and gave me a rebuke that cut deep into my soul. Your aunt Grace came with the impression that

you had only left on a visit.   One morning she brought
me to an account.   I tried to evade, but it was of no
use, and I confessed the whole.   At first I showed no
penitence, but she soon overwhelmed me in confusion!
I told her my regrets and sorrow, and put myself under
her training.   Dear Gwennie, I am deeply sorry for my
conduct, and sincerely ask your forgiveness.   I am
thankful that you disregarded my cruel commands.
To-day Lucas Pugh looks as forbidding to me as he
does to you.   I gladly withdraw all objections to Llewelyn Edwards, who is a worthy young man.   On next
Wednesday, Robin Jones will bring your aunt Grace to
Carnarvon, and I trust that my dear daughter will return with them to her old home.   You can show this
letter to your uncle Morris.

Affectionately your penitent

FATHER."

Grace's letter was very brief.

"MY DEAR GWENNIE:

Your father's letter will explain all.   Your conduct
throughout has been praiseworthy, and your trouble is
at an end.   On Wednesday, of course, you will return
with me to Druid's Grove.

Affectionately your

AUNT GRACE."

With a spirit sweetly calmed, she again joined Mr.
Williams.

"Uncle Morris," she said. "the news was so good,
and, to me, so unexpected, that it completely ove r

whelmed me. I am afraid that my behavior was a little wild."

"It was just right, Gwennie," said Mr. Williams, "and I would not have had it different."

"Papa writes that I may show his letter to you," said Gwennie, "and here are a few lines from aunt Grace."

"Short and to the point," said the uncle. "Grace never indulges in waste words, but has always on hand a good supply of common sense. What beautiful writing, Gwennie! Just look at the graceful curve of that G, and the beauty of that L! Such penmanship, in my opinion, shows something more than mechanical ingenuity. Have you any more letters for me to read?"

"I have one more, uncle Morris, and I have no objection for *you* to read it."

"Oh, no; I don't wish to read that letter. I hope Llewelyn is well."

"He is well and happy, and sends kind regards."

On the afternoon of the following day the familiar equipage from Druid's Grove appeared in front of Morris Williams' mansion. The door of the carriage was pulled open, and the aunt and niece enjoyed a hearty embrace. Gwennie also took her father's faithful servant by the hand, which greatly pleased Robin Jones.

The aunt was conducted into the parlor, where she was gladly received by Mr. Williams, with whom she was on familiar terms.

"Gwennie," said Grace, "my stay at present will be very short. I have only one errand, and that is to take you home to Druid's Grove."

"Nay, Grace!" said Morris Williams, "stay and let us enjoy a little visit."

"Not to-day, Morris," said Grace. "Before long we shall come and make you a good all-day visit. With that promise, we must go. Call Robin in, and let him take the trunks. Now, my dear, put on your things and prepare for a delightful ride."

The trunks were properly deposited, Gwennie gave her uncle a highly demonstrative kiss, and the briefly disowned was on her way to a reconstructed father.

About the time Llewelyn entered the Theological Institute at Bala, Taliesin Roberts, through the influence and under the direction of Mrs. Parry, of Thrush Grove, was admitted as a student into the office of an eminent barrister at Bangor, by the name of Parry Jones, in whose eyes the young man found much favor. Roberts was tall, straight and comely, and was often mentioned in highly complimentary terms by some of the noted lady beauties of the city.

Llangobaith being not far from Bangor, Taliesin was often found under his parents' roof, and he was by no means a stranger at the "shop," where he always found a most hearty welcome.

The day had passed, and part of the night. The lights in the business part of the "shop" had been extinguished. The father, daughter, Mrs. Owen and Taliesin, were seated together in the pleasant parlor.

"Taliesin," said Mr. Edwards, "for some little time you have been a law student. Think you not that this plot against Llewelyn originated at Langobaith?"

"I certainly do," said the young man. "It sprung from the cowardly malice and hatred of Lucas Pugh and John Spike, assisted by those who are more expert in mischief."

"And yet," said Helen, "he utterly fails to find a person at Bala that he cannot call a real friend. There is but one stranger with whom he associates, and in him he has the utmost confidence."

"Aye," said Taliesin, "and that one stranger is a villain in disguise—a hired tool of Lucas Pugh to dishonor your brother."

"Taliesin, you perfectly astonish me!" said Helen. "Papa, what do you think?"

"I think Taliesin is correct," answered the father.

"I am concerned about our boy's personal safety," said Mrs. Owen.

"I am troubled on that score myself," said the young man. "Such is Lucas Pugh's depravity and revengeful disposition, that he would furnish money to carry on even a murderous plan. Llewelyn says that this

13

Jenkins has left Bala for South Wales; but I am of the opinion that even now he is in malicious consultation with Pugh and the Spikes. I have revealed this matter to Parry Jones, and this is his candid conviction. He has given me permission to stay in this vicinity for a number of days, and watch the movements of things. I ask for no higher honor than to bear some part in bringing these depraved wretches to justice and punishment."

"Taliesin," said Helen, with some alarm in her voice, "don't put yourself in the way of these bad men, for they hate you almost as much as they do my brother."

"I will be careful, Helen," said the young man, "but I am willing to run some risk in the interest of one who is so dear to us all. I have no fixed plan, but I am on the watch."

After some more conversation of the same nature, the hour being late, Taliesin took his leave. The night was dark and windy. He was no sooner in the street than he was accosted by a voice quite familiar.

"Robin Jones, is that you?" asked Taliesin, grasping the young man's hand. "Like myself, you are out at a late hour."

"Aye, and so I am," said Robin. "I have been at your father's, and they told me where to look for you. I did not wish to disturb you, and so I have waited for you on this spot."

"It must be something of importance that puts you to all this trouble." said Taliesin.

"You will be the better judge of this when I tell you what it is. First, I have something good to tell you. Gwennie is home again. Her father has asked her forgiveness, and all is sweet."

"Robin Jones!" cried Taliesin, "are you sure that is true?"

"I drove the carriage that brought her home this very day; and didn't I see the master kissing of her?" said Robin.

"It is enough! The news is glorious!" said Taliesin.

"But I have something bad to tell you." Robin went on, "There are some chaps hereabout that wish you ill, and intend to murder Llewelyn Edwards, and you must know it."

"You are a good, faithful friend, Robin!" said Taliesin, "and your faithfulness will not be forgotten. But this is no place to talk about such matters. Come with me," and in a moment he was seeking admission into the room he had so lately left.

"Helen," said he, "I have just met Robin Jones, who has something of importance to tell me in confidence. He also informs me that Thomas Lloyd has repented of his ill-treatment of Gwennie, asked her forgiveness, and brought her home."

"May the Lord be praised!" was Helen's reply.

They were shown into a room, the door was closed, and Robin Jones began:

"Last night I went to see my sister Jane. She is a servant at *Nant y Llyffaint*. I was coming home across the fields, and it was quite late. Not far from Riverside, I heard voices approaching. Not wishing to meet them, I jumped over the high hedge and hid from sight. When they came close to where I was, they stopped, and although they spoke low, I could hear every word. There were three of them; two I well knew by their voices. These were Lucas Pugh and . John Spike. The other voice, which was very rough. I did not know, but from their talk I soon found that it belonged to John Spike's father."

"Didn't we tell you that the stealing trick would fall flat?" asked old Spike; "but like fools, you thought it would be a sure thing. Who the devil would believe that Llewelyn Edwards would steal watches? The other scheme came within an inch of being a success. He went down twice, and would have been nicely out of the way if those cursed students hadn't picked him up. To-morrow night we shall hear all about it from Scroggs himself."

"I have already paid a sight of money," said Lucas, "and I am ready to pay more; but the thing must not fail."

"Fail!" cried old Spike, "Scroggs never fails. Before he gets through, he will put that pious howler eternally out of the way, and of course we shall all be sorry for the sad accident."

"And I am bound that Taliesin Roberts must come in for a share," said John Spike with an oath.

"That will come in all right at the proper time." said the father. "But. John, you must learn to keep your mouth shut."

"At what hour to-morrow night shall we meet Scroggs?" asked Lucas.

"At midnight. in the bower." said Spike. "where he will give us an account of his labors at Bala."

Here the company left. I wanted to run to Bangor and tell you at once, but learning that you were to be at home to-day, I waited."

"Well, Robin, you have discovered an infernal plot." said Roberts. "Already they have tried to murder our friend. and are fully bent on accomplishing their work. To-night they meet again. A thousand pities we don't know the place of their concealment."

"I take it to be some out-of-door place they call 'the bower,'" said Robin. "I dare say. it is far enough from any road or pathway."

"We can now leave, Robin, and enjoy each other's company for at least a mile," said Taliesin; and with another pleasant "good night," they left, and started for their respective homes. In a low undertone they continued their conversation.

When they had traveled about half a mile, Robin came to a sudden stand; but it was only for a few seconds, and starting again, he remarked, "I presume it was nothing, but I thought I saw a faint light." He suddenly stopped again.

"Now, Taliesin Roberts," said he, " can you see a bit of light in that direction, or do my eyes deceive me ?"

Taliesin looked into the far-off darkness and said in a low voice, " I certainly see it ! And now, Robin, tell me the spot as near as you can judge, and see if we agree on the locality."

"I think it is in the vicinity of *Coed y Pant*," said Robin. "There, it has gone out, or out of sight—perhaps into the valley."

"Your opinion agrees with mine," said Roberts. "It may be possible that *Coed y Pant* is the very place where these villains have their 'bower.' Robin, I am going to try to find the hiding place of these incarnate demons. There is no time to be lost. Will you go with me and stand by me ?"

"I will go with you to any spot on earth, and stand by you, even if it should cost me my life!" said Robin.

"Brave fellow!" said Taliesin. " Now for the Valley Woods. I have some knowledge of the surroundings, and will lead. When we get there, we must tread with the silence of a cat. Here we start!"

And at a rapid rate, with their hearts beating with indignant excitement, they started for that unfrequented spot, and before a great while they were not far from the locality where they thought they had seen the light. Instead of moving forward at once into the wooded valley before them, they went around its southern end, and carefully looked down into its depths from the opposite side. Thus they moved slowly and carefully, in perfect silence, for some time. At last, Robin seized Taliesin by the arm and secured his attention. He then, without even a whisper, pointed with his finger downward to the valley. Taliesin saw at some distance a faint light, as if shining through thick branches. With noisless movements they slowly advanced through the thicket, in the direction of the light. Step by step they persevered until they reached the spot. It was a rude cabin, made of tree branches coving a slight frame-work. To their great satisfaction, our two young friends found that they were at the rear end of the structure, and that in case they were discovered, they could make good their escape.

They sat down within a few inches of the cabin, and through very small openings, they had a fair view of the interior. There were four together, and Scroggs seeemed to be the great man of the occasion.

"Let us drink around, and proceed to business." said Lucas Pugh, in rather a strong voice.

"It would better suit me, Mr. Pugh, if you would pitch your tune on a lower key." said Scroggs.

"There is no danger," said Lucas. "I'll defy all hell to find us out !"

"The spot is a good one," said Scroggs, "but your insisting on having a light because you had dropped a knife that was not worth two and sixpence, proves that you are not the safest man for an enterprise of this nature. If we are not pursued by spies, no thanks to you. Among my fellows I stand high, and in this matter my reputation must not suffer. For the present, put that bottle away."

Lucas made no reply, and Mr. Scroggs proceeded.

"The theft movement, on which you boys insisted, utterly failed. I told you it would, and I never would have consented to try it, only as I saw that out of it I could manufacture strength for further movements. I did not blame Mr. Pugh for wishing to accomplish his object without resorting to extreme measures. It would have been far more agreeable to me, and far cheaper for him. I gave the watch movement all the force I could, but it would not work. It was folly to suppose that Gwennie Lloyd would throw off Edwards on the strength of that. In the case of a person of an indifferent character, it would have worked. But out of the movement, weak as it was, I made a grand capital. The way I ridiculed the trick, laughed at its folly, stood by my young friend with tears in my eyes, and poured a stream of indignant eloquence against the vile plotter, rendered me doubly dear to Llewelyn and to all his friends. This proof of my burning friendship made my after movements much more safe. Mr. Pugh soon saw that no half-way measures would answer, and in harmony with his direction, as made known to my chief, and with the knowledge that the sum agreed upon had been promptly advanced, I at once went to work in a more sensible way.

"The boat disaster was well conceived, and carried out to the letter. In a spot where I thought no one could see us, I fell into the lake, and like a stone I went down. I came up, and being unable to swim—ha! ha!—I cried for help. He reached over the side of the boat and took hold of my hands. Then came that frantic pull which brought him into the water as quick as lightning, and he went down like a piece of lead. I then made for the boat, and pushed it off some distance, clinging to the stern. Edwards came up, blowing and struggling, and there I was, longing to save him, but couldn't! Ha! ha! I knew he would come up again, and with tears in my eyes, you understand, I was preparing for a last farewell, when a boat, with two men in it, shot by me like an arrow, and when

Llewelyn came up he was grabbed by one of the students, and taken into the boat. Didn't I inwardly damn those fellows? Edwards, fearing the laughter of his fellow students if the thing should be known, begged of his rescuers to say nothing about it, and they promised.

"That evening, after a most friendly interview with Edwards, I bade him good bye for a few weeks, to visit my father and sister at Cardiff.

"With Miss Thomas, the parting interview was affecting. She believes that Mr. Jenkins is on the very threshold of the kingdom of heaven, and that soon he will be an ornament to the Christian ministry. As a token of affection, I took from her the trifling sum of fifty pounds, which, like a thoroughly honest man, I delivered to my chief, as I have thousands of pounds before. She will not miss her coin for a long time, and when she does find out the deficiency, her friend Mr. Jenkins will be above suspicion.

"You see, gentlemen, that I have been true to my engagements. The lake undertaking was one of my best, and I shall be proud of it as long as I live. I have a project in my mind that cannot fail. It is so ingenious as to astonish myself. As yet it is not fully matured. With the assistance of my chief, I shall be ready to report at our next meeting."

"And when shall we meet again, and at what hour?" asked Pugh.

"On the night of the day after to-morrow, at midnight," said Simon Spike.

"But let there be no light on the hill to look for a two and sixpenny knife," said Scroggs.

"Now let us drink!" said Lucas.

"Yes, pass around the bottle!" said Scroggs. And while this closing ceremony was going on at the "bower," Taliesin and Robin, with beating hearts, were on their way homeward.

# CHAPTER XIX.



The two students who rescued Llewelyn from his desperate condition, had faithfully kept their promise of secrecy. They had also endeavored to believe that it was an accident. In that, however, they were not successful. The more they thought of it, the stronger became their convictions that Mr. Jenkins' movements were deliberately planned, and murderous in their intent.

On one afternoon they were seated on an embankment overlooking the lake, admiring its pacific appearance.

"About there is the spot where we saved Edwards," said Phillips, pointing to a certain part of the lake. "I wonder that such a bright intellect does not suspect foul play."

"It is owing to the wonderful goodness of his heart," said Griffiths. "He is as unsuspecting as a child. He thinks well of every one as long as he possibly can. While this is a noble Christian virtue, yet, when wicked, designing men take advantage of it, it is well to put our friend on his guard. It is evident that he has malicious enemies that seek his hurt, and that this

Jenkins is a hired agent in the interest of these enemies. He has left, and the people shed tears when he departed. But he gave them the consoling assurance that he would come again. If he returns, I fear there will be another *accident*."

"George," said Phillips, "let us have a plain talk with Mr. Edwards. There is no time to be lost."

They were about starting for the town, when the subject of their conversation suddenly joined them.

"Edwards, we are glad to see you!" said Phillips. "We were conversing about you."

"I am glad that you consider me worthy of your attention," said Llewelyn, with a pleasant smile.

"We shall take the liberty of asking you a few questions," said Griffiths.

"And I shall answer them to the best of my ability," said Llewelyn.

"Have you those who cherish toward you feelings of hatred?" asked Phillips.

"I have at least two malicious enemies," was the answer.

"If they wish to hurt you through an agent, can they furnish money?" asked Griffiths.

"As to that, both have abundance of gold," was the reply.

"Have you not suspected that such an agent was seen at Bala?" was the next question.

"When Mr. Jenkins left, I felt as if I had lost a friend," said Mr. Edwards. "I am now well convinced that he is a knave and a murderer. Under this impression, I now seek your advice. I am ashamed that I have been thus duped, and from henceforth I shall be more on my watch."

"My advice is this," said Phillips. "Write to your friends and ask them to be on their watch in regard to the movements of these enemies. In all probability, Jenkins is now in that region, in consultation with his employers."

"My friends are already on the alert," said Llewelyn, "and I have great confidence in their skill."

"Edwards, please keep us posted in regard to this matter," said Griffiths.

"I will certainly do that," said Edwards, and the three students slowly walked together toward the village.

---

After they had left the rear of the bower, it was some time before Taliesin and Robin uttered one word. The complete success of their undertaking gave them wonderful bodily vigor, and they found themselves at Mr. Roberts' mansion before they were aware. So careful was Taliesin in regard to keeping the matter a secret, that he took Robin, at that late hour of the night, into his own chamber, in order to give him instruction.

The parents were somewhat disturbed, but a few words from their son quieted them.

"Hooray, Robin!" cried Taliesin. "we've got them! To-morrow, or rather this morning. I shall go to Bangor and make a full statement to Parry Jones. We shall call for you at the proper time; so now you may go. and don't even mention the thing to a living person until the villains are secured."

"You may trust Robin Jones!" was the answer. as he bade Taliesin good night. and he was soon on his way toward Druid's Grove. Robin's chamber was not in the house proper, but in a small adjoining building. and he was at liberty to go or come at his pleasure, and so his absence or return was not often noticed.

"Well, Mr. Roberts." said Parry Jones. "you must have taken an early start. A little excited. eh? Found out something. I judge. I knew we were on the right trail. Now what is it?"

"Mr. Jones, I would be pleased to see you for a while at your private office, sir." said Taliesin. "I have made very important discoveries."

"Tom." said the lawyer to an office boy. "if any one comes in to inquire for me. you may say that I am engaged for an hour. and am not to be disturbed." and to the private office they went.

The reader is already aware of what the young law student had to reveal. He made a full statement of

what Robin Jones had heard in the field. and of what
they both had heard at the bower

"Nicely done, Roberts!" said the lawyer. "Capital!
There, give Robin Jones that, as a present from me,"
and he threw half a sovereign on the table. which Taliesin took with a respectful bow. The barrister then
took a pen and in a very short time filled a page of
legal paper, folded it and handed it to Taliesin.

" Take that and give it to Justice Ormsby," he said.
" On your way, call on Constable Jarvis, and take him
with you. You will be sworn, and as I am the counsel
for the Crown, I will see that Jarvis has force enough
to tie up the mean devils before they know what is the
matter. Be sure and have Jarvis come with you to my
office."

Taliesin did as directed. The justice read the paper
and remarked:

" This is a very serious case. Your preparation is
very thorough." He then prepared the papers, and
Taliesin, as a witness. swore to their truth.

"Jarvis," said the justice, "take these and proceed
according to your best judgment."

The constable bowed, and with Taliesin went into
the office of the Crown Advocate.

"Jarvis, you have a job on hand that will do you
honor," said the barrister. " Two of those fellows, if
they are not instantly subdued, will fight like devils.

You must take sufficient force to make a sure thing of it.'

"That I will certainly do," said Jarvis, "and your Honor knows what luck I generally have in this line."

"There is not a better officer in the principality,' said Parry Jones, to the great satisfaction of the head constable.

"I presume Mr. Roberts will be glad to give me all the information that he can in regard to the locality," said Mr. Jarvis.

"I shall not only do that, but I shall be with you, and so will Robin Jones," was the reply.

Jarvis then took a blank book out of his pocket, asked several questions and put down the answers.

"Now, Mr. Roberts," said he, "please pay strict attention to what I say. Be near the spot to-morrow morning before daylight. When it becomes light enough for you to see objects clearly, seek the bower and mark the shortest distance to reach it from the hill. Walk it a number of times over, until you are sure that you will know the way in the dark. Notice well the surroundings of their retreat. Select a good spot where we may be safe, and yet near enough to see and hear. Select some tree, stone, or some other object by which you can tell the exact place where we enter the valley. When you leave the woods for home, let it be at quite a distance from the bower. By half-past ten we must be on the ground. See to it that

14

Robin Jones is at your father's as early as nine o'clock. You may look for me and my force soon after dark. I shall come first, the others will follow at short intervals. You have done finely, and I can trust you without the least fear." And Jarvis went his way.

"We can rest assured that he will make a clean job of it," said the lawyer. "In an undertaking of this kind he is in his element. He is cool, strong, and abounding in courage."

"Mr. Roberts," he continued, "we have known that there has been a gang of well-trained, murderous burglars that have long troubled the principality and parts of England, and have so far escaped. I am now of the opinion that this Simon Spike is at the head of the thieving gang. If so, Mr. Roberts, in finding out this villain, you have conferred a lasting favor upon the whole country. This exploit is worth more to you than a thousand pounds. Robin Jones' name also will be favorably known."

"But the thing is not yet accomplished," said Taliesin with a smile.

"Not fully; but it is in such a shape that its complete success is only a question of less than forty-eight hours," said Parry Jones. "You have been deprived of rest; to-night you will find but little sleep, and to-morrow night less yet. Now the best advice I can give you, young man, is to go to bed. In view of what you have to to perform, you had better take this needed rest at home."

# CHAPTER XX.

## THE ARREST.

We have barely mentioned the lady who was known by those who lived in the mountain pass, as "the wife of old Spike." This adjective "old" was not used to show that the person it qualified had reached advanced age, but rather to distinguish one Spike from another one of more recent date. This woman was never seen away from her own premises. She was small in stature, of a sad countenance, and avoided all conversation with her few neighbors. The impression was left on the minds of all that saw her, that she was very far from being happy. The following will throw some light upon the situation:

"Hold your tongue, you blasted fool, or I'll choke the breath out of you!" said Spike, looking at the little woman with the ferociousness of a very cross tiger. "Attend to your own business, will you? and the boy and myself will attend to ours! I say again, hold your tongue!"

"Simon Spike," said the little woman, in a low but firm voice, "I have held my tongue for years, while my heart has been ready to break. I have been your slave; I have run at your command; I have made no reply to your abusive language. At last I have summoned up courage, and I have thrown off fear. I have something to say; say it I will, and don't you interrupt me, at your peril! You look astonished, Simon Spike! I am astonished at myself, and I can hardly believe it is my own voice. With a lying tongue you enticed me away from a good home, and the paths of virtue, into a life of sin and shame. You promised to become my lawful husband, and afterwards you laughed at me and pronounced it a joke. You gave me the charge of your little boy. With him for a while I took some comfort, hoping that he would be a better man than his father. In this I have been disappointed. Already he is rough, and every day I suffer his abuse. After this I learned that I was the mistress of a master burglar. Gold you found in abundance, procured by thieving hands. You are engaged in the same bad business now, if not in something worse, and your son willingly joins in the wicked plottings. What means this absence from home until three o'clock in the morning so often during the last few weeks, and why this close consultation with Scroggs? You think I have not seen him. Curb your anger for a little while longer, Simon Spike! I will soon stop. It is my first utterance and it may be my last. Give up this dreadful way of living. The curse of God is hanging over our heads! Settle down with your son, and lead an honest life, and after so many years, do justice to one that you have degraded and abused. Simon Spike, will you do it?"

The pent-up wrath of Spike now broke loose like a rushing torrent. His face was livid with anger. With gnashed teeth and threatening gestures he poured out a volley of abusive epithets.

"I have been a fool to let your cursed tongue run on so long. Will I 'settle down and lead an honest life?' Ha, ha! I will lead the life I choose, and come home when I please. To-night, again, we go on a pleasure excursion, and to-morrow, if Charlotte Bruce will venture another sermon, I shall have the pleasure of pulling her nose and spitting in her face."

"That is a fair warning," said Charlotte, "and I will take it under consideration," and in her countenance was seen a decided purpose.

------

An hour before the dawn, Taliesin was on the hill overlooking the wooded valley. As soon as daylight appeared, without any delay, he went in search of a convenient passageway. He carefully surveyed every opening. At last he came to what seemed to be an ancient cowpath, and in the loose earth he plainly saw marks of heavy footsteps. He at once concluded that this was the conspirators' entrance, and that it would lead to their secret resort. Far sooner than he expect-

ed, he found himself in front of the structure. His
next search was for a safe and convenient hiding-place.
Here again he was fortunate, for one side of the bower
rested against heavy underbrush, where a number of
persons in the dark could rest unseen. With a strong
pocket-knife he cleared a spot sufficiently large to accommodate the expected company. He then, as directed by Mr. Jarvis, went over the ground several times,
until the whole path was clear to his mind. At the entrance to the valley there was a large stone, which in
the night would prove an unmistakable guide. Having
fully satisfied himself on every point, he left for home,
while most of his neighbors were yet in the embrace
of sleep.

The first arrival at "Cae'r Eithin," in the evening,
was Robin Jones, who was already fully instructed in
the program. Next came Jarvis; and after him, at
short intervals, came four able-bodied men fully armed.
To relieve his parents' mind, Taliesin had partially explained to them the nature of these movements.

"Well, Mr. Roberts," said Jarvis, "first of all we
will hear your report."

"I have made a thorough survey," said Taliesin,
"and am ready to lead you to the spot without the
least trouble. I have also prepared a safe hiding-place
close to the bower."

"You and your friend here are worthy of all praise,"

said the chief constable. "My men are fully instructed. What is said must be said here. Not a word must
be spoken on the way, or even after we get there, until
we rush upon the gang. At a given time, when we
shall have fully learned their future prospects at Bala,
I and my men will fall upon them. Let Mr. Roberts
and his friend Jones follow at their leisure. Now, Mr.
Roberts, we are ready to start. You and your friend
may lead. March!"

They moved rapidly, and with very little noise. They
avoided the road, and went across the fields. They
soon reached the entrance, and in a very short time
they stood by the bower. Jarvis with his men, as far
as the darkness would permit, closely examined the surroundings. He then gave signs for Taliesin to proceed, and in a minute more they were all seated within
a few inches of the cabin, encircled by an undergrowth
which rendered their hiding-place perfectly safe. The
excitement which the occasion produced, measurably
relieved the monotony of their dark and silent retreat.
The time soon passed, and the hour of midnight arrived. Every heart beat a little faster, while each ear
keenly watched for the coming of the conspirators. At
last they heard low voices near by, and the next minute the four villains were within what they considered
their safe council chamber.

A lantern was uncovered, and Jarvis was glad to know

that through the brush he could partially see the plotters, as well as hear their words.

"I feel a little easier now than I did night before last," said Scroggs. "Fortunately, Pugh did not drop his knife, and we had no illumination on the hill."

"That was careless in me, I know," said Pugh, "but we are all safe."

"Now to business!" said Simon Spike.

"I move that the first item be a little inspiration from this," said Lucas, producing a well-filled bottle. "What say you, Mr. Scroggs?"

"We have had a long walk," said the operator. "Yes, pass around the inspiration! Ha, ha! Pugh, that's a good one."

The first item having been disposed of, Scroggs assumed the charge of the meeting.

"Our stay to-night in this quiet spot will not be long. We have but l'ttle to do. For the benefit of Mr. Pugh, for whom I entertain very high regards, and who has not been at all backward in furnishing funds, I will say that I have matured a plan that will in the end give him perfect satisfaction. My worthy chief has given it his full endorsement as a scheme possessing great merit, and has given me some very valuable hints in regard to its faithful execution. Some time may be required to perfect the arrangements, and to make myself doubly dear to my bosom friend. Now let me give you a piece of good advice. When the heart-rending news reaches Llangobaith that by an accidental discharge of a pistol in the hands of Miss Thomas, that Llewelyn Edwards lost his life, let not grief completely overwhelm you. Be moderate in your sorrow. My own grief on that occasion will be frantic enough to answer for the whole company. Oh, how I shall weep! I need not give you the particulars; but I will assure you that it is as neat a thing as I ever produced."

"Mr. Scroggs has not a superior as an operator in the kingdom," said Simon Spike.

"I hope your little instrument will make a sure thing of it," said Lucas. "My father knows nothing of this, and he is too faint-hearted to come up to the scratch. I get the money from mother, who knows all about it. But she cannot give much more without creating suspicion in my father's mind. The final payment will be met when the job is finished."

"Mr. Pugh, it will be but a short time before you will admit that you have had more than the worth of your money. I will also say to my young friend John Spike, that before I return to my field of labor at Bala, I will give him the outlines of a scheme by which he can bring a very fine disaster upon his old schoolmate Taliesin Roberts."

"My revenge will be sure!" cried John, under a degree of inspiration.

"Let us drink all around, and be gone," said Simon.

"Pugh, out with the inspiration!" said Scroggs.

"And let me drink damnation to Taliesin Roberts!" said John.

Jarvis and his men were instantly on their feet. With silent tread they left their hiding-place, and rushed upon the conspirators, while a glare of light filled the bower.

"Surrender as my prisoners, you murderous devils!" cried Jarvis, in a voice that echoed through the wooded valley, while a polished pistol was grasped by each of his men. "Surrender!"

"Damnation!" cried old Spike, "I'll never surrender! Come my men let us fight our way out!" and he made a desperate rush toward the door. The but-end of Jarvis' pistol knocked him senseless.

"Put on his ornaments, Davis!" said Jarvis, "he will raise no objections at least for a while."

The officer placed the burglar's hands in the vicinity of his back and decorated his wrists with heavy irons.

"Who is the next to try the amusing experiment of running away?" asked Jarvis. "Mr. Scroggs, do you wish to indulge in that recreation?"

"My dear Mr. Jarvis," said Scroggs, in the most polite manner, "I have no taste for the absurdities, and in unprofitable amusements I never indulge. I am astonished that Mr. Spike has so far forgotten his common prudence as to rush into seen danger.  I—"

"That will do for this time," said Jarvis.  "Let me see what kind of hands you have."

"With the utmost pleasure, sir.  The ladies pronounce them fair and delicate," was the answer, as he gave the officer every advantage to adjust the iron cuffs.

Pugh and John Spike were completely overwhelmed with terror, and made no resistance whatever.

By this time the prostrate Spike had partially revived, and was anything but amiable in his speech.

"My dear Mr. Spike," said Scroggs, "you seem to be unduly excited.  You are not in possession of that calm tranquility of soul, that a good Christian should manifest in the dark day of affliction."

"Stop your blarney, you infernal fool!" cried Spike. "If my hands were free, you would not dare talk such stuff as that to me."

"Cease thy ravings," said Scroggs in a mild voice. "I am in the same adversity myself; but, with St. Paul, I have learned 'in whatever situation I am, therewith to be content.' "

"You are a devoted Christian, undoubtedly," said Jarvis, "but, it is getting late, your lodgings are at some distance, and we must leave this consecrated spot."

"Adieu! sweet bower, adieu!" said the poetic prisoner.  "Never again shall thy walls resound to the eloquent fiction of Thomas Adolphus Scroggs! Never more shall thy evergreen arches look down and smile upon a merry group eagerly sucking inspiration from the famous rum bottle of the aristocratic heir of Riverside!"

Here the said heir, forgetting himself, and being conscious that his feet were not handcuffed, bestowed a most vigorous kick on a certain portion of Scroggs' corporeal system, which at that moment was the most easy of access.

Mr. Scroggs, being absolutely certain that some solid substance had come in very unpleasant contact with his person, raised his manacled hands to a certain angle, turned about quickly, and with violence brought the iron wristlets against Lucas' head, which laid him prostrate on the ground.

"This must be stopped," said Jarvis, while a slight smile rested on his countenance.

"That was an unfortunate accident," said Scroggs, with a compassionate look.

"It was not an accident," cried Pugh, "and you are a liar!"

"Spike, if you refuse to get up and walk," said Jarvis, "my men will drag you on the ground. Here, Jones and Pritchard, take hold, and start him, while the rest of us follow. Taliesin Roberts, lead us out to the hill."

They started, each officer holding a weapon ready for instant service if required. Spike, after some re sistance, saw fit to walk, and the entrance was soon reached. Here for a while they halted, and Scroggs availed himself of the occasion.

"Behold the memorable spot where the rich heir of Riverside, on the night before last, dispelled the darkness of night, to search for his two and sixpenny pocket knife! Ha, ha! To that blaze we are indebted for this grand entertainment. In honor of that event, forever hereafter let this spot be known as Illumination Hill."

"Mr. Roberts, lead us to the highway, and make the distance as short as possible," said Jarvis; and they started.

"Yea," said Scroggs as they advanced, "let us reach our destination with all speed. My weary eyelids long for repose, and my stomach is becoming an aching void which ruir can never fill. So haste thee on, Taliesin!"

Let it not be supposed that the other prisoners were silent. Far from it. The Spike father belched out terrible anathemas thick and fast. The son spent his vocal strength in hurling bad sounding adjectives at Taliesin, and Lucas poured out curses on the head of Robin Jones.

They had now reached the highway. Jarvis stood on the top of a stone wall and swung his lantern for some thirty seconds.

"What is that contemptible scoundrel at now?" asked Lucas.

"My dear Pugh," answered Scroggs, "I am deeply shocked to hear such an unguarded expression from a youth brought up religiously! 'Speak not evil of magistrates,' is the language of the good book. Alas! I see that the prayers and godly admonitions of your devoted parents have proved unavailing! The swinging of the lantern, is a signal for the horsemen and chariots of Israel, to hasten hither to convey Mr. Jarvis' distinguished guests to that city that has a cathedral, even Bangor, which quietly nestles between the hills."

Scroggs' judgment was correct. A couple of two-horse chariots arrived on the spot with ample accommodations, and the prisoners were properly arranged.

"Mr. Roberts and Mr. Jones, you will save me much extra labor by being present at Bangor, in the morning at ten o'clock," said Mr. Jarvis.

"And ere we part," said Scroggs, putting his head out of the carriage, let me assure Roberts and Jones, that their calm and modest behavior under great provocation, has secured my most profound admiration. If ever in their wanderings they should come near my city residence or country seat, I hope they will call and enjoy my grateful hospitality."

The chariots left, and Taliesin and Robin went to their respective homes.

# CHAPTER XXI.

## A MIDNIGHT QUARREL, AND A FLIGHT.

One night, at somewhat of a late hour, Llewelyn reached his lodgings from an appointment at a Methodist chapel about three miles from the town of Bala. He was no sooner in his room than Mr. Ellis handed him a letter which he had brought from the post office. The familiar handwriting made his heart throb. He fondly gazed at the address, while he admired the beautiful penmanship. "But how is this?" said he, "*Llangobaith?*" and his heart beat quicker. "Is it possible that Thomas Lloyd—well, I'll know in a moment!" And the letter was opened. He read one brief sentence, looked up and cried, "Thank God!" The letter was as follows:

"MY DEAR LLEWELYN:

Wonderful things have transpired since I wrote to you last. I am restored to my dear old home, and these lines are penned in that familiar room that I have called my own ever since I can remember. Three days ago, a little after sunset, my uncle's clerk brought into the house a number of letters, some for my uncle and others for myself. The one from Bala I expected. But judge of my astonishment when I saw one from my father! I opened it, and the first sentence almost

overwhelmed me. With his consent, I enclose it to
you, together with a few lines from my Aunt Grace. I
am very, *very* happy! My cup of enjoyment is running over. The Lord has been better to us than all
of our fears. Papa treats me with a new kind of affection. He is much more quiet and subdued. I fear
that he is not yet a Christian. Let us pray for him.
The wonderful change already wrought, is a proof that
more can be accomplished. I have a sweet hope that
dear papa will yet be a child of God.

I am heartily glad that your Mr. Jenkins has left
Bala. If he returns, as I fear he will, I beg of you not
to admit him into your confidence. I have my strong
fears that he is a base deceiver. Dear Llewelyn, be
very watchful. I have not seen Helen since I came
home, but we shall meet before many hours. May
heaven bless and protect you, is the earnest prayer of
your own dear

GWENNIE."

By this time the young theological student was on
a higher pinacle of enjoyment, according to his best
judgment, than at any former period of his life.

On this same night there had been a large, enthusiastic meeting at the Methodist chapel, for the purpose
of relieving the house of worship from an embarrassing debt. The effort had been highly successful, and
the sum realized quite large. Among the liberal sub-
scriptions was one from Miss Thomas for fifty pounds.
This lady was proverbially liberal in all worthy enter-

prises, especially those directly connected with the gospel.

The next morning Miss Thomas met Llewelyn in one of the passages, and smilingly said—

"Mr. Edwards, we greatly missed you last night, and you lost a highly interesting meeting."

"I am sure of that," said the young man. "I am very happy to hear that the effort was such a grand success."

"O, I am delighted!" said the young lady, while her animated countenance gave clear evidence of the joy of her heart. "I had the pleasure of handing in my name for fifty pounds, and I know by experience that 'it is more blessed to give than to receive.'"

"At that, your share of blessedness must be large," said Edwards, "for your giving is quite extensive."

"It is not worth mentioning," said Miss Thomas. "But the little I do give affords me much pleasure. Mr. Edwards, seeing that you go to the Institute, will you be so kind as to hand my subscription to Professor Davies, who is the treasurer?"

"I will do so with pleasure, Miss Thomas," said Llewelyn.

"Thank you. I will run into my room and get it. I laid by that sum for that very purpose some time ago," and she left.

15

She was gone a long time, and at last she asked Mr. Edwards to come up stairs.

He found her in the sitting-room, with a reflective look upon her countenance.

"I have arrived at another mysterious event in my life!" said she. "That gold watch transaction remains a mystery. I have now discovered that fifty pounds have been taken from a locked drawer in my desk!"

"Miss Thomas," said Llewelyn, with perfect calmness, "your watch was found in my possession, and I would be pleased to have every article moved from my trunk in your presence."

"If the money is in your trunk, it was put there by the same thieving hand that took the watch," said Miss Thomas. Let the knowledge of this matter be confined to us two; at least for the present. I want no uproar or excitement. For our own satisfaction, you may examine the trunk."

This was carefully done, to the perfect satisfaction of the young lady.

"I have plenty of money in the bank," said Miss Thomas, "and my subscription will be promptly paid, but not to-day."

"Miss Thomas," said Mr. Edwards, "pardon me if I ask you a few questions, for this is a serious matter. Have you any remembrance that at any time, say within two months, you mentioned this subject of church debt, directly or indirectly, to any person, or in the presence of any person?"

Miss Thomas hesitated a moment, and said, "I mentioned this thing to Mr. Jenkins, and gave him a hint that if he wanted an object worthy of his benevolence, it was our church debt."

"And what did he say?"

"O, he seemed to be interested at once, as he always was in everything that was good," said Miss Thomas with a moderate sigh.

"Did you tell him that you intended to give something yourself?"

"Yes, and if I am not mistaken I told him that I had laid by a sum for that purpose. But, has not this questioning in regard to Mr. Jenkins a strange appearance, Mr. Edwards?"

"I was sure you would think it strange," said Llewelyn, "and you will think it more so when I tell you in all sincerity that I fully believe that this very Mr. Jenkins that you and I have so confided in, and looked upon as a perfect gentleman, is a thorough scoundrel, an accomplished thief, and a would-be murderer."

For a while Miss Thomas looked on her young friend in utter astonishment. She turned pale, and then her color returned. At last she spoke—

"Mr. Edwards, I have always looked upon you as a man of deep sense and good judgment, and I exceedingly regret that anything has transpired which compels me to change my opinion."

"Your regret cannot be greater than my own, Miss Thomas," said Llewelyn, "for I hold your favorable opinion in very high esteem. I have expressed to you my firm convictions. I am fully persuaded that it was his hands that took your watch and put it in my trunk, that it was he who wrote that letter to the Carnarvon *Herald*, and that it was he who stole your fifty pounds."

"But in the matter of the watch, did he not eloquently and with tears in his eyes declare you innocent? And did he not ridicule the plot as silly and ludicrous? And did he not on that occasion endear himself to us all?" asked Miss Thomas.

"That he did," was the reply. "But he had accomplished his double purpose. First, under a guise of truth he could slander me. Again, it gave him a fine opportunity to blind our eyes as to his true character, by becoming my eloquent champion and defender. In this last he was eminently successful; and in this, as far as I can see, was the only strength of the plot· Jenkins is in the employ of others, who pursue me with deadly malice."

"Of your enemies I know nothing," said Miss Thomas, coldly. "Of Mr. Jenkins I have some knowledge; and I cannot believe your monstrous theory for one moment. Mr. Edwards, is it not possible that of late your studies have been too hard, and that your mental powers have been too heavily taxed?"

"My studies are not burdensome," said the young man, with a broad smile. "I think, Miss Thomas, I am in my right mind, and I believe also that the sequel will prove that my theory is correct."

"Let this answer for the present," said Miss Thomas, pleasantly. "Please say nothing about this interview or the lost money, and I will keep the same silence. In regard to Mr. Jenkins our opinions greatly differ. You believe him to be a thieving knave, and I believe him to be a true gentleman."

----

While the exciting scene was going on at the bower, and while the conspirators were being secured by the strong arm of the law, an uneasiness and sleeplessness had crept into the magnificent bed-chamber, in which, on downy pillows, were found the heads of Mr. and Mrs. Evan Pugh.

"I cannot account for his absence from home night after night until such late hours," said the husband, with evident feeling. "I thought at first that he staid at the Red Lion; but Mrs. Owens assures me that he does not stay there. I cannot see into it, and he must explain the matter to my satisfaction."

"Lucas knows what he is about," said his wife,

sharply. "He has not forgotten the dirty insult heaped upon this house. And are you not aware that he has vowed vengeance against the shop boy, and sworn that that howling Methodist shall never wed Gwennie Lloyd? Lucas knows what he is about, and so do I. Evan Pugh!"

"Am I to understand that you encourage that boy in anything for which he would be arrested if it was known?" asked Pugh.

"You may understand what you choose," said the wife. "Llewelyn Edwards will be disposed of to my perfect satisfaction, and we must all lament the painful *accident.*"

"My God!" exclaimed Pugh, suddenly leaving his bed. "This is something I never dreamed of! A mother and son plotting against the life of an innocent man! Heaven save us! Get out of that bed in one moment and dress you!" and he hastily put on his own garments.

"I have always said that I married a fool!" said Mrs. Pugh, while she remained unmoved upon the pillow.

"At that time I was indeed a fool!" said the agitated husband. "But I was not aware that I was bringing with me to Riverside a woman that would connive with murderers."

The lady of the house was no longer in bed, but on the floor, and resorting to her common mode of war-

fare, she was about to hurl a water pitcher at the head
of her husband, when for the first time in his life he
came to the conclusion that he would use new tactics.
He suddenly snatched the pitcher from her hands, and
gave her a proof of his bodily strength in the shape of
a violent and prolonged shake. Indeed, he was conscious of a degree of enjoyment in the new exercise.
It increased in violence until the aggressive party cried
for quarters.

"There!" said Pugh, proud of his first victory. "Let
that answer for the present. Now put on your garments and prepare yourself to answer some questions."

The new process had produced a wonderful change
in the little lady, and to her own astonishment as well
as that of her husband, she found herself in the very
act of obedience.

"Now, Mrs. Pugh," said the master, "according to
your own confession you have given countenance to
a most villainous scheme. From whom besides does
Lucas receive advice?"

"I shall answer no questions, Evan Pugh!" said his
wife, with returned courage. "I feel much more like
spitting in your face. Lucas will be home in a few
minutes, and he may answer you as much as he
pleases."

"If this devilish thing should be found out, it would

result in your transportation for life, if not in your death on the gallows," said Pugh.

"But it will not be found out," said Mrs. Pugh. "It is in the hands of those who understand their business."

"Aye, business worthy of demons!" said the husband.

Just then they heard the sound of approaching carriages. They listened, and the horses stopped in front of their gate.

"What can this mean at such a late hour of the night?" said Pugh, in evident alarm.

Heavy knocking was heard below. They both went down, and the husband opened the door. Standing before him he saw a man with a lighted lantern in his hand and heavy pistols in his belt.

"This is an untimely hour to call, Mr. Pugh," said Jarvis, "but I could not well come sooner. I have under arrest a gang of murderous conspirators, who have aimed at the innocent life of Llewelyn Edwards. Among them I find your son. The others are Simon Spike, his son, and an accomplished knave by the name of Scroggs. Their hiding-place was found, and their guilt has been learned from their own mouths by reliable witnesses. They will be examined before Justice Ormsby this morning at ten o'clock. I thought it was best to let you know it."

"Mr. Jarvis, I am shocked and crushed!" said Pugh. "I knew that my son was often out late at night, and it gave me uneasiness, but it never entered my head that he was engaged in mischief."

"Your son assured his fellow conspirators in my hearing that his *father* knew nothing about it, and that *he* was wholly ignorant in regard to the large sums of money furnished him to carry forward the plot."

It is possible that Mr. Jarvis had a purpose in thus emphasizing the word "father." At any rate, Pugh gave it that construction, and said—

"Mr. Jarvis, I thank you for the information, terrible as it is."

Thus ended the interview. The constable left for the carriage, while Pugh closed the door and joined his wife in the parlor.

"Well, you have heard all," said the husband, with some severity. "You have furnished Lucas money to reward a villain, with the full knowledge of what was going on! Without any delay you must escape, or in the morning you may be arrested and shut up in jail. And now before you leave, if it will give you any satisfaction you may spit in my face."

Here the wife broke down, and gave vent to her feelings in hysterical weeping, freely mixed with very bad language. She soon recovered her composure, and with a desperate resolution on her countenance said—

"Our scheme has miscarried!  Now, Evan, if you think I am worth saving from prison, give directions and I will follow them."

"Pack your trunks at once!" said the husband.  "You must be in Carnarvon by five o'clock to take the coach for London.  I will give you a good supply of money.  Keep your face veiled until you are out of the Principality.  Settle in London, and keep away from your relatives in other parts of England.  Write to me regularly, and I will address you by the name of Jane McKnight.  I will dispose of my property as soon as I can, and join you at the Metropolis.  You have acted most wickedly.  But in this Gwennie Lloyd business I was not without blame myself.  Put your things together, and Tom Williams will soon have the carriage ready."

"Betty " was called to assist, and a plausible reason given.  The trunks were soon ready.  At three o'clock in the morning Mrs. Pugh bade a sudden adieu to her Welsh home, and at five she was inside of the royal mail coach on her way for London.

# CHAPTER XXII.



Early in the morning Bangor was thoroughly excited. The news of the wonderful arrest had quickly spread throughout the city. Women ran to and fro, and men gathered in groups on the street corners. To hundreds, Lucas Pugh and John Spike were well known. The nature of their offence was but slightly understood, but they had been informed, that at ten o'clock the prisoners would be brought before Justice Ormsby. Long before the hour the public room was crowded, and so would have been the passages, only as they were kept open by the police.

There was a noise of a crowd outside, and presently Jarvis, and his assistants, brought in the prisoners. With the exception of Scroggs, who still maintained his strange hilarity, they appeared angry and defiant. Able counsel had been procured. The warrant was read, and Parry Jones before examining the witnesses, briefly addressed the Court.

"May it please your Honor, in the evidence we shall present, the Court will learn the nature and origin of the most cowardly, malicious and depraved conspiracy, that has ever disgraced the pages of history. It was against a young man of as pure a character as ever breathed the air of the principality. While these conspirators were taking their parting drink, at their plotting place, Mr. Jarvis and his assistants claimed them as their legal guests, adorned them with wristlets, and gave them a free ride to Bangor. Here they are, your Honor, and we are ready to proceed with the examination."

Robin Jones gave in his evidence with clearness and simplicity. Taliesin followed. The Justice remarked, that at this stage it was not necessary for the prosecution to produce any more testimony, and asked the advocate for the defence if he wished to speak.

"The evidence is of such a nature, your Honor," said the lawyer, "that at present I have nothing to say. When they are brought to trial, it shall be my pleasure as well as my duty to see that, as prisoners, they have all their legitimate rights. That is all, your Honor."

Justice Ormsby then remarked, "From the evidence advanced, I am compelled to commit the prisoners. The officers will now see that these four men are taken and lodged in jail, to await the action of the grand jury."

The prisoners were removed, and were soon on their way to the county jail.

During the examination, a young man of comely appearance was seen near the Crown Advocate, busily engaged in writing, who, as soon as the men were committed, rushed out of the court room with eager haste. In a few minutes after this, the same person was seen on one of the swiftest horses, sweeping along towards Carnarvon at the rate of twenty miles an hour. He was the Bangor correspondent of the Carnarvon *Herald*, and this was the day of publication.

In the afternoon, the *Herald* made its appearance, and the excitement it produced may be judged from the following heavy heading:

"STARTLING NEWS FOOM BANGOR! AN INFERNAL PLOT DEFEATED! THE WOULD-BE MURDERERS OF LLEWELYN EDWARDS BROUGHT TO GRIEF! LUCAS PUGH, SIMON SPIKE, JOHN SPIKE AND THOMAS ADOLPHUS SCROGGS, (the Bala "Jenkins,") LODGED IN CARNARVON JAIL! THE HEROIC CONDUCT OF TALIESIN ROBERTS AND ROBERT JONES!"

Then followed a long article, in which was given the full particulars, ending thus: "The praise of Taliesin Roberts and Robin Jones is on every tongue. Through their untired efforts by day and by night, a gang of villains have been arrested, and in all probability a most worthy young man saved from a violent death."

Morris Williams was one of the first to see the startling article. He was not demonstrative, like some others, although deeply agitated. "And this villain wanted Gwennie for a wife, did he?" said he to himself, and hastened to the post-office.

"Mr. Stevens," he asked, "what time will the next regular mail reach Bala?"

"About this time on the day after to-morrow," was the answer.

"Thank you," said Mr. Williams, and then left for the office of the *Herald*.

"I should be glad to get fifty copies of this day's *Herald*, Mr. Jones," said Williams.

"We published a large edition, and we can accommodate you," was the reply.

"Please send them over to my house as soon as you can, for I am in a hurry," said Williams, and off he went.

"Tom, now see how quick you can get ready my horse and chaise. I wish to be off without any delay. I will not be home until to-morrow night; and then you will be on hand to take good care of 'Black Jim.'"

"Yes sir," said the young man, and he made haste for the stable.

"Black Jim," was the finest horse in Carnarvon; and many of the gentry envied Mr. Williams, as they often witnessed "Jim's" graceful form and grand speed. Large offers had been made for the noble animal, but the uniform answer had been, "The horse is not for sale."

The chaise was already at the door. Presently Mr. Williams came out, and threw a large bundle into the vehicle.

"Tom, take this note and this paper and leave them at the livery stable office."   He then seated himself in the chaise, took the reins, and Jim proudly trotted out of the city in the direction of Llanllyfni.

———

In the parlor at Llwyn y Derwydd, there were together Thomas Lloyd, Grace and Gwennie.

"Papa," said Gwennie, "don't you think that for a number of days, Robin Jones has acted somewhat strange and mysterious?"

"I certainly do, Gwennie," said Lloyd. "His cheerfulness is gone, and he is absent minded. At times he seems to be indignant. At one time when he thought perhaps that no one was near him, I heard him indulging in what sounded like a defiant laugh, while his fists presented a very threatning shape."

"I don't feel easy about him!" said Gwennie. "Recently, I think he has been out until late hours. This is so unlike Robin Jones! Papa, what reason did he give for going to Bangor this morning?"

"He said that Taliesin Roberts requested him to go on very important business."

"That certainly was a good reason," said Gwennie. "When Taliesin requests his presence, it must be either in Robin's interest or for the good of some one else."

"Tom, would it not be well for us to question Robin

in regard to this trouble?" asked Grace. "We might be of some help to the good fellow."

"I think it would be well," said Lloyd. "But here he comes, and there is certainly a great improvement in the appearance of his countenance. Gwennie, if you wish to question him, you had better invite him in."

Robin came up from the road toward the house with a lively step, and with such an animation of countenance, which they had not witnessed for several days.

Gwennie rose and stood in the door. "Well, Robin," she said, "and you have got back. You have had a long walk, and you must be tired."

"I am not tired the least bit, Miss Lloyd," said Robin. "I never in my life came from Bangor to Druid's Grove so easy and in so short a time."

"I am very glad to hear it, Robin. I want you to come into the parlor, for we have a few questions to ask you."

Robin entered the parlor with some diffidence. It was a room where men-servants never visited. Gwennie noticed some signs of embarrassment, and said—

"Sit down on this chair, Robin, and be just as much at home as if you were in your own room."

"You are very good, Miss Lloyd," said Robin, "and I am ready to answer any questions as far as I know."

"Robin, we have thought that for some days you have not appeared exactly like yourself."

"And you have thought right, Miss Gwennie," said Robin, "and it is a wonder that I did not behave a good deal worse. When I tell you what the trouble was, you will say that Robin Jones behaved pretty well."

"Robin, why did you not let us know about this trouble? We might have helped you."

"I think you could not have helped me a bit, Miss Gwennie," said the young man. "And that is the rea son that Taliesin told me to be sure and not mention it to you nor any one in the house, until we got through. I can tell you all about it now, Miss Lloyd. It will shock you a good bit, but it will not kill you."

"Go on, Robin!" said Gwennie with wondering anxiety.

Just then a boy on a horse suddenly stopped in front of the house, jumped from the saddle, rushed to the open door and knocked. Gwennie met him.

"Mr. Morris Williams, from Carnarvon, sent me with this paper for Miss Gwennie Lloyd."

"I am that person," said Gwennie. "Will you not come in?"

"I thank you, Miss Lloyd," said the boy, "but I must return at once." And so he left.

"What can there be in the *Herald* of sufficient importance to require a special messenger?" said Gwennie, as she slowly opened the paper.

16

"I think you will learn in that paper what was the trouble with Robin Jones," said the faithful servant.

Gwennie's eyes soon fell upon the startling article from Bangor. She instantly dropped the paper, and in a voice of deep agitation. with uplifted hands, cried out—

"Oh, papa, papa, papa!"

Thomas Lloyd jumped to his feet in a moment, and in a soothing tone asked—

" What is it, my child ?"

" Oh, papa. papa!" cried Gwennie. "It was dreadful!"

" Is any one killed?" asked her Aunt Grace.

"No, but they were going to murder him!" cried Gwennie, with tearful eyes.

" Murder who?" cried her father, in a voice of alarm.

"Take the paper, papa, and read that terrible heading."

Thomas Lloyd took the paper, glanced at it for a few moments, and turned pale.

" In the name of Heaven, what is it?" cried Grace.

"I will give you the heading." And in trembling accents he read the dreadful words.

'"It is no wonder, dear Gwennie, that you were so terribly shocked!" said the aunt, fondly kissing her. "But how thankful we are that their wicked plot has been defeated!"

"May the name of the Lord be praised!" said Gwennie.

Thomas Lloyd then read the article aloud to its close, while the rest listened with intense interest.

"Gwennie," asked her father, "did Llewelyn tell you anything about this lake disaster?

"Not a word, papa!"

"In that he acted wisely," said Grace.

"Now, Miss Gwennie, you understand why I behaved a little strange," said Robin Jones.

"Oh, Robin, you have behaved most nobly!" said Gwennie, with joyful tears in her eyes.

"I cannot see that I have done anything that should make the people cry in the streets of Bangor, 'Hooray for Robin Jones!' And only think, Parry Jones made me a present of half a pound!"

"And here is another present of half a pound," said Thomas Lloyd, while the astonished Robin took the coin.

"And here, Robin, take that from me," said Grace," handing him a crown.

"And, Robin, take that from me!" said Gwennie, as she earnestly kissed his cheek.

Robin, with all his power of endurance, was not proof against such wholesale demonstration. He broke down, and wept like a child.

"Now, Robin," said Gwennie, "you can go and eat

your dinner." And, rising, she continued, "I will see that you have a meal worthy of the occasion." And she left the room.

"And, Robin," said Thomas Lloyd, "after dinner, you need not go to work. You have slept but very little this week, and I would advise you to go to bed."

"I thank you, master!" said Robin, as he left to enjoy a feast, in the merits of which Gwennie was interested.

The daughter soon returned to the parlor. Her father was again looking over the paper from Carnarvon.

"Ah!" said he, "here is something in writing." "On the start for Bala with 'Black Jim,' twenty-four hours in advance of the mail, I have fifty copies of the *Herald* for free distribution. Will be home to-morrow night.

UNCLE MORRIS."

"Well done, Morris!" said Lloyd in all sincerity. "That is a wise movement."

"Just like all the rest of his movements," said Grace Lloyd, with an expression of countenance that, for her, was a little unusual.

They left the parlor. The brother went into the garden, where he sat down for deep reflection; the sister to see that Robin Jones was provided with abundance; and the daughter to her room, and prayed to that "Father that seeth in secret."

# CHAPTER XXIII.

TWO LETTERS.

As intimated in another chapter, repeated burglaries had been committed in various parts of North Wales at different times, in such a manner that the authorities, with all their skill, had utterly failed to find the perpetrators. It was now believed that the chief of this gang was in custody, and the sheriff at Carnarvon, without any delay, sent two officers, in behalf of several parties that had been robbed of money and valuables, clothed with full authority to make a thorough search at "Raven's Nest," and the premises. On their way they made some inquiries at a house in the mountain pass, and were informed that the men were seldom at home, but that the woman never left the "Nest." They went forward and reached their destination. After repeated calls and knockings, no one answered. They tried the door, and found it unlocked. They went in, and the interior presented a scene of strange disorder. It was a mixture of squalor and finery, destitution and opulence. It was evident that no presiding genius was on the throne in the management of that household. They moved into a small room, which showed some degree of order; and on the table was a letter which had

an outside fresh appearance.  It was unsealed, and in
a fair, legible hand it was directed, "Simon Spike."
One of the officers took the letter and read the following :

"Simon Spike, you have abused your slave for the
last time.  Long have I suffered your cruel tyranny.
With lying lips and fair promises, you enticed me from
my home.  A thousand times have I purposed to leave
your accursed service, but until now my resolutions
have failed.  Your abusive language to-night strength-
ened my courage.  I am on the point of leaving the
premises of the most abominable wretch that ever
cursed the earth.  Your house abounds in stolen goods.
When you come home to-morrow morning from your
wicked conspiracy, you will find me gone.  With my
departure will disappear, also, from Raven's Nest a
large sum of gold.  Ah, Simon Spike! you thought
that your submissive slave knew nothing of your money
depository.  I have known the passage for years, and
the secret spot where you leave the keys.  You will
see that I have not taken all ; that would be too heavy.
I have taken as much as I can conveniently carry.
This gives me some compensation for years of degraded
service rendered Simon Spike, the great burglar chief,
the lying villain, and murderous plotter, for whom the
burning fires of an endless hell will be too good.
What did I hear the other day from you and Scroggs,
in regard to young Edwards, when you thought that I
was far away?  It was *murder!*  There is preaching
for you, Simon Spike!  Now please 'lead me by the
nose and spit in my face.'  I am glad that my educa-

tion reached a fair point before I ever saw a devil in human shape. It is to that bit of learning that you are indebted for this letter, and that I am indebted for the pleasure of cursing you on paper. The balance of the gold I had a good mind to throw into the depth of the well, but I have left it in the coffer. I have been careless enough to leave your secret door open. Go down and shut it quickly, and learn that Charlotte Bruce is not such an 'infernal fool' after all.

Ha, ha!"

"A good discovery, Williams," said Thomas Lewis. "This letter puts us on the right track, and is a crushing evidence against the prisoners," and he carefully put it in his pocket. "Now for a thorough search. The letter says 'go *down* quickly.' So the treasures are below, and the door is open."

They went down into the cellar, and in a corner they came to an opening into a dark passage, dug even with the floor. They procured a light, and pursued their way until they reached a small, square room at a distance of about fifteen or twenty feet from the opening. Here, as they expected, they found treasures. In one small coffer was about £500 in gold. In a larger coffer, or rather chest, was found a great quantity of valuable articles, in gold and silver, of almost every description. On many of these were names and initials of owners, and on some the coat of arms of the houses to which they belonged.

Seeing nothing more in that secret place, they carefully secured the chests, and made further search, but they found nothing of value that had the appearance of being stolen goods. The sheriff's seal was put on the treasures, they were taken to the ready vehicle, and conveyed to Carnarvon to await further developments.

———

Miss Thomas was in her parlor. In her hand was a letter which she had just read, and in her eyes there were unmistakable tears. Those tears were a mixture. The prevailing ingredient was sympathy. There was some affection, and a few grains of indignation. The reader will better understand the young lady's feelings when they have read the epistle.

"CARDIFF, Sept. —, 18—.

MY DEAR MISS THOMAS:

In harmony with your kind consent, and my own glad promise, I now attend to a most pleasant duty. I found my father, sister and aunt all well, and the ado they made over my return was altogether more than I deserved. My long absence explains the warmth with which my return was hailed. Miss Thomas, the day is lovely. Our residence stands on an elevation, and these lines are penned in an upper room. From my window the scene is inspiring, and to many it would be perfectly enchanting. I look upon the broad bay, stretching into the expansive ocean, while a hundred sails dot the blue waters. To these scenes I have long been accustomed, and they possess an enduring charm. But far sweeter to me were the quiet scenes of Bala, with its charming environs, than anything Cardiff can afford. Those few weeks spent in your delightful little town will forever remain in my fond memory as the most happy in my history. They were also, I trust. the means of a foundation of a better life. My early training. I am sorry to say, was not strictly religious. My mother was a quiet woman, and a modest Christian. My father, although an excellent man in many respects, is somewhat skeptical on the subject of religion. That is one reason why my own views of Christian doctrine have not been more positive and fixed. Never have I witnessed the practical workings of Christianity in so beautiful and clear light as at Bala; and I think I left you a much better man than when you first saw me. I trust that I shall yet be brought into the full light. I consider Mr. Edwards the finest specimen of young manhood, physically, intellectually and morally, that I ever saw. I have seen, also, at Bala a high perfection in womanhood. I will mention no name, for fear it may not please you.

My sister Helen sends her love in her own impulsive way, as the enclosed lines will show you. A friend of mine, Mr. Burt, is about to start for the north, and he will post this letter at Carnarvon. My kind regards to friends, especially Mr. Edwards. Hoping to see you again before long, I remain

Your sincere friend,<br>JOHN JENKINS."

The small note from the sister, written in a neat, delicate hand, was in this wise:

"MY DEAR MISS THOMAS:

John has said so much about you since he came home, that I feel as if I was well acquainted with you. I have fallen desperately in love with Bala, and with its good people, especially with you and Mr. Edwards. There! I have said it! Never mind, I will not call it back. Oh, Miss Thomas, I do hope my dear papa will let me come to Bala with John.

　　　　　　Yours truly,　　　　HELEN JENKINS."

"To think that this pure-minded and noble young man is regarded by Mr. Edwards as a thief and a knave is perfectly shocking!" said Miss Thomas to herself. "I cannot endure it! I think this letter will cure him of his cruel suspicion. As there is nothing in it of a confidential nature, I will ask him to read it; and if it will not make him blush, then I am mistaken," and she put the letter in her pocket to await the hour of her triumph.

About the time when Miss Thomas was shedding tears over Mr. Jenkins' letter, there was something of a sensation in front of the "Bala Hotel," caused by a certain arrival. The personage that made his advent was not the cause of this wonderment, for in his personal appearance he did not much differ from other gentlemen. Neither did the chaise in which he rode create any particular excitement; for finer and more costly vehicles they saw almost every day. It was the horse he drove that drew both their attention and admiration. Never had they seen a horse to equal him; and if "Black Jim" was conscious of the praise bestowed upon him, he certainly must have felt proud. But he was not long on exhibition.

"Take this horse, my man, and see well to his comfort, and you will lose nothing by it." said Morris Williams.

"When I bring him out, sir," said the man, touching his cap respectfully, "you will be sure that David Jones knows what is good for a horse." And the fine beast was taken into comfortable quarters; while his master was ushered into a well furnished little parlor.

"If you have any orders, sir, they will be attended to with great pleasure," said the landlord.

"I have a young friend at the Institute by the name of Llewelyn Edwards," said Williams. "I will thank you for sending him this card."

"That will be done without the least delay, sir," said Mr. Hughes. "Mr. Edwards is a young man that we all greatly respect."

"I wish to dine with Mr. Edwards at one o'clock," said Mr. Williams. "Please to furnish the dinner in a private room."

"With great pleasure, sir," said the proprietor, and left.

In about fifteen minutes Llewelyn came, and it was evident from his countenance that he had some fears.

Mr. Williams took his hand in a friendly manner, and remarked, "Llewelyn, I am glad to see you. How do you do?"

"I am quite well, Mr. Williams, and am very glad to see you at Bala. I hope you bring no tidings of evil."

"Well," said Mr. Williams, "I hardly know what to say to that. Yes, I think I bring tidings of evil; but don't take it much to heart, for evil as it may be, it partakes of features that call for thanksgiving."

"I trust that no calamity has befallen any of our friends," said Llewelyn exhibiting a degree of nervousness.

"Our friends are all well, and very happy I should judge," said Williams. "I have brought with me the Carnarvon *Herald* about twenty-four hours in advance of the mail. In it you will find an article in which your own name is mentioned several times." And he handed the young man the paper and pointed to the page.

Llewelyn read the startling heading and at first was so agitated that he bowed his head on the table by which he sat. He soon mastered his feelings and said:

"Mr. Williams, I have for some time believed that I was the subject of a plot, and that Jenkins was a villain. But little did I think that their evil design would so soon be unveiled." He then read the whole article and said :

"I have no vengeful feelings, but may the Lord's will be done! It is well for the safety of the community that such characters are shut up. May heaven bless my ever faithful friend, Taliesin Roberts, and the kind hearted Robin Jones! I wish that you had brought twenty copies of the *Herald* with you, so that the Bala people might see Jenkins in his true character."

"I think you will find more than twenty copies in this package Llewelyn," said Williams, as he handed him the large bundle. "Open it, and let these copies be at once distributed among those of your citizens that you may choose to mention. Now speak the names, and I will write them on the papers."

This was soon accomplished to the entire satisfaction of the two friends : and the papers were put into the hands of faithful and competent carriers.

"Now, Llewelyn." said Williams. "we have got along nicely. At one o'clock we dine together in this hotel. This will give us ample opportunity for confidential conversation."

"I would be most happy to have you as my guest, Mr. Williams," said Edwards, "but if you have made a different arrangement, it is all right. Please excuse me for a while, and let me inform my people that they need not expect me to dinner."

"Yes, go and return at your convenience," said
Mr. Williams.

Llewelyn picked up a copy of the Carnarvon *Herald*,
and was soon on his way toward his boarding house.
Miss Thomas stood in the door with a triumphant
smile on her countenance.

" Mr. Edwards, if you are not very busy I would be
pleased to see you at my parlor for a short time."

"I am at your service this very moment," said
Llewelyn, and together they went into Miss Thomas'
room.

"Mr. Edwards," said Miss Thomas in her politest
manner, "do you still entertain those cruel opinions
which you expressed in regard to Mr. Jenkins at our
last conversation?"

"I have had no reason for changing my mind, Miss
Thomas," was the reply.

"I think I have something here that will give you
reason for changing your mind," she said, producing
Mr. Jenkins' letter.  "Will you be so kind as to read
it carefully and then tell me what you think?"

"I certainly wi'l if you so desire," said Llewelyn
with a peculiar smile.

Miss Thomas closely watched him as he read, and
was pleased to see unusual excitement in his countenance, while mentally she said: "I have him at last."
Llewelyn finished the reading with a heavy sigh.  .

"It is no wonder you sigh, Mr. Edwards," said Miss Thomas, "we are all liable to fall into error, but that *you* should fall into such a monstrous mistake is to me a wonder of wonders. Of course you are now thoroughly convinced."

"Yes, Miss Thomas, I am thoroughly convinced," said Mr. Edwards. "I am thoroughly convinced that this letter was never written at Cardiff. I am thoroughly convinced that his residence on the hill, his Mr. Burt and sister Helen are purely fictitious. I am thoroughly convinced that Mr. Jenkins is an unmitigated liar, a scoundrel, thief, and would-be murderer. I am thoroughly convinced that Miss Thomas is duped a little worse than I was myself, and that it will not be long before she will see things in their true light."

"Mr. Edwards," said Miss Thomas, while paleness gathered on her countenance, "if you have got through with Mr. Jenkins' letter I will relieve you from what must be a burden." She took the letter and tenderly put it in her pocket. "I am not deceived in Mr. Jenkins, but I am bitterly deceived in you; and from henceforth I must drop from my list of friends a person that can use such vile language against a person that I so highly esteem."

" Your language is plain, and I can not fail to comprehend its meaning," said Edwards. "With the views you have of Jenkins your language may, perhaps, be justifiable; but before you erase my unworthy name from the list of your friends, will you do me one favor ?  At your request I read Mr. Jenkins' letter.  At my request will you read an article in yesterday's Carnarvon *Herald ?* "

" Most certainly I will ! " said Miss Thomas somewhat sharply, " give me the paper."

She was seated on a sofa, and the *Herald* was handed to her.

" Show me the article," she said in a voice denoting irritation.

" You will easily find it on the second page by its startling heading," said Llewelyn.

The heading was read, and with a shriek she fell over on the sofa.  Mrs. Ellis, passing through the hall, heard the cry and was instantly by her side.

" What can ail Miss Thomas, Mr. Edwards ? "  asked Mrs. Ellis as she bathed the young lady's temples.  " Did she hear some bad news ? "

" She saw something in the paper that greatly shocked her," said Llewelyn.

By this time Miss Thomas had partially revived, and, being unwilling to exhibit weakness in a certain direction said :

" I am so nervous ! and it is so dreadful !  Mr. Edwards, I have greatly wronged you ; and when I get my strength I will make suitable confessions and ask your forgiveness."

"Ask no forgiveness of me, Miss Thomas," said the young man. "For weeks I was deceived myself, and only through the importunity of my friends was I brought to see my mistake."

"Please say nothing about this foolish fainting," said Miss Thomas. "Be kind enough to leave the paper here. You need not stay. I will see you again in regard to this matter."

After explaining to Mrs. Ellis that he was to dine with a friend at the hotel, Mr. Edwards left.

"Now, Miss Thomas, for pity's sake, do tell me what is all this about," said Mrs. Ellis.

"Here, read this article to me clear through, heading and all," said Miss Thomas, "and then you will find that my fright was not all for nothing. Now go on while I lay me down and listen. Why don't you read?"

"May the Lord of Heaven have mercy upon us!" cried Mrs. Ellis, dropping the paper. rising up, and wringing her hands in a paroxysm of excitement. "Oh my dear Miss Thomas, it is no wonder that it upset you! Mr. Jenkins a villain after all!"

"Yes, and a thief!" cried Miss Thomas.

"And an intended murderer!" said Mrs. Ellis. "Oh how the guilty wretch deceived us all! I will try and read the dreadful article, but I tremble like a leaf from

17

head to foot." And so she read, occasionally stopping to make remarks.

"Well," she continued, "the old adage says '*Drwg y ceidw'r diawl ei was*,' (the devil gives his servant but a poor protection). Let us be thankful that—"

"Mrs. Ellis, what is the matter outside?" asked Miss Thomas. "The people act as if there was an alarm of fire!"

Mrs. Ellis looked from the window and asked a neighbor passing by what it meant.

"There is startling news in the Carnarvon *Herald* in regard to the narrow escape of Mr. Edwards from being murdered on our lake; and forty copies have been distributed in town. The people are almost wild; and no wonder," said the man, and went his way.

# CHAPTER XXIV.



On his way to the hotel Llewelyn met Phillips and
Griffiths, who had saved him on the lake. Now that
the secrecy was over, it soon became known to the
citizens who were Mr. Edwards' deliverers, and their
names were on every lip.

"Come with me to the hotel, and let my friend
Williams from Carnarvon have the pleasure of grasping
your hand ." Said Llewelyn.

"With pleasure," said Griffiths. " We are anxious
to see the man who brought us the good news twenty-
four hours in advance of the mail. The Bala people
appreciate his kindness, and he must receive some
token of our gratitude."

"Mr. Williams, I have brought with me my two kind
deliverers—Mr. Phillips and Mr. Griffiths."

"Gentlemen, it gives me great pleasure to see your
faces and take you by the hand," said Mr. Williams.

"And we most sincerely thank you, sir, for bringing
us the news with such unusual speed. Your great favor is warmly appreciated by our citizens," said Mr.
Phillips.

"It has given me no trouble that is worth mentioning," said Mr. Williams; "and if it had, the pleasure ti has afforded would entirely overbalance it."

"At what time must you leave us, Mr. Williams?" asked Mr. Griffiths.

. "I must leave at have-past two," was the reply.

The two young men then left, saying they would see him again before he would leave the town.

The confidential conversation between Williams and his young friend was long and pleasant. They branched out into the doings and circumstances of days and years gone by; and the time passed away delightfully. Mr. Hughes furnished a most excellent dinner, and assured the gentleman from Carnarvon that this day would long be remembered by the inhabitants of Bala.

The hour at last arrived for Mr. Williams to leave. When about to go, Phillips and Griffiths called again at his room.

"Gentlemen," said Mr. Williams, "my short stay among you has given me much pleasure. Should you come to Carnarvon, be sure to call on me."

They now left the parlor and walked into the front of the hotel. They were no sooner seen than a loud "Hooray!" went up from some two hundred people.

"What means this, Llewelyn?" asked Morris Williams in perfect astonishment.

"You will learn in a moment what it means," said

Llewelyn.   Presently a gentleman stood on a table in the midst of the company, and said :

"As citizens of Bala, we have thus assembled with but little consultation, to express our thanks to our worthy friend, Mr. Morris Williams, for bringing to our town, in advance of the mail, the good news contained in the Carnarvon *Herald*.  We wish Mr. Williams a prosperous journey home.  (Loud cheers.)  We also express our thanks to Thomas Phillips and George Griffiths, who saved our friend Edwards from impending destruction.  (Cheers for Phillips and Griffiths.)  We also thank those young heroes, strangers so us. Taliesin Roberts and Robert Jones.   (Tremendous cheers.)  And now three Hoorays for Llewelyn Edwards!"  (A wild demonstration.)

Mr. Williams was now loudly called for.  He stood on the steps and said :

" Ladies and gentlemen, I am no public speaker. These two noble men who saved my young friend from the jaws of death, are worthy of all praise!  As for myself, your words express far more than I deserve.  You have my warmest thanks.  And now, good bye!"

He stepped into his chaise, put half a crown in the hand of David Jones, took the reins, and "Black Jim," in splendid style, amid a grand shout, was on his way to Carnarvon.

At a little later hour, on the same day on which was witnessed the exciting scene at the parlor of Druid's Grove, mentioned in another place, Morgan Edwards and Helen were sitting together in their comfortable parlor. The aunt was absent on a short visit.

"Llewelyn is convinced at last that his Mr. Jenkins is a villain in disguise," said the daughter.

"Yes; and for him he uses very strong language," said the father. "I am led to think that he has some evidence of Jenkins' villainy beside that matter of the watch."

"Papa, I am afraid that my brother is in danger of bodily harm!" said the sister in a trembling voice. "Lucas Pugh hates him with all the malignity of his depraved heart, and he has sworn that he shall never be the husband of Gwennie Lloyd."

"Llewelyn is far safer at present than when he confided in Jenkins," said Mr. Edwards. "He will now be on his guard, and others are on the watch in his interest. Above all, I trust that an overruling Providence will cover him with her protecting wing."

"I am almost sure that the secret communication of Robin Jones three nights ago, was something in regard to this matter," said Helen. "It was— But, papa, here comes Taliesin at an awful speed! I hope he brings no bad news!"

Taliesin gave his panting steed to a boy, rushed into

the house without ceremony, and threw himself into a chair.

"Taliesin," cried Helen, "what is the matter? You don't act like yourself!"

"Perhaps not," said the young man. "However, under the circumstances, my behavior is excusable."

"Taliesin Roberts, what has happened?" asked Helen in a very serious tone. "Have you heard any bad news from Llewelyn?"

"I have not." was his reply. "I came straight from Carnarvon, and the whole town is in a whirl of excitement over an item of news from Bangor."

"And does the news affect us, Taliesin?" asked Mr. Edwards.

"You can judge for yourself." said Taliesin, as he handed Morgan Edwards a copy of the Carnarvon *Herald*. "You will find the article marked on the second page."

Mr. Edwards read the heading, while his face showed great agitation.

"Oh, Taliesin, what *is* it?" cried Helen almost in agony.

"Be calm, my child!" said the father. "To us the news is not bad. I will give you the startling caption."

Helen fell on her knees, bowed her head on her father's lap, and gave vent to her feelings in sobbing, which continued for some time.

When the rush of feeling had subsided, Mr. Edwards read the article aloud.

"Helen, you can easily excuse my strange behavior."

She made no reply in words, but she looked upon him through her tears, and never before had she been able to concentrate so much love into one look. Taliesin felt its power and was of the opinion that the happiness of those moments was not much inferior to the joys of heaven.

After a long conversation, in the course of which he gave them to understand that Morris Williams had gone to Bala, Taliesin got his horse and hastened to his father's house and there indulged in what he greatly needed—sound sleep.

Before the close of day, the news had spread far and wide. At Llangobaith men and women ran to and fro in all directions in a high state of excitement. In front of the Red Lion there was a crowd of people indulging in loud talk and violent gestures. Rejoicing and indignation were found in equal quantities. Thus things continued, more or less, for several days.

------

Evan Pugh kept within the walls of his own residence. The calamity had fallen upon him with terrible weight. Still, there was in his countenance a defiant, angry appearance. He still felt an undiminished hatred of Llewelyn and Gwennie. He came to the conclusion that he would either sell Riverside or secure a trusty tenant. He would then leave the country and mingle among strangers where he would not be known as the father of a felon.

Affairs at Druid's Grove were progressing favorably. In the light of the recent terrible developments, Thomas Lloyd still more clearly saw the enormity of his offence against his daughter, and fairly shuddered as he viewed the awful gulf into which he had endeavored to hurl her. The reflection lowered him in his own estimation, while it revealed Gwennie's superior judgment. He did not express himself very freely, but it was evident that his nature was undergoing a rapid transformation. The past seemed to him as far worse than a failure. The retrospective view was humiliating, and he was honest enough to confess to himself that in point of moral goodness he was exceedingly deficient. The idol at whose shrine he had worshiped with such uniformity for so many years, had not only lost its former charms, but appeared to him now horrid and repulsive. He closed his eyes from beholding its frightful visage, and solemnly vowed that never again would he pay homage to Mammon. Men whom he had despised rose before his mental vision, with whom he compared himself, and the result to him was anything but flattering. Even Methodists and other Dissenters, drove him completely into the shade. His great zeal for the Established Church he saw was but a sham, wholly destitute of a single holy purpose, or worthy motive. He was a prisoner at the bar of his own conscience, under heavy charges, which were all sustained, and he pronounced himself guilty. He was sorry, but at this time his sorrow was not thoroughly evangelical. His repentance, as yet, was not "toward God." But he was progressing in the right direction. His former imperiousness had disappeared, and he showed a fair degree of humility. He looked upon Gwennie from a new standpoint. In addition to his restored natural affection for his child, he loved her for her grand moral perfections. Such transformations are not common occurrences, especially in those persons who are Mammon worshipers. They generally wax worse and worse, until at last they reluctantly leave their accumulated treasures and pass away to the great hereafter. Thomas Lloyd was an exception to the rule, and in that light let him be considered.

The affectionate intimacy between Helen and Gwennie was becoming closer and sweeter from day to day. They were very often in one another's society, and each looked to the future with joyful anticipations.

At Bala, Llewelyn's popularity was on the increase, chiefly on account of his pulpit power. He was also rendered more dear to the people by his narrow escape from the malice of his enemies.

Miss Thomas, in her own estimation, was greatly humiliated. She knew that before Llewelyn she had betrayed a degree of regard for Jenkins that could not be well explained on the score of simple friendship. She had lost fifty pounds, but to her that was a trivial calamity compared with the fact that she had given a thorough villain the highest seat in the sanctuary of her heart, and that another person had witnessed the proof of it.

In a subsequent conversation she had said to Mr. Edwards—"In view of this matter, I abhor myself in dust and ashes! The hard words I spoke to you, and the *manner* in which I defended that wicked deceiver, must have astonished and grieved you. You are in possession of a secret known to no other person at Bala except myself. But such is the confidence that I have in you that I am sure you will not expose the weak judgment of a woman that has been too confiding."

"Miss Thomas," said Mr. Edwards, with much feeling, "you judge yourself too severely. I have seen nothing in your behavior for which you need offer the least apology. You may rest assured that any conversation between us in regard to this man will be considered sacred."

"Thank you," said Miss Thomas. "In this I have learned a lesson that will prove valuable in the future. Satan's agents, as well as their master, can transform themselves into angels of light."

# CHAPTER XXV.



In those days the Calvinistic Methodist ministers of Wales were itinerants—not over small circuits like the Wesleyans, but under the direction of the Association they traveled over extensive fields. They were very much of the time away from home, while their appointments were well understood by the churches several weeks in advance. Sometimes a young unordained man would be put on the plan with his more experienced and older brethren.

These men usually preached from fifteen to twenty times a week, and at most of the places their congregations were large. Even in the heat of harvest the farmers, with their men servants, would, for a while, leave the field and hasten to a neighboring chapel to listen to one of these noted ministers. For this luxury, however, they would willingly work harder, earlier and later, so that there was no temporal loss in the premises.

These traveling preachers were supported by the voluntary contributions of the churches. At Llangobaith they were always well rewarded, while from weaker societies they received but little.

Among the Welsh, even until to-day, the notices are given out by an official of the church, who is *y cyhoeddwr* (the announcer). At the close of the morning service, on one Sabbath, Robert Ellis said: " You will be glad to hear, as I am glad to announce, that on next Sabbath, Providence permitting. our young friend, Llewelyn Edwards, will preach here morning and evening."

To nearly all present this was unexpected. and every countenance beamed with gladness. His recent escape from the malice of his enemies, together with his fame as a preacher, rendered his name at this time exceedingly attractable.

The thrilling events of the few months which had passed rendered Llewelyn's arrival at his father's house deeply affecting, and the reader's imagination can do better justice to the occasion than the pen of the writer.

The student was received by Thomas Lloyd with genuine warmth. He well knew that Llewelyn had full knowledge of all that had transpired between him and his daughter, and this caused him some embarrassment, but he was really glad to see his anticipated son-in-law. Of Gwennie it is only necessary to say that her deportment was easy and worthy of her sound sense and warm heart. Grace, also, being yet at Druid's Grove, was delighted to welcome her young friend.

Sabbath morning came, and at an early hour Thomas

Lloyd, the exclusive churchman, seemed to be fully ready for service, although in the parish church Mr. Rowlands would not officiate before two in the afternoon. Gwennie noticed this early preparation with a degree of interest. Presently the daughter and her aunt Grace started, when Lloyd promptly joined them, and together they walked slowly toward the place of worship.

As they progressed, it became evident that "Siloam," on this Sabbath, would not be able to accommodate the hundreds that from all directions were bending their way thither. By the time our friends from Druid's Grove reached the chapel it was well nigh filled, although they were a full half hour early. Extra seats were brought in, and every available spot was filled. At last the young minister, accompanied by the rest of the family, made his appearance. With some difficulty he reached the pulpit. The sight of Llangobaith's favorite deeply touched the audience, and with the remembrance of recent events, there were tears in many eyes. No more could possibly get into the building, and a large number were under the necessity of remaining without. The day, however, was fine, the windows were open and the people, with but few exceptions, were able to hear the preached word.

The preliminaries were conducted by Griffith Jones, from Bangor, a most worthy unordained minister. Af-

ter the opening prayer and singing, the young herald
stood and announced his text—"The Lord reigneth let
the earth rejoice."—Psalm 97, 1.  He was somewhat
pale and slightly embarrassed, but he well knew that
under God he was master of the situation.  At first
he went on in a conversational style, and beautiful sen_
tences fell over his lips as easy as the running rivulet.
He gathered inspiration as he went.  He dealt in
weighty theological truths, but in a way familiar to the
congregation.  His sermon abounded in pertinent illustrations.  His imagination was lively and his language
perfect.  He was earnest, pathetic and emotional.  As
he advanced the interest continually increased, and old
fashioned shouts of "Diolch i Dduw!" (Thank God)
were heard from many lips.  He closed the Bible and
the audience feared that he was going to sit down, but
to their joy he still continued, entering sweeter into the
Welsh melodic "*hwyl*."  He soared like the English
lark, chanted in his upward flight, and closed amid a
halo of glory.

In this morning service the presence and appearance
of Thomas Lloyd caused much astonishment.  For
years he had been known as an open despiser of the
"sects," especially the Calvinistic Methodists, and on
no occasion would he enter a chapel.  But far more
than his simple presence at "Siloam," his evident emotion took the notice of the people.  In vain he strove to

hide his feelings.   Unbidden tears forced themselves to
view.   Was it any wonder?   In the one who stood before him in that pulpit he saw a young man whom he
had despised and hated, while his covetous admiration
had centered on a villain into whose polluted embrace
he had endeavored to force his own lovely daughter.
Here, with other things, were materials for the production of penitence, and among those repentant sinners
that cause " joy in heaven " was Thomas Lloyd.

In the evening the ministry was equally powerful.
The closing appeal to the young people was attended
with great effect.   As is customary among the Welsh, at
the close of this evening service, the members of the
church were asked to tarry, with all others who were
willing to take upon them the yoke of Christ.   A number of these remained, and among them was found the
bowed head of Gwennie's father.

---

The day for the trial of the conspirators at last arrived, and in view of the overwhelming nature of the
evidence for the prosecution, it was generally believed
that their attorney would advise them to plead guilty.
This conviction served, in a measure, to moderate the
excitement.   Still there was an immense throng at the
commodious court house.   The country people, especially from the vicinity of Llangobaith, were present by
the hundreds.   From Bala, also, there was a large num-

ber, and many who had suffered from burglary had come to have a look at Simon Spike and Scroggs.

The four prisoners were marched in under strong guards, and seated in their appropriate place. Spike, the elder, looked angry, and faced the audience with a defiant frown. Lucas Pugh endeavored to do the same, but failed. John Spike gave further proof of his depravity by vulgarity and profane levity. Scroggs seemed to be at perfect ease, and gave the audience an excellent imitation of amiability and politeness. Under peculiar disadvantages, as far as his costume was concerned, he had taken pains to appear well. He smilingly looked around on the large audience and bowed in a style that would have done honor to royalty.

The court, amid perfect silence, proceeded with its business. The indictment was read, and Judge Tudor politely asked the attorney for the defense, what, in behalf of his clients, he wished to plead.

The talented advocate arose and said, "May it please your Honor, in view of the overwhelming evidence that is in the possession of the advocate for the Crown, the prisoners at the bar plead guilty. We trust that this pleading may somewhat modify the sentence."

The advocate for the prosecution then respectfully submitted that the court proceed at once and pronounce the sentence.

The Judge rose and said, " The prisoners will stand
18

up." He then proceeded, "Simon Spike, Thomas Adolphus Scroggs, Lucas Pugh, and John Spike, you plead guilty to an awful indictment; a conspiracy to take away the life of an innocent man. Your plot well nigh succeeded. The whole movement shows a depth of depravity, perfection of iniquity, ripeness in villainy and fiendish cruelty seldom equaled in the anna.s of crime. I will not disturb the delicate and modest feelings of some persons present by referring to the origin of this base conspiracy. It is enough to say that it is the offspring of cowardly malice. You, Simon Spike, in consideration of a large sum of money paid and promised by Lucas Pugh, sent a well-trained villain to a distant town, who worked himself into the confidence of a most worthy young man, in order to take away his life under the guise of an accident. This having failed, you met together again, and were about to try another murderous scheme. Your talented counsel hopes that your pleading guilty may modify the sentence of the court. Your pleading has no virtue. The evidence is overwhelming. A recent change in the law, however. is in your favor. If this trial had transpired a few years ago, Carnarvon would have witnessed the hanging of four guilty wretches. But fortunately for you, if not for the community, that law has been abolished. The sentence of the court is, that Simon Spike, Thomas Adolphus Scroggs. Lucas Pugh and

John Spike be transported to His Majesty's penal col
ony in New South Wales, and there be subjected to
hard labor during the whole period of their natural
lives."

The sentence was received with thundering applause,
and the four culprits were taken back to the prison.
The court adjourned to two o'clock in the afternoon,
and the assembly dispersed, well satisfied with the result of the morning session.

Nearly three years had passed away since that morning when Llewelyn Edwards, amid the well-wishes
of friends and relatives, left his home for the Bala Theological School, a period crowded with weighty and
startling events, with some of which the reader is acquainted. He had diligently pursued his studies and
had won the high regards of his instructors. At a late
meeting of the Association for North Wales. after a
thorough examination, in experience, doctrine and dis-
cipline, he was elected to sacred orders, the ordination
to take place at the " Gymanfa " (yearly meeting) at
Llangobaith. This was well understood, and throughout all that region it was looked for with more than ordinary interest. In the meantime Llewelyn had left
Bala, and was once more a happy inmate of his father's
home.

At these ordination meetings there were always a

large number of ministers present, and many sermons delivered. To the church officials it was evident that their chapel, although large, would not hold one quarter of those who would attend, and they very wisely made excellent arrangements for an out-of-door meetin . A few rods from the chapel stood a number of tall trees, whose wide spreading branches formed an excellent shade. Here a large platform was erected, and as many seats prepared as they could well secure. The long expected period at last arrived. On the afternoon of the first day the " Gynadledd " (Conference) was held in the church edifice, and so was the preaching meeting in the evening.

Among the celebrated pulpit orators of the occasion were Ebenezer Morris, Ebenezer Richards and John Elias. These were stars of the first magnitude, which, at that time, with many more, blazed in the ministerial firmament of the Calvinistic Methodist Church. Their names, even to-day, among the Welsh, are familiar as household words. Besides these, there were present other eminent ministers. In those meetings they often stood before an audience of eight or ten thousand, who "were astonished at" their "doctrine," for like their great Master, they taught as those "having authority." While the Welsh Calvinists of the present day can point to men in their regular ministry who are far in advance of the fathers in intellectual culture, it is doubtful whether they have any that surpass those we have mentioned in genuine pulpit oratory—that oratory that moves and thrills the masses.

At an early hour of the second day the people began to come "as clouds and as doves to their windows." The first to preach was a young man of fine appearance and excellent pulpit ability; and, considering who was to follow him, he succeeded well in securing and retaining the attention of the thousands present. Still, there were many on the outskirts that walked to and fro.

The first speaker having sat down, John Elias stood, and in harmony with custom, gave out one stanza to sing—

> "Dysgwyliaf o'r mynyddoedd draw,
> Lle daw im' help 'wyllysgar."
>
> ("Up to the hills I'll turn my eyes,
> From whence my help shall come.")

After the singing, in his own impressive manner, he announced his text, "Whom God hath set forth as a propitiation." His very appearance had a magnetic power. His clear voice reached the remotest in the assembly. As he advanced with his grand theme, the atonement, the standing multitude came nearer the stand and closer together. No more walking about or idle conversation. All were wrapt in the deepest attention. The speaker soon became animated. His great soul was inspired. The throng swayed under his burning eloquence as a field of wheat is swayed by the breeze. Copious tears fell, while shouts of praise from hundreds echoed among the trees. Thus, for an hour, the vast concourse was oblivious of everything in heaven above or on earth beneath, save the sublime truths presented by this famous Welsh pulpit orator.

In the afternoon, before a still larger audience, Ebenezer Richards preached one of his characteristic sermons, which in many respects was not inferior to the second sermon in the morning. He had a wonderful facility of expression, unlimited command of words, and a most loving spirit.

At the close of this service, Llewelyn Edwards, with a number of other young men, surrounded by some forty ministers, was solemnly ordained to the full work of the Christian ministry. The grand address of the occasion was by the eloquent and venerable Ebenezer Morris. He also preached the last sermon in the evening, from the text, "The way of life is above to the wise, to escape hell beneath." His majestic presence, commanding voice, melting pathos, peculiar delivery and tremendous earnestness, swept every thing before them. A single emphatic word from his lips would roll over the people like a wave. At this time, he represented the sinner's course as a downward career, until at last he reached the awful "*beneath!*" and with this one word in his inimitable manner, he thrilled the audience.

The union of Llewelyn and Gwennie took place at the parish church. It was conducted quietly, and in the presence of a few invited guests. Thomas Lloyd spared neither pains or expense to render the occasion delightful and highly respectable. On this day he was a happy man. He looked upon the young minister with love and pride, and upon his daughter as "blessed among women." They were to remain at Llwyn y Derwydd, and Gwennie rejoiced to know that she was still to enjoy her dear old home.

Druid's Grove had already become a welcome retreat to the weary itinerant; and he who had for so many years treated them with contempt, was now glad to sit at their feet, and learn from their lips more fully the way of truth. In his religious experience Thomas Lloyd was humble and penitent. He chose a low seat and refused all official honor. He was liberal in his contributions for the support of the ministry, and benevolent in almsgiving.

Llewelyn, being now in the regular itinerancy, was much of the time from home. Soon he became known throughout Wales as "Edwards of Llwyn y Derwydd." Gwennie was noted for spirituality and her cheerful labor in every enterprise affecting the interest of the church.

# CHAPTER XXVI.



Evan Pugh was now never seen at Glan 'r Afon. It was generally believed that he had joined his wife in some part of England. His farm was managed by an agent in Bangor by the name of George Price. Before Pugh left, he had secured a tenant in the person of John Trevor, to whom he had given the use of everything as it stood, for a reasonable rent, for the term of two years, with the understanding that in the interval the farm would be for sale. John Trevor, by his kind disposition and upright walk, was much beloved in the community. He had an amiable wife and one daughter, a brilliant lady of eighteen.

For several months Riverside, with all it contained, had been advertised to be sold at auction. This notice was well circulated, not only throughout Wales, but also in the most prominent of the English papers. At that time the sale of a farm was not a common occurrence in the Principality. for nearly all belonged to some large estate, owned by some rich landholder. It was generally expected that this valuable property would be purchased by the Hon. Ashton Smith, and added to the "Vaenol" estate. The sale was to be on the premises, and the appointed day arrived. At an early hour the people began to gather; some from curiosity, and many with the intention of buying. It was evident from the conversation that many of those present, were from England. A printed list of all the personal property was freely distributed among those present, and ample time was given for examination. The whole was to be sold, and each bid was to include the whole property.

It seemed to the agent that all who had an intention of bidding had already arrived, and the auctioneer was requested to proceed with the sale. Chairs had been placed in a semi-circle in front of the house, while the "orator of the day" faced the company from a higher position. He was not one of those dispensers of cheap nonsense that are so often seen in that fraternity. A fluent speaker he was, but before those rich men his speech was dignified, and his language choice.

"Gentlemen," said he, "I will not insult your intelligence by claiming for this property undue value. In this matter every one of you is a better judge than myself. I am cheered by this conviction, and I am sure that this magnificent farm, with all that is mentioned in the bill, will bring a sum that will nearly equal its value. I base this opinion upon your individual judgment, as well as your individual ability. We shall not hurry matters in a business of this importance. You will be calm and deliberate. In bidding please speak out plainly and distinctly, so that there shall be no mistake on my part. Now we—."

Here he suddenly stopped, observing in the road close by a very fine carriage drawn by a span of spirited horses. They turned, and with full speed they came up toward the house. The animals gave signs of having traveled in haste. The coachman hurriedly opened the carriage door, and a full bearded gentleman, of youthful appearance, finely dressed, came out and, with much ease of manners, took his seat within the half circle.

"The gentleman is in time," said the auctioneer. "I presume he knows all about the property and the terms of the sale."

The new comer simply bowed.

"I now ask how much am I offered for Riverside, embracing one hundred and fifty acres of choice land, with this fine residence and all its rich furniture; all farming utensils, with barns, carriages, horses, sheep' cattle, and many other things too numerous to mention. What is the first offer?"

"Five thousand pounds," said the Vaenol agent.

"That is certainly a bid," said the auctioneer, with a smile, "and I will not despise the day of small things."

Six thousand was the next.

"I Thank you, but gentlemen are respectfully request-ed not to indulge too freely in playing. Go on!"

Then the bidding began to be lively, the Vaenol man showing much interest. By degrees it ran up to twelve thousand pounds, while the talented salesman enter-tained them with very ingenious remarks. Hitherto the gentleman that arrived late had taken no part in the bidding, and seemed to view things with indiffer-ence. The bidding was still progressing, although slowly. It had reached £12,500, and it was the bid of Ashton Smith's agent. No one seemed disposed to go higher.

"Now, gentlemen," said Mr. Gibson. "I have no fault to find with your bidding. If no more is offered, Thomas Ashton Smith will have a fine addition to his estate, and that at a great bargain. Shall I have any more ?  12,500 once, 12,500 twice, 12,500 three—"

"£13,000!" cried the young gentleman that arrived last.

This caused some merriment among a number of the bidders, while the Vaenol agent looked somewhat dis-turbed.

"I am offered £13,000," said Mr. Gibson. "Now you begin to see things in their true light. Next!"

"£13,500!" cried the Vaenol agent.

"£14,000!" cried the young gentleman.

"Now that begins to look like it!" said the auc-

tioneer.　"Glan 'r Afon begins to be appreciated.　Do
I hear any more from Vaenol?"

"Vaenol has got through!" said the agent, with
somewhat of a flushed countenance.　"I am not au-
thorized to go any higher."

"£14,000 I am offered for Riverside, with all its
grand advantages.　Gentlemen, your superior judgment must tell you that this property is worth more
money.　But it must be sold.　Fourteen thousand
pounds!　Must I be compelled to sell this earthly paradise, the most lovely spot in the vale of Llangobaith,
for fourteen thousand pounds?　Now is your last
chance!　Once, twice, t-h-r-e-e times—and—*sold!*
What is the gentleman's name?"

"You may call it Thomas Wynn," said the young
man with perfect ease.　And inasmuch as I am a stranger to you all, I will relieve you from all embarrassment by paying the agent a small sum now.　He will
please call at my rooms at Penrhyn Arms, at Bangor,
on the day after to-morrow, and he will find that his
money will be ready."

"How much does Mr. Wynn wish to advance?" asked
the agent.

"You may write me a receipt for two thousand
pounds," was the prompt reply.

"Much less would have answered," said the agent,
as he took the money.　The receipt was quickly writ-

ten and given to the young gentleman, and the sale was over.

When most of the people had dispersed, John Trevor, the tenant at Riverside, in a most respectful manner, approached the purchaser and said:

"Mr. Wynn, if you have not already a tenant in view, sir, I would be very glad to remain at Riverside. I think Mr. Price will say that he finds no fault with my management."

"In Mr. Trevor I have found a most excellent tenant, Mr. Wynn," said the agent.

"Then if Mr. Trevor wishes to remain," said Mr. Wynn, "he may have the place for one year at the same rent that he pays you, if that meets his mind."

"It meets my mind, and deserves my thanks," said Mr. Trevor. "If you will please to accept our humble offer, we shall consider ourselves highly honored if you tarry with us until to-morrow, or longer if you can. This will give you an opportunity to see the farm and all its surroundings."

"I think I shall accept your kind offer," said the stranger. "I will give my coachman a few directions."

"Robert, you may return with the carriage; and day after to-morrow, at ten o'clock, I want you to be here again to take me to Bangor. Let the horses return slowly. Take my valise out, and give it to Mr. Trevor."

The coachman bowed, removed the valise, took his
seat, and the carriage rolled away

Mrs. Trevor and Miss Nellie seemed at first a little
embarrassed in the presence of the rich new master,
but his ease of manners and cheerful conversation soon
gave them perfect relief.  To them it was a matter of
some astonishment that a person who could command
his thousands should make himself so much at home
in the family of his comparatively poor tenant.

After a conversation of half an hour after dinner,
the new master proposed a walk through the farm,
which proposition met the hearty wish of Mr. Trevor.
They started, and it was not long before they came
near "Pren y Góg," the humble cot of Evan and Margaret Jones.

"I don't consider this little hut of any benefit to this
property, nor an ornament to the farm," said Mr.
Wynn.  "How came Mr. Pugh to permit such an un-
sightly looking building as this to remain standing?"

"I have heard," said Trevor, "that his father, before
he died, gave express orders that Evan Jones was not
to be disturbed as long as he wished to stay, and pay a
reasonable rent.  It is true, Mr. Wynn, that the *house*
is no ornament; but those that live in it, sir, are considered very bright ornaments in this vicinity.  Some
ornaments in the shape of children have been found in
that house, one of which is in the bottom of the sea,

sir. It would touch the heart of this neighborhood to the quick to see Evan Jones and his wife turned out of house and home."

Mr. Wynn was silent for a while, and then said, "Let us take a look at the interior of this old jewel casket. You have made me anxious to see this Owen Jones."

"*Evan* Jones, sir," said Trevor. "He is seldom home during working hours. His good wife, perhaps, you can see."

"There was no one at home except their youngest daughter, Mary, who looked with astonishment at one of her visitors.

"Good afternoon, Mary," said Trevor. "All alone, I see?"

"Yes, sir," said Mary. "I don't know what the people will think. Mr. Lloyd has invited father and mother, Jane, Will and myself to Druid's Grove to tea this afternoon. Robin, with the carriage, has taken my parents. Llewelyn Edwards is home, and Mary Humphreys is there from Bangor, and Gwennie sent me word this morning that I must be sure and come. It is not often that poor people, like of us, are treated in this way by their betters."

"In this, Thomas Lloyd has shown a clear head and a good heart," said Trevor. "Mary, this is Mr. Wynn, who has just purchased Riverside."

"My dear father troubles himself a good bit for fear

he shall have to leave," said Mary, with some trembling in her voice. "It is a poor old house, but to us it is the dearest spot on the green earth!" ar d looking at Mr. Wyn' , she continued: "Here, sir, we children were all born. In and about this poor hut, we laughed and sung, and shouted and ran, when we were little boys and girls. How our dear Dick used to climb to the very top of yon tree, and say he was going to be a sailor—" And here poor Mary had to stop, overcome with the fond memory of the departed.

"Well," said Mr. Wynn, "and did Dick became a sailor?"

"Aye, that he did!" said Mary, "and the poor boy was lost on his first voyage!"

"That was very sad!" said Mr. Wynn. "But, Mr. Trevor, we must go." And looking at Mary, he said: "Young woman, I will give you my word that your father will not be disturbed, and while I am owner of Riverside he will have no rent to pay."

"May the blessing of heaven rest upon your head, sir!" cried the girl, breaking into a sob, while the two men walked away.

"Mr. Trevor," said Mr. Wynn, "I am becoming somewhat interested in this family, and I am sorry we did not find the parents at home. I am disposed to do something for their comfort. Think you that Mr.

Lloyd's family would take it kindly if we should call there for a short time this afternoon ?"

"The family would be delighted to have a call from the new master of Riverside," said Trevor. Whenever you choose to start, it will give me great pleasure to drive you there."

"Thank you !" said Mr. Wynn, "let us start in about an hour—that will be about four o'clock," and they slowly walked toward the house.

"John," said Mrs. Trevor, "Nellie has had an urgent invitation to make a short visit at Druid's Grove this evening. Mary Humphreys is there and must return to Bangor to-morrow. You know that if there is any person on earth that Nellie loves, it is Mary."

"Let her go, by all means," said Mr. Trevor. "And by the way, Mr. Wynn and myself are going there in less than an hour, and Nellie can ride with us."

"That will be nice," said the wife. "I will tell her to get ready."

Mr. Trevor went out to give some orders to his men. When Mrs. Trevor returned to the room, she smilingly remarked :

"While Mary Humphreys' name is of no importance to you, she is very dear to all in these parts on account of her many excellencies. Mrs. Lloyd took the little orphan into her family and treated her with the tenderness of a mother. She gave her school advantages,
19

and when she was seventeen, sent her to Bangor to learn to be a dressmaker, and in eighteen months from that time she was considered the most accomplished in that line in the city. But it is her kindness and amiability that makes her such a favorite. She is in her element among the poor, and deeply attached to those who were her playmates. There is one family that she seems to love above all others—that of Evan Jones. She insists on calling the old people father and mother. It would be a wonder if they were not called to meet her at Druid's Grove to-day."

"They have gone there," said Mr. Wynn, "and from the daughter I learned the sad fate of poor Dick."

"Since you have come to that," said Mrs. Trevor, "I may as well say that that is the grand secret of Mary's love for the family. Dick Jones was her lover, and a bright young fellow he was, and so kind to his parents. His sad fate almost killed his mother, while poor Mary Humphreys wept in secret. To a few she revealed the depth of her sorrow. Half a dozen of worthy young men have since then sought her hand, but all in vain. The image of her lost Dick is so stamped upon her heart that no power can erase it. She looks for some spiritual reunion in heaven."

Trevor now came in, and Nellie being ready, they were soon on their way. The daughter, by this time, as will be seen, had conquered her embarrassment, and was in a good frame of mind for a pleasant chat. Nellie Trevor had the name of being quite entertaining in conversation.

"If Mr. Wynn is so unfortuate as to be a batchelor," said she, with her pretty smile, "I think he will be in danger of falling in love when he gets to Llwyn y Derwydd. A word of warning may set him on his guard."

"And is it not quite possible, Miss Trevor, that the great calamity may overwhelm me while on the way there?" asked Mr. Wynn.

"It is barely *possible*, but not at all probable, that Mary Humphreys may meet us on the road," said Nellie, "so you may reserve your power of resistance until you reach the end of the journey. Then, Mr. Wynn, you must be on your watch, or you will be a bound captive."

"Your mother gave me a brief sketch of this wonderful Mary Humphreys," said Mr. Wynn. "I judge that she must be a very interesting person, and that you have some reason for setting me on my guard."

"You will see more clearly the reasonableness of my caution," said Miss Trevor, "when I assure you that to fall in love with Mary Humphreys will be a fruitless performance. She has sacredly and forever consecrated herself to single life."

"She may yet, possibly, change her mind," said Mr. Wynn.

"Not unless Dick Jones is raised from the dead!" was the emphatic reply.

A sharp trotting pony soon brought them to Druid's Grove. The sight of Trevor's carriage brought out Thomas Lloyd, Gwennie and Mary Humphreys. Miss Nellie attended to the introduction in an easy, graceful style.

" Mr. Wynn, we are heartily glad to see you !" said Mr. Lloyd, " and we are sure that you will give us the pleasure of your company for a few hours this afternoon and evening."

"I thank you for your cordial invitation," said Mr. Wynn. "I understand that you have company, and I only fear that I shall intrude."

" Don't mention such a thing. my dear sir !" said Lloyd. " A few friends have come together who will be very glad to see the new master of Glan 'r Afon. Trevor, Robin Jones will take care of the horse. Now let us go in," and to the house they went.

# CHAPTER XXVII.



### SOME EXCITEMENT.

Gwennie and Mary Humphreys went with Miss Trevor up stairs, where Helen Edwards awaited them, and, as a matter of course, the conversation turned upon the new master.

"What a magnificent looking person, Mary," said Mrs. Edwards.

"If his goodness corresponds with his looks, he is a noble specimen of a man," said Mary.

"We cannot judge of his moral character on a few hours' acquaintance," said Miss Trevor. "He has all the appearance of a perfect gentleman. I think if he had less beard he would resemble Taliesin Roberts. What say you, Helen?"

"I only say that the comparison pays the stranger a very high compliment," said the young lady.

"We shall not disagree on that, Helen," said Miss Trevor, smiling. "for you have the handsomest lover in the parish."

"But are we treating the illustrious stranger with re-spect by shutting ourselves up in this room?" asked Mary Humphreys. "Let us go down and help to entertain him."

"That is well said, Mary," said Gwennie. "You go down, girls, and I will run into Llewelyn's room and acquaint him of the grand arrival."

So they went down, and Mrs. Edwards hurried to the minister's study, where he was busily engaged on a sermon for *Sasiwn y Bala* (Bala Association).

"Now, my dear," said Gwennie, putting her soft hand on his head, "lay aside your books and papers for a little while, and go down with me to be introduced to the new owner of Riverside."

"That I will, Gwennie, with pleasure. I shall be right glad to form his acquaintance," was his reply, and together they left the study.

"Mr. Wynn, this is my husband—Rev. Llewelyn Edwards," said Gwennie.

They cordially shook hands, and entered at once into a general conversation. The company was not divided. Evan Jones and his wife were present, with all their children, except Robin, who was attending to some outside duties. Mr. Wynn rendered himself highly agreeable. His remarks ran smooth and easy. The venerable pair from Pren y Gôg were delighted with the frank manner of the rich stranger. Mary had already informed them of his kind remarks at the house, and they were sure that in the new owner they had found a friend. In about an hour, tea was announced, and in the most friendly manner, they sat around the table. The meal being over, they again united in the parlor, and the new master was the great centre of attraction. It soon began to get dark, and the candles were lighted.

"My daughter Mary informed me of your very kind remarks to her at our house, sir." said Evan Jones. "I had my fears in regard to the matter. I did not know into whose hands I would fall. We dearly love the old spot where we brought up our children. There are a score of sweet but sad memorials about the premises that remind us of our dear Dick! Yes, Mary told you, and I need say no more. To think that we can still remain there, and that without rent, has almost overcome me, sir! My dear, good wife, does not look as she did three or four years ago. The sad fate of our poor boy almost crushed her!"

"Oh, he was such a kind, dear lad!" said the mother, wiping away her tears. "His letters from Liverpool were so religious. I would not part with them for the whole of Glan 'r Afon. He was in the church ever since he was fifteen. I am sure that he safely reached his home."

"Pardon us, dear sir, for introducing a subject that cannot be interesting to you, but when we begin to talk of poor Dick, we don't know how to stop," said Evan Jones.

"Do you know the name of the ship in which he sailed, and the name of her captain?" asked Mr. Wynn.

"O, dear, yes!" said Evan Jones. "He sailed in the ship Bombay, bound for the East Indies, and commanded by Captain Bradley."

Mr. Wynn suddenly arose and said: "Mr. Edwards, I would be glad to see you alone for a few minutes."

"Please walk with me into my study, Mr. Wynn," said Llewelyn. They went, and the door was closed after them.

"I wonder what he wants with Llewelyn?" said Helen Edwards.

"I think he wishes to convey, in writing, all right and title of Pren y Gôg to Mr. Evan Jones and his wife Margaret," said Nellie Trevor.

"Nellie is always devising liberal things," said Mary Humphreys.

"Mr. Trevor," said Gwennie, "has Mr. Wynn told you where he is from?"

"He has not," was the answer. "I should not wonder if he is a relative of Sir Watkyn William Wynn."

"I think it is a great pity for such a fine man to cover his face with hair," said Margaret Jones.

"Mother," said Mary, "don't you know that all the pictures we have of Jesus Christ show him with a heavy beard? But you don't think any less of the Saviour on that account?"

"No, my child, I don't," said the mother. "Neither

do I think, less of Mr. Wynn. But when he talks so nicely, I would be so glad to see his mouth."

Just then Llewelyn returned with a very peculiar expression of countenance. His eyes were tearful and his face pale.

"My dear husband!" cried Gwennie, rushing toward him in evident alarm, "what is the matter? Is Mr. Wynn sick? What *is* it?"

"Don't be alarmed, Gwennie: I have no bad news to relate," said her husband, while every eye in the room rested upon him, and while every ear was watching for further developments. "Since I left this room I have received some startling revelations, and now I wish to make them known to you, as Mr. Wynn revealed them to me. They concern Evan Jones and his family mostly. Mr. Wynn has lately returned from the East Indies, from Bombay, and gives me the most positive assurance, not only that Captain Bradley is alive, but that Dick Jones also was saved from the wreck, and is now alive and well."

Here was a scene! The father, mother, sisters, and indeed the whole company, as by a sudden shock, rose to their feet. Exclamations broke forth from almost every lip. The mother ran to Llewelyn, seized him by the arm, and cried: "Is it true? Oh, is it *true*? *Is* my Dick alive? Do *you* believe it, Llewelyn? Answer me that before you say another word! Do *you* believe it?"

"Thank God!" cried Llewelyn. "Margaret Jones, I know that Dick is alive and well! Try and govern yourselves, for I have much more good news to tell you. Mr. Wynn sailed from Bombay with Captain Bradley, and landed in Liverpool only two days and a half ago, and he declares that Dick was one of the cabin passengers!"

Here was another scene, far exceeding the first in demonstrations. There was a mixture of joyous weeping and laughter. Mary Humphreys, who, until now, had manifested entire calmness, broke down with emotions and buried her face in Gwennie's lap.

" *O Llewelyn anwyl !*" cried the mother. "A oes genyt fwy o newyddion da?" (O, dear Llewelyn! have you any more good news?)

"Yes, I have, Margaret Jones," said Mr. Edwards, "and may God give you grace to bear it. It seems that Dick arrived in Bangor at the same time as did Mr. Wynn, and in some manner has contrived to get into this house. I have seen him with my own eyes, and he is now up stairs."

Here was a scene that far exceeded the two previous. "Now, order!" cried Llewelyn. But there was no order. All was happy confusion. "O, let me see my boy!" cried the mother, with arms extended.

"Now I will go after Dick Jones, and then you may enjoy yourselves over him as your feelings may dictate," and he left the room.

By a struggle, they kept back for a few moments the torrent of feeling that was almost irresistable. Footsteps were heard descending the stairs. The door was partially opened, while Llewelyn stood in it and said:

"Mr. Wynn has disappeared, but Dick Jones remains. Walk in, Dick, and make yourself at home!"

And the tall form of the new master was seen rushing into the extended arms of an almost bewildered mother. "*O fy mam anwyl!*" (O my dear mother), he loudly cried, as he pressed her sinking form to his throbbing bosom. Then the rest of the family clustered around the restored one and covered him with tears and kisses. Trevor laughed and wept. Nellie ran and kissed Helen Edwards, and then both together embraced Mary Humphreys. Thomas Lloyd cried like a child, and Gwennie, leaning on the bosom of her husband, looked up to heaven with thanksgiving. When Dick was released from the grasp of his relatives, he made his way to Mary Humphreys. Their eyes met, and those glances were crowded with intense affection, and that mutual grasp told a story of undying love.

After a while silence was restored, and the young man thus addressed the company:

"I am not in a frame of mind to speak at length.

For three years I have been to you as one dead. You have wept over my sad fate. Now that I am restored, you naturally wonder why I did not write to you and acquaint you of my almost miraculous escape from an awful shipwreck. I will only say now, that such were the circumstances that rendered this impossible. My story is full of interest, but it is long, and I will not touch upon it to-night. I would gladly embrace the opportunity, if offered, to give a full narrative before the public, in the shape of an address. In this I could put myself right before the community, and it would save me the trouble of explaining the matter to individuals."

"Richard," said Llewelyn, "on what evening can you give us the narrative at Llangobaith? The people will receive it as a great favor."

"On any evening you may see fit to appoint," was the answer.

"Then I will take upon me the responsibility of saying that on next Wednesday evening, Richard Jones, formerly of Pren y Gôg, will give a narrative of his shipwreck, rescue and adventures in the East Indies, at the Methodist chapel, in Llangobaith. The meeting will be publicly announced on next Sabbath. And now, as some of the company must soon leave, it is highly proper that this extraordinary event should close with prayer. Let us now all kneel before the Lord."

They bowed in grateful reverence, while the pastor, in language of pathetic earnestness, offered up thanksgiving for the kind Providence that had watched over their young friend. A holy atmosphere filled the room, while the face of Margaret Jones shone like that of an angel.

The father and mother now departed for home. The sisters also left with beating hearts, while the sweet impressions of their brother's kisses rested on their animated cheeks

"Now, Mr. Richard Jones, formerly of Pren y Gôg," said Miss Nellie, "if you are responsible for the promises of that fine looking Thomas Wynn, with whom I came pretty near falling in love, we have a claim on you for the night at Riverside."

"You certainly have, Miss Trevor," said Richard, "and I shall most gladly accompany you and your father home. 'I was a stranger and ye took me in.'"

"Yes, I think that is the way it reads," said Nellie, with a smile, "and to show your gratitude, you have ' taken in ' a dozen of us."

Amid the hearty cheers and good wishes of the company, they started for Glan 'r Afon. Miss Trevor was uncontrollably happy. This showed itself in sudden fits of alternate laughter and sobbing. " O, papa dear, isn't this glorious ?" she cried. " Yes. Dick Jones *is* risen from the dead, and some one *will* change her mind!"

"Nellie, I am afraid you will not sleep much to-night," said her father.

"*Sleep*, papa! I don't wish to sleep! I would like to sail on this beautiful stream of happiness, without interruption, for a week! But, dear papa, I shall soon be myself again." They had reached home.

"Well, Nellie," said the mother, "I presume that you had a pleasant time?"

Nellie could not control herself. Perhaps she did not try.

"O, Mother, *mother!*" she cried, "I have such good news to tell you. I have been half crazy ever since I found it out. Dick Jones has come back, and we have seen him!"

"Nellie Trevor," said the mother, "I think you are a little more than *half* crazy!"

"Mother, dear, it is no wonder you don't believe it," said Nellie, "but I am telling you the living truth! I appeal to Mr. Wynn."

"Mrs. Trevor," said the new master, "your daughter is telling the simple truth. Dick Jones has certainly returned from India. She has seen him and conversed with him."

Mrs. Trevor now sat down completely overcome with emotion.

"Mother, I have been laughing and crying for two hours," said the daughter, "and so have all that were at Llwyn y Derwydd."

"How does he look, Nellie?" asked the mother, mastering her feelings.

"O, he looks a nobleman all over!" proudly answered Nellie.

"And where did you leave him?" asked the mother.

"We didn't leave him! We brought him along with us. and, mother dear, here he is: no longer Thomas Wynn. but just Dick Jones of Pren y Gôg. the new master of Riverside!" and she ran around the room clapping her hands.

Mrs. Trevor hardly knew what to do or say. and so Richard came to her relief.

"I hope you will pardon me. Mrs. Trevor. for this bit of deception. It did not continue long, and it had a very happy ending. I had a hard struggle to keep it up as long as I did. and I am very glad that it is over. Mr. Trevor and your daughter will tell you, in my absence, how things went at Druid's Grove. and on next Wednesday evening I am to give a public narrative, at the chapel at Llangobaith, of my shipwreck, escape and stay in India.

Mrs. Trevor rose, gave Richard her hand, and said: "We thank the Lord for your wonderful escape, and most gladly welcome you to your home and friends!

I know you must be tired ; your room is ready whenever you wish to retire."

The young man thanked her, bade them good night, and went to his room.

The next day the whole family, with the addition of Mary Humphreys, met together at the old familiar homestead, and there they had another joyful meeting. In all the principality of Wales there could not be found a happier company. In the evening, Dick and Mary went to Druid's Grove. The next morning he sent word to Riverside to have the carriage call at Mr. Lloyd's. and so about ten o'clock it came. Good wishes were exchanged, and they were on their way to Bangor.

The news that "Dick Pren y Gôg" had returned from the East Indies a rich man, and that he was the owner of Glan 'r Afon, spread like wild-fire throughout all that region of country. The fact that for three years he had been considered dead, added much to the enthusiasm. It was the great theme of conversation among old and young. Crowds visited the humble residence of Evan Jones to inquire about him, and were satisfied with the assurance that they would hear all about it from his own lips, at the chapel, on Wednesday night.

"Siloam," on the appointed evening, was crowded to its utmost capacity. A most earnest prayer was offered

by Llewelyn, while heartfelt responses freely resounded throughout the congregation.

The speaker was appropriately introduced to the
audience, and, although at that day, cheering in a
Welsh chapel was not encouraged, for this once those
sacred walls echoed with loud applause.

# CHAPTER XXVIII.



"Ladies and gentlemen," said the speaker, with a smile on his countenance, "you well know that Dick Jones is not a public speaker. You do not expect eloquence or philosophy. You have come together to hear the plain narrative of one brought up in humble life, and a stranger to the higher branches of education.

Our voyage was rough throughout. We first encountered a severe gale at the head of the Bay of Biscay, which lasted forty-eight hours. I greatly enjoyed the sea, and almost welcomed the gales. We had rounded the Cape of Good Hope, and were east of Madagascar, entering into the Indian Ocean, when we were overtaken by a dead calm. This continued for two days when, to the joy of all, one morning about six o'clock, a fresh breeze blew from the west, and the Bombay was again on her way. At the close of that day the western sky showed signs which Captain Bradley did not consider favorable.

'What do those fellows in the west say to you, Mr. Bigelow?' asked the captain, pointing to the clouds.

'They tell me that they are busily engaged in work-

ing up a storm that will overtake us, sir,' said the first
mate.

'You are correct, Mr. Bigelow,' said the captain.
'Send the men aloft at once and reef the foresail and
close reef the main-topsail.'

The order was given, and we ran aloft and everything
was well secured. The wind was gaining in strength
every hour, and already it was tempestuous. Other
sheets were closely reefed, and by morning the Bombay
presented a bare appearance. The sea was in a perfect
fury, and thus it continued and increased in wildness
throughout the long day. Darkness overtook us, and
such darkness I had never witnessed. It seemed as if
the firmament, in all its horrid blackness, had fallen
and was crushing us. Daylight, such as it was, again
appeared. It only revealed a more terrible sight than
that of the day before  At seven in the morning, our
galley was swept overboard, and at ten the topsail was
carried away. Owing to the entire absence of the sun,
it was impossible to know how far we had drifted. The
storm was yet in the height of its madness.

'Starboard watch, man the pumps!' cried the second mate. 'Shake her up lively, my lads!'

'Aye, aye, sir!' we heartily responded. We joined in
our familiar pumping choruses with as much heartiness
as we did in fair weather. In half an hour the water
gained upon us, and the officers found out, to their ut-

ter consternation, that the ship had sprung a leak! For hours we continued at the pumps, but to no purpose, and by order of the captain we were commanded to go aft. He met us with a cheerful countenance, and thus addressed us:

'My men, I have called you here to thank you for your noble sailorlike behavior during this long and stormy voyage. To all appearance, the Bombay is about to be lost. We shall do our duty to the very last moment, and when it comes to the worst, we shall meet our fate like men. Now, Mr. Bigelow, you may order one watch to the pumps and the other to have in readiness the long boats.'

Every man was swift to do his duty. The leak gained upon us in a fearful manner.

' Mr. Bigelow,' said the captain, in hurried words, 'let the lead be thrown overboard! By the looks of those waves, I suspect we have no deep soundings.'

This was done, and ' six fathoms!' was sung out.

' Captain Bradley, we are close on breakers! Shall we drop an anchor, sir?' cried the first mate.

' Let go the starboard anchor!' cried the captain.

In a moment the anchor was dropped. But the violence of the storm, and the immense weight of the ship, caused the anchor to drag. Presently the ship's stern struck with a fearful violence, and the mizzen mast, with a terrible crash, fell overboard. By this time the anchor kept the ship from drifting, while it continued to beat violently against the breakers. The boats were quickly supplied with water and provisions, as well as with quadrants and compasses. We were divided into three parties under the command of the captain and the two mates. I was to be in the boat with the captain.

I knew we were about to leave the ship. I ran to the forecastle, opened my chest, seized my little Welsh Bible which my mother gave me the day I left home, put it in an inside pocket of my waistcoat, locked up my chest, put the key in my pocket and joined my companions.

The boats were soon in the water, and the Bombay was abandoned. We soon found that our condition was well nigh hopeless. How our companions of the other boats were doing, we could not tell. By reason of the darkness, the captain was no longer able to see the huge waves. and was less effective at the helm. Our boat's side became partially turned to the wind. a huge billow took it, and in a moment we were upset. It was so sudden that there was no struggle. When I came up I could see the boat with its bottom upward, and in a moment I lost sight of it. I could see none of my companions, and I did not hear any cry. I was a good swimmer from early childhood, and I kept myself afloat without much trouble. I know not how long I had thus drifted, when I found myself in contact with a piece of wreck, which evidently was not a part of the Bombay. I eagerly clung to it and found that much of it was under water. With a great effort I reached the upper portion and was able to sit down. Suddenly the wind ceased, and before a great while I could see the stars. At last the morning dawned, and the sea was much more pacific. After some hours, I could dimly see in the southwest what resembled land, and I was glad to know that I was drifting that way. I took out of my pocket my soaked Bible, read the 23d Psalm, aud committed myself to the tender care of the Shepherd of Israel. Onward my piece of wreck slowly moved, and I was more sure I was in sight of land, and that it was not far away. My spirit greatly revived, and I drifted along for another hour. Soon my heart leaped for joy! Not far away I saw a large canoe, paddled by two men, approaching. I was saved! They were natives, strange in features and language, but at the moment I hailed them, as angels from heaven. Their countenances denoted compassion, and I knew they were friendly. In about two hours we reached the shore.

The appearance of things indicated that this little groupe had but recently reached this remote, desolate little island. I learned after this that they had fled from the violence of some hostile Indians. They were low in the scale of humanity, and yet possessing a kind disposition. The women and the children at first shunned me, but soon, however, concluded that I belonged to some tribe of the human race. I was able to make them understand that I was very hungry, and the men put before me some pieces of fowl, fish and rice, which, under the circustances, proved quite palatable.

It was about two weeks after I landed, that in company with Lago, a lad who, perhaps, was twelve years of age, I wandered until I came to the brink of a rivulet. Through its clear water I saw a number of shining substances. I went into the water and found that they were pieces of solid gold, without any mixture of dross. I became excited over my discovery. The lad looked upon me with a smile, and seemed to pity my folly. I carefully marked the spot and we returned home. I showed my host the gold, and he treated it with more indifference than did the boy.

The next morning the two men who had rescued me started in the same canoe on a fishing excursion, while I went in search of more gold, which I found in rich abundance. In the afternoon I returned and deposited my treasure in a hollow stone, without any fear of its being stolen. The men were returning, and near the shore. In one end of the canoe there was an elevated something, over which the men had thrown a covering. I met them at the landing place ready to render them assistance, and there, to my utter astonishment, I found

*my own familiar sea chest!*  I clapped my hands in
perfect ecstacy.  As well as I could, I informed them
that the chest belonged to me, and that it had floated
from the wreck.  They understood me.  The inmates
of the cabins were given to understand that the box
was mine.  I took the key, which I had carefully kept,
put it in the lock, the chest was opened, and I found
all my things perfectly dry!  The man at Liverpool
who had made it assured me that as long as it was kept
locked not a drop of water could enter it.  I first
brought out my violin, put the instrument in tune, and
played ' God Save the King,' which perfectly delighted
the whole company.  I then played on the clarionet.
The overhauling of the articles took some time.  I gave
them a large number of presents, with which they were
greatly delighted.

Without much change in my mode of proceeding, I
remained with this people for two years.  I imparted
to them some instruction in the preparation of food and
the cultivation of rice, which they slowly adopted.  I
now anxiously longed for civilization and home.  I gave
up gold gathering, being well satisfied with the sum
deposited in my chest.  Borga well knew that I was
daily watching for a sail, and had promised to help me
whenever I desired assistance.

One morning we sat together on an elevation near
the shore.  I took my excellent telescope and surveyed

the ocean, and to my great joy my glass brought to view a vessel in the distance, and it was evident to me that it was nearing the island. In about half an hour it became visible to the naked eye. I asked Borga to leave for home, and have the canoe in readiness. He left, and I remained on the hill for another hour. I then hastened down to join the men. My two friends assisted in bringing out my chest, which, by the way, was quite heavy. The rest well understood what was going on. There were tears in their eyes, and Laggo fairly sobbed. He had become greatly attached to me, and I had taught him to play several pieces on the violin. I had also taught Kroonah to play on the clarionet. I again opened my chest, and gladly parted with everything I could spare. I handed Laggo my violin and asked him to play for me once more. The poor boy, with tearful eyes, played 'God Save the King,' and with quivering lips, handed me back the instrument.

'O, no, Laggo!' I said, 'the violin is yours for ever! Keep it in remembrance of Dick Jones.'

The boy's countenance plainly showed the depth of his gratitude. I then gave my clarionette to Kroonah, which he took with many gestures of thanks. I then gave my telescope to Borga. He was overjoyed, while the women and the smaller children rejoiced in their wild heathen fashion. I closed my chest and had it carried into the boat. With moistened eyes and a choking sensation, I parted with the women and children, jumped into the canoe and took my place at the helm, while the men pulled at the oars.

We pointed due west, and when about five miles from our starting point, I judged that we were near the ship's course. I asked Borga for the glass. I put it to my eye, and the first object I saw was the British flag waving in the breeze!  'It is enough,' I cried, with much feeling. We again started. The mammoth proportions of the ship filled my men with terror. I assured them that they had nothing to fear, and they calmed down. At a point, which I considered suitable, I stood up and cried at the top of my voice—

'Ship ahoy!'

'Aye, aye, sir!' was the laughing answer. 'And who are you. and what is the name of your ship?'

'I am an English sailor, once shipwrecked, picked up by Indians, and carried to a well nigh desolate island,' I cried out.

'You have an honest face,' said the man, ' but shipwrecked sailors are not in the habit of swimming ashore with their sea chests on their backs.'

'It is a strange story, sir,' I said, 'but as sure as I am a Welshman, this chest was picked up in two weeks after the ship went to pieces.'

'And what was the name of your ship?' was the next question.

'The Bombay, sir,' I replied, 'commanded by Captain Bradley, as able and kind a master as ever walked a quarter-deck.'

'Correct, my man!' he answered, in a loud voice, as he threw over the side the ship's ladder. 'Now bring your craft along side. Two of you men get that chest aboard and give it a careful handling. Now be lively.'

'Aye, aye, sir,' and it was safely on deck.

I tried to persuade the Indians to go on board to see the wonders of the ship, but they refused. I bade them farewell, and they pulled away with desperate speed. I looked after them from the ladder on which I stood, waved my hat, and then sprang on board.'

The man who had spoken with me was a fine looking Englishman, while the finished sailor was visible in his every movement. He invited me to his room.

'Well Richard,' said he, (he had seen my name on the chest), 'I should like to hear a little more of your history.'

'I will give it most gladly, sir,' I said, and did so, but said nothing in regard to the gold.

'This ship is the Borealis, and it belongs to Bombay, where we are bound,' said he. 'Please remain here for a short time. I will report you to the captain, who is very busy with some papers. I am the first mate, and my name is Bonner,' and he left for the cabin.

'What has been going on, on deck, Mr. Bonner,' asked the captain. 'Has any one boarded us?' (This I learned afterwards.)

'Two Indians brought us an English sailor, sir, who relates an exciting adventure,' said the mate. 'I think he tells a true story.'

'I should like to ask the fellow a few questions myself,' said the captain. 'Bring him to the cabin, Mr. Bonner.'

The mate returned, and to the cabin I went, feeling a little uneasy.

The chief officer, with his back toward us, was busily engaged with his papers.

'Captain Bradley,' said the mate, with some emotion. 'This is Richard Jones, formerly of Liverpool, who claims acquaintance with the captain of the Bombay.'

The captain turned around, jumped to his feet, and in a moment I was in his arms! We both wept like little children. The mate also was affected. He bowed, and left.

Then followed a long recital of our respective escapes. The captain, after remaining in the water some time, saw the longboat close by. By this time it had been righted. By an effort, he found himself once more in his boat. When the storm subsided he unfastened a pair of oars secured to its sides, which he used to good advantage. He also found water and biscuit in the locker, and at the end of three days was picked up by a schooner bound for Bombay, where he was quickly furnished with the Borealis by the same owners. He had not heard anything from the unfortunate crew, and he presumed that all had been lost.

'And now, my dear Richard,' he said, 'my next voyage will be to England. I start in about four months. From this moment until, with the consent of Providence, I land you safely in Liverpool, you are to be my guest.'

'Captain,' said I, 'I am not worthy of such honors, but I will obey orders.' I then related to him my gold enterprise.

'Heaven bless you!' said he, 'your little island has made you rich. There is now a great demand for un-coined gold, and at Bombay you can easily exchange it for coin or bills of exchange. Bless my soul! Richard, we have been driven two hundred miles from our course, or you would never have seen the Borealis in these waters. It is hardly ever a ship heaves in view of your island, and it is a wonder that you saw us.'

Nothing could exceed the kindness I received from Captain Bradley. His home in Bombay was my home. The owners gladly took my gold and gave me in exchange coin, and bills of exchange on the Bank of England.

The day arrived for the Borealis to sail. The captain's wife and son were to accompany us, and all were in fine spirits. The anchor was weighed, and before a prosperous breeze our noble ship was ploughing the waters of the Arabian Sea.

In six months from the day we left Bombay we anchored in the Mersey. In Liverpool, during my short stay there, I received the same kind treatment from Captain Bradley.

One day, at my hotel, I chanced to take up a Liverpool paper. In large letters I found the familiar name 'GLAN 'R AFON.' I read the notice. The place was to be sold to the highest bidder, and that in less than forty-eight hours. I hurried to the bank, took what I thought a sufficient sum to pay for Riverside, and hastened to secure a passage for Wales. I reached Bangor on the morning of the day of sale. I procured a conveyance and reached the spot in time. The rest you know. The little deception I played for a few hours, was the hardest mental effort of my life. Our meeting in the evening at Druid's Grove was an event never to be forgotten. Now that I have reached my native land, I intend here to remain until I leave for that 'bourne from whence no traveler returneth.'

I thank you for your presence, and the kind attention you have paid to my unadorned story."

When the narrative was ended the audience gave

vent to its feeling in rapturous applause. Llewelyn Edwards, in behalf of the throng, thanked the speaker for his interesting address, and declared the meeting closed.

Then came such hearty greetings as were seldom witnessed in any country. The people would not leave without grasping the hand of him whom they had mourned as dead.

# CHAPTER XXIX.



### ECCENTRICITY.

Druid's Grove had now become a point of great attraction to the Calvinistic Methodist ministers; not only as the residence of Llewelyn Edwards, but also on account of the cordial welcome they received at the hands of Thomas Lloyd, who was never so happy as when entertaining these laborious men of God. Aside from its yearly Associations, this body held meetings on a much smaller scale every six weeks in different parts of the country, at which, besides preaching, they arranged the local appointments and other matters. One of these meetings was held at Llangobaith on the week following the one on which our young friend from India delivered his narrative. On the morning succeeding this meeting, there were some half a dozen ministers seated in the commodious parlor of Druid's Grove, enjoying a friendly visit before starting again for their various fields of labor. Their countenances denoted cheerfulness, intelligence and humor. No class of men enjoy each other's society in a familiar, friendly chat, more than do gospel ministers. Many of the early dissenting ministers of Wales were exceedingly eccentric, and the peculiarities of these pioneers were often made the theme of conversation among the preachers in their social intercourse. This genial gathering at Druid's Grove had drifted into this strain. Some of the incidents and sayings mentioned partook largely of the ludicrous, but on that account they were only the more acceptable.

"Yes," said Rev. John Thomas, "old Sienkin, in the main, was a good preacher, and secured good congregations. But he was unsafe. Sometimes he would drop suddenly from the finest thoughts into the most laughable absurdities. He was at one time preaching on the prodigal son. In dwelling on the father's love for the erring boy, his language was very touching and pathetic, and his hearers were much affected. But when he came to the 'fatted calf,' he was not quite so fortunate. "I shouldn't wonder at all, my brethren," he cried, in his own peculiar tone, "if that dear father had kept that very calf *for years and years*, waiting for his son to come home!" At this, the mirth of the audience became uncontrollable, to the great disappointment of old Sienkin, who looked for tears and not laughter.

"What did that uncommon levity mean during a part of my sermon, Robert Davis?" he rather indignantly inquired of one of the brethren, after the meeting had closed, "and I rather think that you joined in it yourself."

"I did, indeed," said the man. "We were laughing
21

at that wonderful 'fatted calf,' that was so accommodating as to remain a tender veal for 'years and years.' "

Sienkin saw the point, pronounced himself an *hen ffŵl* (old fool) and declared the levity to be perfectly justifiable.

"Perhaps of all the preachers we had in the principality, no one was more peculiar or eccentric than Robert Thomas," said Rev. John James, "and there were but very few that were more talented in the pulpit. Yet, in many things, he seemed to be as ignorant as an infant. At one time he published a very small volume of his poems. He ordered one thousand copies, and he got the impression that this would be an enormous quantity. He would often inquire, with deep anxiety, how they could be brought from the publisher's, at Bala, to Ffestiniog. 'I wonder,' said he, 'if the four horse wagon of *Rhyd y Fen* can bring them all at once?' Then addressing his wife, he said: 'Sarah, you must empty that large clothes press; we can put many of them in that. And then you can move the things from that long shelf in the kitchen. We shall need it only for about two weeks; by that time the books will be sent to the subscribers. And if we need more room, we can move the parlor table and pile them in that corner.' That is the manner in which this great man dreamed about the bulk of a thousand very small volumes of his poems."

One afternoon the hired servant of Rhyd y Fen brought in his arms a good sized bundle, and said: "Here is something from Mr. Saunderson, Bala, for Robert Thomas."

"But where are the rest, my good man?" asked Mr. Thomas, in astonishment. "Why should he send these few copies?"

"That is all he gave me," said the man, "and he said nothing about any more."

"Well," said Robert Thomas, "you can bring them all next time. Tell your master I would be very glad to get them. even if for once he should not bring any flour."

"Robert," said Mrs. Thomas. "the book, you know, is a small one, and they may be all in that bundle."

"All in that bundle!" cried Robert Thomas, out of all patience. "Sarah, you have lost what little common sense you ever had! A *thousand* 'Gleanings from the Field of Boaz,' in that little bundle!"

He opened the parcel. and to his utter astonishment he found a thousand copies. The clothes press was not disturbed, the long shelf was not molested, the parlor table remained as it was, and Robert Thomas humbly apologized for the reflection he had cast upon Sarah's common sense.

"How about that spider, Mr. James?" asked a young minister by the name of Hugh Evans.

" That was at *Pant Glas*, near Bala," said Mr. James.
"He was in the middle of a splendid sermon, when he
spied a small spider descending by his web from the ceiling and approaching the front of the pulpit.  The preacher at once spread out his open hands, ready for execution,
but kept on preaching with all his might, with his eye
fixed upon some object, which the congregation did not
see.   At last those open hands came together with such
a force as to make the walls of the chapel ring, and the
poor spider was no more.  'There,' said the minister,
in a lower tone, as between parenthesis, 'that is the
end of *him!*'  He then, without the least embarrassment, finished his discourse."

"This is certainly very amusing," said Rev. Morgan
Griffiths, "and I could well enjoy it for an hour longer,
but I shall be under the necessity of leaving very soon,
so let Robert Thomas and the spider end our stories."

"Just a minute longer, if you please," said Levi
Thomas.  "Mr. Jones, who was it that called the Gla-
morganites Salamanders, and what were the circumstances ?"

" O, that is soon told," was the reply.  "You see,
David Evans, from the north, had been in the land of
flames and furnaces preaching, and when he returned
from the south, some of the ministers asked him if he
had had good success in Glamorganshire."

" Well, yes, upon the whole, but not at first," said

he. "I had a sermon upon the burning of Sodom and Gomorrah. I preached it repeatedly, but every time it fell perfectly flat. You see, those old Salamanders were so used to fire that it didn't affect them at all. But I had a sermon on the *deluge* that took splendidly, and produced a wonderful effect."

The company now arose, and after an affectionate parting with the family at Druid's Grove. the itinerants went their way toward their respective appointments.

---

We will not undertake a description of that unspeakable bliss that filled the devoted hearts of Dick Jones and Mary Humphreys since they had been restored to each other; those hours of unmixed pleasure in telling over the joys and sorrows, hopes and fears. clouds and sunshine, they had experienced since that night. over six years before, on which they parted with tears at the kitchen door of Druid's Grove.

Soon after completing the business with Pugh's agent, Richard made an arrangement with Mr. Trevor to make his home at Riverside for the present The house was commodious, and there was abundance of room to spare. This gave much satisfaction to all concerned. To Mr. Trevor it was a financial gain, and the boarder was near his family, and in the midst of his friends.

In Wales, among the festivals of the year, none compares in importance with that of Christmas. It is so now, and it was so then. The festivities were not confined to the day proper; they began before, and continued after. It was a season of general rejoicing and happy greetings. The well-to-do remembered the poor, although in many instances, on the part of many, this was sadly neglected. Within the surroundings of Llangobaith, there were quite a number of needy parents, who could not enjoy a Christmas dinner with their little ones, even on a small scale, unless they were remembered by some benevolent heart.

Just then there was in that vicinity, at least one such heart. He well remembered a little boy, many years before, whose heart had often beat with joy as Mrs. Lloyd, or some other benevolent person, would send to Pren y Gôg materials for merry Christmas in the shape of flour, a dressed goose, with, some times, pairs of shoes for little destitute feet. Yes, he thought of that time with a tear in his eye, a smile on his lips, and a very good purpose in his heart.

"Very well," said the master, after a long conversation with Trevor. "Let him bring, to-morrow, from Bangor, twenty baskets, into each of which you can put a dressed goose, a piece of bacon, and a small bag of flour; for which I shall have the great pleasure of paying you a good price."

"All that will be strictly attended to, Mr. Jones,"
said Mr. Trevor.

The baskets were well filled and labeled ; and on the
day before Christmas, Robin Jones of Druid's Grove,
and John Pritchard of Riverside, with their respective
conveyances, started on their benevolent mission, with
the instruction  to make no explanation, but simply to
say that the baskets were presents as well as their con-
tents.

# CHAPTER XXX.



CHRISTMAS EVE AND "PLYGAIN."

On *Nos Nadolig* (Christmas Eve), above all other
eves in the round year, the young people, with a fair
sprinkling of those older in years, would assemble in
different neighborhoods and spend the most of the
night in innocent mirth.   Their amusements were various.   One feature was the making and pulling of
*cyflaith* (molasses candy.)   At what period this custom
began, we cannot tell; but it is ancient as well as universal.   To see a boy or a girl among the peasantry on
Christmas day, without a good supply of taffy, was an
unusual sight.   The writer remembers, with lively
emotions, the delightful features of many a *Nos Nadolig*
in Llanddeiniolen over fifty years ago.   In these gatherings there was also what was termed *codi afalau
o'r dwr*, or bobbing for apples.   A good number of
fair sized apples were thrown into a large tub, half
filled with water.   A very slight touch would cause
the fruit to sink below the surface, and to secure an apple by simple suction was not an easy matter, and the
effort would cause much merriment.   When a victory
was won, the prize was handed over by the fortunate
swain to some favorite maiden, who would accept the

compliment with blushing delight. They had another laughable performance. A string was fastened to the ceiling, and the other end to a short stick in such a way as to balance an apple at one end and a lighted candle at the other. To snatch the apple with the lips, and yet escape the candle, was the aim of the competitors, and in the great majority of efforts the candle would come in contact with their hair, and create bursts of laughter. After a wholesome repast, the company would generally settle down into hearing and telling stories. The most popular of these were of the ghost and fairy type, or anything that had a touch of the supernatural.

It was about two weeks before Christmas, and Gwennie thus addressed her father:

"Papa, I would be delighted to give Robin Jones, during these Christmas holidays, some special proof of the high estimation in which we hold him. Let him. at our expense, on next Christmas Eve, entertain his friends at our commodious kitchen. Let us provide for them a good supper, and this will please him much more than anything we can give him in the shape of a present."

"This strikes me favorably," said Mr. Lloyd, "and you may tell Robin that it is for his sake."

"Thank you, papa!" said Gwennie, and she went and revealed the matter to Robin, who was deeply affected by the sudden news, and especially the motive that prompted the movement.

That *Nos Nadolig* at Druid's Grove surpassed in enjoyment anything of the kind ever known in the vicinity of Llangobaith. The company was large, made up of choice young men and maidens from the surrounding peasantry, with a few older friends. The usual features were fully carried out, and gladness beamed in every countenance. Occasionally, the family went in to smile upon their youthful hilarity and to assure them of a cordial welcome.

After an abundant feast, the tables were cleared, and the closing feature was story-telling. There were those present who were perfectly at home in that line, and were never found without a fresh supply.

"I'll give you *Llwyn y Nefoedd*," (Grove of Heaven), said Ellis Thomas. "There was in the olden times in *Clynog Fawr*, in Carnarvonshire, a very pious monk. He often spent hours together in meditating on the splendid scenery of the heavenly world. He also had one longing desire to have while yet below, one glimpse of the better land. One day, about vesper time, the question arose in his mind, 'Can the bliss of heaven retain its sweetness and freshness to all eternity? Will not the period arrive in the great hereafter when even the melody of the upper sanctuary shall become monotonous?'

With these questions in his mind, he was slowly walking along the banks of a silvery stream not far from the monastery. Nature was retiring to rest, and the feathered songsters in the grove had well nigh ceased their melodious warbling. He slowly pursued his way, while his thoughts were full of heaven. The stream hastened toward the ocean, and the monk penetrated farther into the beautiful grove. Presently the most delightful warbling music fell upon his ears. He sat down beneath the shade of a green tree, and fell into a blissful trance. The melody continued, and time sped on. The monk was oblivious of all below, and in heavenly ecstacy he listened to the strange music. At last he heard a voice, 'Sleeper, arise!' He arose, and after some wandering in the grove he found his way out. To his astonishment, he found that all things had changed. The old monastery was there, it is true, but every house, cot, wall and stile had been moved since he saw them last. He went into the monastery, but no one knew him, and he knew no one. He was treated kindly and conducted to a soft seat. His venerable appearance commanded respect. In utter bewilderment, he looked around him and cried out:

'*O, Arglwydd Dduw, pa le mae'm pobl?*' (O, Lord God, where are my people?)

'But who art thou, and where hast thou been?' asked a priest.

'I am a monk of this monastery,' was the reply. 'One short hour ago, as it seems to me, I went to yonder grove, and in listening to some wonderful bird melody I fell into a heavenly trance. I awoke, and what means this strange transformation?'

'And what is thy name, venerable father?' asked the priest.

'This morning they called me Father Ignatius,' said the old monk, gazing around in wonderment.

'Ignatius!' cried the priest. 'There was such a monk here long ago, who mysteriously disappeared and was never found.'

'Give me a few of the circumstances!' cried the stranger, with deep feeling.

The priest took from a shelf an ancient manuscript, and read, 'On an afternoon in the month of August of that year, Father Ignatius, a most devout priest, left the monastery. He was last seen in the vicinity of a grove near by. He never returned, and as no trace of him could be found, it is believed that he was miraculously carried up into heaven, for he had one longing, abiding desire to see the glory of the heaven y world.'

'And when did that take place?' asked the old man.

'That was over two hundred years ago!' was the answer.

'To me it seems but one brief hour!' said the monk. 'But I am weary and need rest.'

'But thou needest food also,' said the priest.

'Nay, I simply need rest,' was the answer.

He was conducted into a comfortable bed-chamber, and when they sought him they found but *a handful of dust!*"

"If you don't object to a goblin story, and a pretty rough one at that," said *Twm y melinydd* (Tom the miller), I will give you *Bwgan Llanegryn* (Llanegryn goblin.)

"About fifty years ago, the good people of this place in Meirionethshire were most unmercifully treated by some unseen monster. The pious Lewis Williams lived in the vicinity of the trouble, and had often witnessed the antics of this abusive devil. Mr. Williams was a fearless old gentleman, and fully trusting in the Lord, he was not afraid of a goblin. Now I will give you his own words—here they are: 'While with others in a field belonging to this haunted house, binding wheat, some invisible power followed us, untied every sheaf, and scattered the grain in all directions. This was done three times right before my eyes, on days when there was not a breath of wind.' This is what Lewis Williams said. Well, after this he thought he would go to the haunted house to sleep, hoping to put an end to this goblin disturbance. But here he found no peace. Sometimes the noise would be under the bed, again above his head, and often the pillow would be snatched away. At times the whole house would be violently shaken to its foundation. So on this night he found no rest. But Lewis Williams was not disposed to give up the contest. And so on the next night he went with a candle and a Bible. He made his way to the room where they were mostly troubled, thinking of spending the night in reading the word of God and in prayer. But long before midnight the invisible something came on with more fury than ever, and in spite of Bible and prayer, he began to throw things about in the most spiteful manner. The room was filled with very offensive odor, and Williams was obliged to retreat.

After this the family sought the assistance of old Mr. Lewis, the vicar of the parish, for it was understood that he could master any devil out of perdition. He came, and it was said the conflict was terrible. His sister, who kept house for him, told her neighbors that he reached home in a dreadful plight; that his garments had to be hung out for days to be purified from their sulphurous and Satanic smell, and that his flesh for a long time savored of brimstone. But after that night, the inmates of the haunted house were not troubled; and that is the story of *Bwgan Llanegryn.*"

Here the festivities of that Christmas Eve came to an end. The company was greatly pleased, and Robin Jones stood higher in their estimation than ever. The hour was late, and the company dispersed, in order to enjoy a brief rest before the meeting in the parish church in the morning.

Among the religious features of Christmas at that time was the *Plygain*, for which I find no single English word. It means very early in the morning. At Llangobaith, this Christmas meeting had been held for generations. It commenced about five o'clock, and continued until daylight. The gathering was highly popular, owing to the joyous event it commemorated and to the attractive melody it presented. In every published volume of the old Welsh bards we have a goodly number of *Carolau Nadolig* (Christmas carols) in a variety of metres. For weeks before the event the best vocalists of the community had prepared themselves in this branch, and it was generally understood who were to sing at the Plygain.

On this occasion the church was beautifully decorated, while hundreds of lighted candles presented a grand illumination. The officiating clergyman read the morning service, with additional lessons and prayers suitable to the "Nativity." After this came the singing of carols.

Never had there been known a Plygain at Llangobaith in which the poor people showed such cheerful countenances. The remembrance of those well

filled baskets at home rendered their morning meeting
doubly valuable.    The last carol was sung, the meeting
of the early morn was over, the congregation was dismissed, and a perfect shower of " Merry Christmas !"
fell at once from a hundred lips.

# CHAPTER XXXI.



The winter was over. Nature smiled in beauty. The meadows were dressed in living green. The lark merrily warbled in his majestic ascent. The thrush poured forth its sweetest strains, while the woods rang with the sound of melody. The joyous day had dawned on which the new master of Riverside and Mary Humphreys were to be united in holy matrimony.

The old church at Llangobaith had never been so gaily decorated. Evergreens and flowers, woven into beautiful mottoes, abounded throughout the building, while on the outside the bridal party was to pass under spacious floral arches, on a pathway strewn with roses. All along the road from Druid's Grove to Llangobaith, at short intervals, there were inscriptions worthy of the event.

The expected procession at last appeared. It was fine; as much so in equipage as Bangor and Carnarvon combined could make it. They soon reached the church, and in perfect order they entered it. Then followed the concourse, and the edifice was thronged. The bride was given away by Thomas Lloyd. The ceremony presented no new features, but the peculiar in-

22

cidents connected with the history of the bridegroom, gave the service a peculiar effect. They were pronounced "husband and wife together," in the name of the Holy Trinity.

When the party again reached the open air, and the restraint was removed from the throng, a grand shout of good cheer went up from five hundred voices, while banners waved and church bells rung. The carriages were soon occupied by the guests, and all were ready to start. In an instant the horses were released from the bridal carriage, when a company of broad shouldered young Welshmen seized the vehicle, and thus the united twain were conducted from the church to the residence of Thomas Lloyd, where preparations had been perfected on a large scale for feeding the gathered throng. And on that evening, when the last gleam of daylight had vanished from the western sky, there were seen such illuminations as never before had been witnessed in that part of North Wales. Bonfires were kindled on every hill, while along the sides of the adjoining mountains the ascending flames were visible until a late hour, and the people at last had found the coveted opportunity to show their kind regards for Dick Jones and Mary Humphreys.

---

Llewelyn Edwards had been away from home for about two weeks, engaged in his itinerant labors, preaching twice every week day, and three times on the Sabbath. He was closing one of his meetings on an afternoon in the old and historical town of *Harlech*, when a letter was put into his hand. At once the seal was broken, and while the congregation was singing the last hymn. he read the following :

" My Dear Llewelyn:

Papa is very sick. He was taken down a week ago. Dr. Evans thinks that you had better come home without delay. The fever is very high, and of a malignant type. His case is considered as highly critical. Our trust is in the Lord.

Affectionately,

Gwennie."

Llewelyn gave the audience to understand the nature of the message, and said that he would immediately return. His appointments would be filled by others, to whom he would send word at once. And the congregation at Harlech was dismissed.

On the afternoon of the next day, Mr. Edwards reached home. By the tearful eyes of his wife, he knew that the sick man was no better. With silent steps they entered the chamber where, under the influence of a burning fever, the father was restlessly tossing about. By a table sat Dr. Evans preparing some powders. Grace was present, paying the strictest attention to every direction that fell over the physician's lips. Mrs. Richard Jones was also there like a ministering angel,

moving about quietly and systematically. Her husband, also, and Mr. Trevor were near at hand to render
any assistance within their power. Anxious days and
weary nights passed away, and there was no improvement. When lost in delirium, the sick 'man would
sometimes refer with horror to his past behavior, call
himself a cruel father, and beg of his daughter to come
home. But far oftener would he find himself with the
brethren at "Siloam." "No!" he would cry, "confer
no office on me, for I have persecuted the church of
Christ!" Once or twice he mentioned his wife. "Sarah!"
he cried, "you were right, and I was wrong! Never
mind, Gwennie is safe!"

At the end of fourteen days, the fever subsided, but
so fearful had been its ravages that there was no hope
of a rally. He was calm, conscious, and fully aware
that he was passing away. While he was yet able, he
bade them all an affectionate farewell, and smiled in
view of his approaching departure. He continued to
sink, and at last, without a struggle or a groan, the
spirit of Thomas Lloyd passed away to the great hereafter.

The funeral was very large. At the house a most impressive sermon was delivered by Rev. John Elias, who,
although comparatively young, had already set the
country ablaze by his wonderful ministry. At the
church, the rector read the usual burial service, and the

mortal remains were laid in their last resting place by the side of her who had gone before him into the "Bright Forever."

He left a carefully prepared will, by which Gwennie received a large sum of money, with much personal property. A liberal sum was left to the Methodist society at Llangobaith, the interest of which would go for the support of the ministry. To his most faithful servant, Robin Jones, in view of special services rendered the family, he left fifty pounds, with smaller sums to several other servants on the farm and in the house.

---

"Robin Jones," said Llewelyn, one morning. "I am no farmer, as you well know. If you are willing to remain here and superintend this farm, I will do well by you. I have but little confidence in the judgment of any of the other men."

"I am very thankful to you, Mr. Edwards," said Robin, "but my brother has made different arrangements. I am to have the charge of Riverside on very favorable conditions."

"You have my hearty good wishes!" said Llewelyn. "But I must have a competent hand to superintend Druid's Grove. I presume that Trevor, ere this, has secured a place?"

"I think he has not," said Robin. "Trevor is a perfect farmer, and Mrs. Trevor is a splendid housekeeper, and she would be such a company for Mrs. Edwards."

"Robin, you are a philosopher, as well as a farmer," said Llewelyn. "I will at once try and secure their services. There is another member of the family that you have not mentioned. Perhaps that Nellie would not object to remain where she is, if she was properly approached. Eh, Robin?"

Robin colored, and with some embarrassment, as well as ingenuity, he replied—

"Nellie has never been known as a servant, and I doubt if Dick would ever approach her on that subject."

"That is well turned, Robin," said Mr. Edwards. "I will go and see Trevor this very day."

———

"I should be so sorry to leave this vicinity and go so far!" said Nellie Trevor, with tears in her eyes, as she and her mother sat together. "We have been so happy, and we have such excellent friends."

"There is no certainty that your father will go, dear," said the mother. "He has ten days to think of it. Before that time expires, an offer may come that will not take us so far away."

Just then Llewelyn and Gwennie drove into the front yard. The mother and daughter rushed out to meet them, and to give them a cordial greeting.

"Mr. Jones and Mary have gone to Bangor," said Mrs. Trevor.

"I know they have," was the reply. "Our errand to-day is with Mr. Trevor and his family. Is your husband at home?"

"He is, and will be in the house in a few minutes," said Mrs. Trevor.

Presently Mr. Trevor came in with a smiling countenance, and assured his friends that he was very glad to see them.

Mr. Edwards then very briefly stated the object of his visit, informed Mr. Trevor what he would do for him, and asked if the offer and terms suited him.

"With many thanks, I accept your very liberal offer," said Mr. Trevor, "and I know my family is greatly relieved."

"And so we are!" cried Nellie, while joy beamed in her face. "O, I was so afraid that we would have to go far away from this dear vicinity, where we have so many kind friends."

"Well," said Llewelyn, "I have but little time to spare. I must leave home to-morrow morning to be away for some time. We shall have to start."

"And between this and your leaving Riverside, be sure and come to see us often," said Mrs. Edwards, addressing the family.

"I shall often pay a visit to my future home," said Nellie.

"Of your father and mother we are pretty sure," said Mrs. Edwards, "but you may meet with a better offer and give us the slip." And amid very pleasant feeling, the company separated.

"And Robin Jones is to have the charge of this noble farm," said Trevor. "Heaven bless him! It could not go into the hands of a more worthy young man."

And Nellie, as if remembering something she had forgotten, ran up stairs.

On that evening, it was no wonder at all that Robin Jones took more pains than usual with his toilet. Of late he had been much in the society of Nellie Trevor, and but few knew it. It was so fortunate! He could, of an evening, go to Riverside, and the people would naturally suppose that he went to see his brother. The twain had often been in the parlor, without molestation, for long periods, when the young man would be perfectly charmed with the spontaneous brilliancy of the young lady, while his heart throbbed with emotions. He looked upon her as far above him, and shrunk from the important avowal, and the weighty question. On that night he had come to the firm resolve that he would conquer his timidity and know his fate. His toilet being finished, he started, and on the road he pondered in his mind whether it was best to study a few set sentences in which to present his ardent desire. He very wisely abandoned the thought, and trusted himself to the inspiration of the moment.

Nellie expected him, but knew nothing of what was coming, although her keen eye could easily discern that Robin Jones was laboring under some embarrassment.

A gentle knock was heard at the door. Nellie was instantly on her feet, to answer it, and Robin was ushered into the very room where his courage had so often failed him. And for fear that it might so prove again, he thought that without delay he would open the subject.

"Well, Nellie, you look very cheerful and happy."

"I am very happy, Robin, and I have a very good reason for it," said Nellie. "We are going to Druid's Grove. Isn't that glorious? O, I was so afraid that we would have to go far away. I am as happy as a soaring lark! How does it affect you, Robin?"

"Well," said the young man, "as far as your father and mother are concerned, it is grand, and it pleases me ever so much. But for a particular reason, which, by your permission, I will tell you, I hope that *you* will not leave Riverside."

"Why, Robin, you talk strangely!" said Nellie, blushing in spite of herself.

"Rather strangely for me," said Robin. "My reason may be somewhat selfish. You must judge of its merits and act accordingly. Nellie, for a long time I have loved you most ardently, but owing to my natural timidity, I have not avowed it until this moment. I am aware that I am greatly your inferior, both in intellect and education. I am but a plain farming young man, and in asking for your hand, I am taking a bold step. I am about to take the charge of this farm, which my brother gives me, on terms that are wonderfully favorable. My earthly prospects are bright, and now in all sincerity and love, I ask Nellie Trevor to be my wife."

Nellie did not fall into a delicious trance, nor gently lean upon his bosom and sob, nor sweetly refer him to her father. She did not indulge in a number of other things which we often read of. It was not Miss Trevor's style.

"Robin, you undervalue yourself, and I don't like it!" she said. "Inferior, indeed! It may be possible that I can do a number of things that you cannot, such as washing and ironing, make bread and talk nonsense. But what about plowing, sowing, reaping, and harvesting? Yes, Robin, I will be your wife. I love you dearly, and—"

The rest of the sentence, whatever it intended to be, was interrupted by a certain movement on the part of the young man, which seriously interferred with Nellie's utterance. This interruption the young lady promptly resented by an infliction of the same chastisement on Robin Jones.

They were betrothed. Gwennie's pleasing prophecy had been fulfilled. Nellie Trevor met with a better offer, and Riverside was to be her future home. Her parents were happy over it, and Robin's relatives were delighted. The wedding was quiet. There were no bans published, and it took the community by surprise. Both were general favorites, and showers of blessings were invoked to rest upon their heads.

# CHAPTER XXXII.



Mr. and Mrs. Trevor, according to agreement, went to Druid's Grove, where they remained for many years. happy themselves, and conferring happiness on others.

Llewelyn Edwards increased in popularity, and was a power in the Calvinistic body as long as he lived. Years ago he died in good old age, all covered with glory, while weeping thousands followed him to the tomb. Two years later his loving companion joined him in the better land. They had three children. The youngest is to-day a shining light in the ministerial heaven. The sister is the companion of a venerable D. D., and the other brother is enjoying a happy evening of life at Llwyn y Derwydd.

Taliesin Roberts became an eminent counselor and attorney, and with his beloved Helen, settled at Carnarvon, where he had large practice and great influence.

Morgan Edwards remained at the "shop" until the death of his sister. He then sold his property at Llangobaith, and at the earnest request of Llewelyn and Gwennie, made his home at Druid's Grove.

Dick Jones, without delay, made extensive repairs at Pren y Gôg, where his parents continued to live for many more years, happy in the society of their children, amid peace and plenty. He, himself, remained at Glan 'r Afon as long as he lived, while Robin carried on the farm. At an advanced age the two brothers, with their companions, passed away, leaving a large property to their children and relatives.

Morris Williams, after having been a widower for many years, received in return for his own the warm affection of Grace Lloyd, with whom he lived many happy years.

Mrs. Parry, of Thrush Grove, remained a widow until Arthur became of age, and was married. She then was united in marriage to Mr. John Williams, of *Ty Mawr*, a gentleman mentioned in another part of our story.

Dick Roland remained in the service of Arthur, and at last married Jane Jones. They would have entered into this state much sooner, but it was hard for Dick to make Jane believe that he was really in earnest. At last, still having some doubt, she consented to go with him to church, and to her perfect delight she found that for once he was not joking. The coachman's married life was happy. They remained in a neat cottage on the place as long as they lived.

Miss Thomas, of Bala, was married to one of the Professors at the Institute, and was noted through life for her deeds of charity.

In about four years after the departure of Evan Pugh from Riverside, the following appeared in the Carnarvon *Herald*, copied from a London paper:

" A shocking case of suicide took place yesterday at Grosvenor Square.  For some years, a lady calling herself Mrs. McKnight, had occupied rooms in the house No. 50.  Where she came from, and under what circumstances, no one knew.  She seemed to have abundance of money, and her rent was regularly advanced.  Not long after she had occupied these rooms, she was joined by a gentleman who was thought to be her husband.  He was not at all communicative, and gave evidence of a troubled mind.  It was plain that their domestic relation was not happy.  Boisterous language on the part of the woman, was frequently heard, and she was often under the influence of liquor.  For the last few weeks her husband, if husband he was, had not been seen.  It is thought that her constant violence and drunkenness had driven him away in despair. Yesterday morning a lady of an adjoining room, who was on familiar terms with Mrs. McKnight, went into her apartment, and beheld a most shocking sight.  On the floor, with her face in a pool of blood, lay the woman, with her throat cut from ear to ear.  In her hand was a razor' and on a stand near by a brandy bottle nearly empty. On the lady's person were found papers and correspondence which clearly prove that her real name was Mrs.

Evan Pugh, and that she had long resided at Riverside, in North Wales. What may have been the reason for hiding under a false name, we cannot just now tell; but the once proud mistress of a beautiful country residence, came to a terrible and disgraceful end."

THE END.

# TESTIMONIALS.

taken up, will be hard to lay down till the last page is finished.
It is a work of rare merit.  The spirit of it is true and elevating.
Its perusal will afford much pleasure and instruction.

H. W. BENNETT.

*From Benjamin F. Lewis, of Utica, N. Y.*

REV. E. W. JONES :

*Dear Friend*—I read every word of "Llangobaith," and thoroughly enjoyed it from first to last.  I read several chapters to
my aged mother, and it would have done you good to see with
what pleasure she listened, and to hear her approving exclamations, as some of the scenes brought back to her incidents in her
early life.  The book contains much valuable information worked
into an absorbingly interesting story, especially interesting on
account of the insight it gives of the moral and religious phases
of social life in our dear native land.  The pure tone of the book
should make it a welcome addition to every family library.

BENJAMIN F. LEWIS.

*From Prof. Apmadoc, of Utica, N. Y.*

REV. E. W. JONES :

The reading of "Llangobaith"—a charming name by the way
—gave me unmixed pleasure.  You have interwoven in your
story so many unique Welsh customs and characteristics, that I
feel confident will delight a large number of readers who heretofore were strangers to the Welsh character.  Many of the incidents in your readable work recalled to my mind similar ones that
actually occurred in and around my native town.  I believe that
among the most difficult tasks of a story writer, are the true con-
ception, and the delineation of character, and the successful
working out of a strong plot to a thrilling climax.  Allow me to
congratulate you on your success in this respect.  Your characters are natural—they speak for themselves.  The variety of
matter introduced, the many incidents showing the religious
warmth and tendencies of the Welsh people, and the racy style of
the whole narrative, will command, I predict, a large number of
readers.  Wishing you much and immediate success,

I remain very cordially yours,        W. APMADOC.

*From Rev. F. H. Beck, Pastor of First M. E. Church, Utica, N. Y.*

"Llangobaith" is a most charming story, written in a style that will interest, please and instruct the reader. The characters are true to nature, and exhibit that keen insight of men the author possesses, which has already given him favor as a writer. The story will delight the Welsh people, who in thought will be transported to the father land. Americans also will read it with interest, as it will give them an insight into Welsh character and customs, and a better idea of the geography of that historic land. I commend the work most heartily to the patronage of the reading public, and hope it will be widely circulated.     F. H. BECK.

---

*From Rev. Wm. R. Griffith, Pastor of the Welsh M. E. Church.*
*Utica, N. Y.*

**MY DEAR BROTHER:**

I thank you for the privelege of reading the MS. of Llangobaith. With it, I have spent happy hours amid the charms of "Cymru Fu" (Wales of the past.) It's like a museum rich with the relics of gone-by days. I was permitted to listen to the pulpit giants of eighty years ago, and to witness the social customs of the fathers. In publishing this incomparable work, you confer a great favor upon your nation and the world. In it we find a beautiful combination of the serious, the comic and the religious; and all of an instructive bearing. The characters are as natural as nature itself. You have not only given them form, but also *life*. The book will be popular.